I0846730

A New Flower in the Yukon

Sharon Poppen

SORIANO
RAGAZZO
PUBLISHING

Soriano Ragazzo Publishing

A New Flower in the Yukon

© 2024 by Sharon Poppen—All rights reserved. No part of this book may be reproduced, distributed, or transmitted in any form or by any means, including photocopying, recording, or other electronic or mechanical methods, without the prior written permission of the publisher, except in the case of brief quotations embodied in critical reviews and certain other noncommercial uses permitted by copyright law.

Published by Soriano Ragazzo Publishing, 2620 Clarke Dr, Lake Havasu City, Arizona 86403, Contact: Sorianoragazzopublishing@outlook.com

ISBN: 979-8-89890-017-5

LCCN: 2026902996

Disclaimer: This is a work of fiction. Names, characters, organizations, and incidents are products of the author's imagination or are used fictitiously. Any resemblance to actual persons, living or dead, or to real organizations, events, or locales is purely coincidental.

Cover design and interior layout by Soriano Ragazzo Publishing, Tina Harden

Contents

Also by

Sharon Poppen

Abby–Finding More Than Gold
    A Passage Through Secrets
    Moose Rides and Wedding Rings
    Regardless
    Hannah
    Mama Played for the King
    Finding Amy
    Irish Girl
    Just for You

<u>Farrell Family Saga Book Series</u>

After the War, Before the Peace–Book 1
Lita–Going Home–Book 2
Deborah's Story–Book 3
The Woman Between–Book 4
Stephen's Boys–Book 5
The Band–Book 6
Peace by Pieces–Book 7

Cast of Characters

<u>Main Characters</u>
Malie Iona
Brian Stockton

<u>People in the Yukon</u>

Devon MacDonald–CMP Sergeant Major
Peggy Moynahan Martin–Miss Lucy's Bar Owner
Elmer Martin–Peggy's husband
Patrick Finley–JP Transit Owner
Kathleen Finley–Patrick's wife
River Finley–Patrick's brother
Blair Finley–River's wife

<u>People in Hawaii</u>

Jake Bennett (alias Bill Jones)–Flyin' Hi Bar Owner
Ruby Kent–Flyin' Hi Barmaid
Gus–Flyin' Hi Bartender
Detective Harrison–Oahu Police Dept.
Detective Bader–Oahu Police Dept.
Ronald Phillips–Attorney

A New Assignment

1947 WAS PROVING TO be an extra cold winter. But after the recently ended world war, the peace and optimism cherished by those who had served and those who had kept the home fires burning was encouraging them to make up for lost time and not worry about low temps and snow.

As Constable Brian Stockton made his way to the Whitehorse Canadian Mounted Police station, he couldn't help but notice all the relaxed smiles shared by the people making their way to work, school or shopping. It was just what he needed to override the memories of his time on Iwo Jima. At the door to the station, he paused to enjoy the atmosphere of this quaint wilderness town. He'd been in Whitehorse just short of a year, but the citizens and his fellow Mounties were making him feel like it was a place he could eventually call home. With a smile on his face, he headed inside.

It was a few minutes before eleven a.m. and his tour didn't start until two p.m., but he enjoyed the company of the other Mounties, and he had nowhere else to go. He hung his pea coat and Stetson under his name above the row of pegs near the door and headed for the break room. On his way, he stopped by his sergeant major's desk to lay the report he finished at home last night on his desk. As he set it down, he noticed the unopened envelope that had been sitting there for a few days. It wasn't like Sergeant Major Devon MacDonald to leave anything undone.

He was tempted to pick up the envelope to see where and who it had come from. He even glanced around the empty office, then his better judgement surfaced. Brian turned and headed for the break room for some coffee with his fellow officers.

The station hours were six a.m. to ten p.m. when they had no prisoners in their small, two-cell jail. Sgt. Major Devon Mac-Donald usually opened the office and often stayed until it closed. The other three officers rotated their eight-hour shifts with one starting at eight a.m., one at ten a.m. and the final shift starting at 2 p.m. The office was closed from 11 p.m. to 8 a.m. most nights with MacDonald on call. When the jail did have an occupant, shifts were rotated to a twenty-four-hour duty roster.

"Morning," Brian said as he made his way to the coffee pot.

"Morning," said Sgt. David Gibson as he sugared and creamed his large cup of coffee.

"Morning," mumbled his fellow constable, Ron Kennedy, through a large bite of a maple long john.

Brian, Dave, and the sergeant major were all about six foot tall with lean, muscled bodies. Ron was only five-nine and carried some extra weight, mostly around his waist.

When Brian's cup was filled, he asked, "Where's the major?' When there were no citizens or criminals around, the men often shortened the title to just major.

"Don't know," said Gibson.

Brian shook his head. "During the past year, he's always here when I arrive. For a while I thought he lived here."

"I practically do," agreed MacDonald as he hung his hat and coat on the rack, then headed straight for the coffee.

Dave, who had worked with MacDonald for several years, smiled and nodded as he saluted his senior with his cup of coffee. "Morning, major."

Ron and Brian also nodded and said their good mornings.

Turning to head back into the office with his cup of black coffee, MacDonald asked, "Any calls come in this morning?"

"No. All quiet so far," said Dave. "You get any calls during the night?"

"No," said MacDonald as he settled into his desk chair. "I'm just late. No excuse."

Gripping their coffee cups, MacDonald's subordinates made their way to their desks. Just as each sat down, the phone rang.

Dave answered the call. "Whitehorse CMP."

"Dave?"

"Yes, Philomena, what's going on?" he asked the local telephone company operator.

"Call came in from Adele. She said Rocky's drunk again and hitting her, but before she could tell me more, the line went dead."

Dave was already on his feet. "On our way," he said, then hung up. "Ron, let's go." He turned to Devon. "Our town drunk is at it again."

"Why the hell doesn't she divorce him?" grumbled Devon.

Dave put his hand to his heart, and in a mock feminine wail, he said, "'Cause I love him when he's sober."

Devon uttered a brief laugh as Dave and Ron grabbed their Stetsons and coats from the rack by the door.

"Call Bertie and tell her we'll be needing a couple meals for the next day or two," said Dave as he and Ron headed out the door.

"Want me to call Bertie?" asked Brian.

"Please," said Devon as he picked up the report Brian had set on his desk earlier.

Brian dialed a nearby diner under contract to supply meals to prisoners in the CMP local jail. "Hi, Bertie. Brian, here. Looks like Rocky is coming to stay with us for a few days. We'll need some meals." He listened, then said, "Not sure when, but probably by noon, so figure on lunch and supper for today and at least a breakfast for morning." He listened, then said, "Thanks," and hung up.

Having turned in yesterday's report on a minor disagreement at the local general store between the owner and a local miner, Brian had nothing to do. Sitting at his desk was not what had signed up for. He needed to keep busy. After a look out the window, he decided to get some exercise by taking a patrol walk along the Yukon River docking area.

"Major," he said as he stood up and turned to see the major set his report down. "If you don't need me, I think I'll take a patrol walk along the shoreline."

"Sounds like a good idea."

Brian grabbed his coat and hat, then headed out. As he closed the door, he noticed the major had picked up the unopened envelope and was tapping it on his desk as if trying to decide whether to open it or not. It was so unlike the major and it was really making Brian curious. Still, it was none of his business, so he left the office without another word.

The crisp air and the bright sunshine, with not a hint of wind, brought a smile to Brian's face. It sure beat the heavy air and humidity of the South Pacific where he'd spent his war years. As he walked along, the Christmas decorations along Front Street brought memories of Vancouver, where he had been born and lived until heading down into the States and joining the Navy when the war broke out. The smiles and laughter of a young couple and their three children threatened to sour his mood as more memories of his family came to mind.

His father had owned a fishing boat that alternated between commercial fishing with a small crew and captaining day-trip fishing for tourists. The commercial fishing catch was sold to the fresh fish vendors along the docks. The tourists had come up north for some halibut fishing. Both Brian and his older brother Joe grew up on the boat, and it was probably why both of them were drawn to the U.S. Navy when the war broke out.

His mother, originally from Phoenix, Arizona in the States, was a homemaker who spent her days cooking, cleaning, doing laundry and canning a variety of fruits and vegetables for sale to the tourists on his father's fishing jaunts. Although becoming a Canadian citizen years ago, she retained her U.S. citizenship and passed it on to her sons.

Life had been good for Brian before the war, spending time with his family, whether on the boat fishing or enjoying home-cooked dinners every evening in the midst of his very close family.

Then, the war broke out, and he and Joe joined the U.S. Navy. Joe was killed when his ship was bombed and sunk in the Pacific during an air attack by the Japs. His parents were killed aboard the family fishing boat. When the boys had left home, his mother helped his father with the daily fishing trips. A late summer storm broke out with heavy rain, thunder, and deadly lightning strikes pounding all of Vancouver. When charred pieces of the boat were found floating in the water after the storm ended, it was assumed his parents had died from a lightning strike to their boat.

When Brian was discharged, he came home to an empty house. Finding peace and a return to any kind of normal life was hampered by all the family memories that surrounded him in the family dwelling. Walks along the dock where his father's boat had docked at the end of each fishing trip didn't help. The memories were there, too.

One morning while sitting in the local coffee shop, he saw an ad in the paper for recruits for the Canadian Mounted Police. He'd never been involved in any sort of police work, but he decided that something totally new was his only chance to move beyond the pain of losing his entire family. He sold the family home, applied to the CMP, attended the twenty-six-week training session, then was sent to Whitehorse in the Yukon for his first assignment.

Now, as he walked along the Yukon on this sunny day, he smiled. He still had his family memories, but this new occupation in this new territory enabled him to dwell on the good parts of the memories and not on his loss. By the time he had made his tour of the docks and was making his way back to the station, he could actually enjoy the Christmas decorations.

Opening the door to the station, he heard the familiar voice of Rocky ranting about injustice, claiming innocence and wanting something to eat.

"Shut up," ordered Devon, "or I'll cancel lunch."

"You can't do that," roared Rocky.

"Try me. Or, just quiet down and take a nap to sober up."

"Go to hell."

Devon picked up his phone and pretended to dial a number. "Bertie, never mind about bringing a lunch by for Rocky. And, just bring a bowl of soup broth for supper."

"Hold it," pleaded Rocky. He stretched out on the cell cot and ran his finger over his mouth as if zipping it shut.

Devon smiled as he spoke into the dial tone. "Bertie, ignore what I just said. Your regular lunch and supper meals will be fine." He hung up the receiver and looked up at Brian. "Good walk?"

"Yes, sir. All is well along the shoreline."

"Good to hear."

"Where are Dave and Ron?"

"Lunch over at Bertie's."

Brian sat at his uncluttered desk and looked for something to do. He glanced over at Devon and found him toying with the unopened envelope. This time his curiosity won out. "Bad news?" he asked.

Devon smiled. "Probably not. It's from my mother up in Dawson City."

"Never been there."

"Middle of nowhere."

"They live there for a long time?"

"No, they had a sheep farm just over in Ibex Valley. My younger sister married a miner from up in Dawson. Once the grandkids started coming and the sheep farm got too much for Ma and Da, they moved up there so they could be close to family."

Brian looked at the unopened envelope. "Ah, family."

Devon knew about Brian's background and his loss of family. Brian's words got him thinking. He knew his mother would be relaying all the good news about his sister Blair and her family, and her good news about his brother Ian, his family and his successful fishing boat business. Trouble was, she would always close with her concerns about Devon's single life and how he rarely made it home for a visit. But, looking over at Brian, he accepted that he was lucky to have such a loving family. Some heavy snoring broke into his thoughts, and he glanced over to see Rocky sound asleep, stretched out on the small cot. He opened the envelope and began to read.

Brian felt like he was intruding, so he headed for the break room and another cup of coffee. About the time he felt he could go back to his desk, Dave and Ron arrived with a lunch tray for Rocky.

After quietly placing the lunch on the floor near the snoring Rocky, the Mounties sat at their desks. Dave worked on the paperwork for Rocky's arrest. Ron read the newspaper, and Brian grabbed his copy of the CMP Rifle Competition manual and tried to get interested. He was surprised when the major suggested Brian accompany him on a patrol walk around town.

The men grabbed their hats and coats, then headed out. After walking about a block in silence, the major began to share the contents of his letter.

"My Ma says the winter up in Dawson has been fairly snowless. They're hoping for that to change by Christmas."

"Well, it's still a week away, so maybe it will come."

Devon nodded.

"Are you going up there for Christmas?"

"Haven't been up there for a few years and hadn't planned on it."

"That why you hesitated on opening the envelope?"

"Sort of."

"Well, sir, I think you're lucky to have family. I can tell you that if I had anyone, I'd be asking for some vacation days to spend Christmas with them."

Again, they walked along in silence as Devon thought about the call from headquarters a couple days ago regarding a Mountie presence in Dawson City. It would be a one-man operation to establish what was needed in a small community so far north. Devon knew his folks would want him to take the assignment. He loved and appreciated his family, but his life was in Whitehorse. He may not have settled down and started a family, but he had made friends, both male and female, who were now almost family. He was a member of a couple local clubs that did some hunting, some ski treks, and lots of relaxing at a bar alongside wilderness bachelors like himself. He had a good life.

He glanced over at Brian, and a thought came to him. Perhaps Brian would fare well in Dawson, having daily interaction with the small local population. They walked along, nodding and offering the occasional wave to the townsfolk. As they were about to turn back toward the station, Devon pointed to a snack vendor along the docks.

"How about another cup of coffee? I've something I'd like to discuss with you."

Brian was surprised at the offer, then quickly concern set in. His first official work appraisal was about due. He felt good about his performance over the past year, but police work was new to him and he could only hope he'd lived up to the major's expectations. Brian nodded and followed him down to the vendor.

Once they had their coffee, Devon directed them to a dockside bench. He wasted no time. "So, young constable, what do you think of your time as a CMP?

"Well, to be honest, I didn't know what to expect. Most of my life has been on the water in one way or another. This past year has surprised me in many ways. I really enjoy my work. I'm glad I was assigned to your station, and I feel like, for a rookie, I've done okay."

Devon smiled. "I should have started by telling you that this is not your yearly appraisal. This is just two cops sharing info about their work."

Brian exaggerated a deep sigh of relief, then laughed. "Good to know, sir."

Still smiling, Devon went on. "Well, in answer to your thoughts on being a rookie, I can tell you that I, and your fellow Mounties, feel you've done a good job."

"Thank you, sir."

"So, do you think this is your career for the long run?"

"I do."

"Good. I hate training new Mounties." He laughed. "Now, let me ask you about this issue with water. Has it been tough for you to limit yourself to a calm boat ride up the Yukon, now and then, versus the beauty of the wide-open ocean?"

"Surprisingly, not tough at all. The variety of wildlife amid the wooded areas and the snow topped mountain vistas provide much more beauty than the vast, flat scope of the ocean. I've found I haven't missed it at all."

"Glad to hear it." He studied Brian for a few moments, then made a decision. "Brian, I got a call the other day from headquarters about opening a one-man station up in Dawson."

"Sir, that's good news for you. Your family would love it."

Devon smiled. "Yes, they would. But I'm pretty settled here in Whitehorse, as are Dave and Ron. They and their families have been here for years. No, the three of us prefer our assignments here in Whitehorse."

What Devon was tacitly offering was not lost on Brian. His mind was awhirl with all the changes, possibilities, and losses he'd have to face if Devon was truly offering him the assignment. He waited for the major to go on.

"So, that leaves you to consider for the assignment." Devon took a sip of his coffee as he assessed Brian's body language. He detected only interest, not concern. "Would you be interested?"

"Sir, do you think I'm ready for such a responsibility?"

"Look at me, Brian," said Devon. The men locked eyes so Devon could look for any sign of concern or hesitation. Finding none, he eventually smiled. "Yes, Brian, I believe you are ready."

A broad grin crossed Brian's face. "Thank you, sir. When is this new assignment going to start?"

Devon stood up and extended his hand.

Brian stood and extended his.

"Right now," said Devon as the men shared a confirming handshake.

Life in the Yukon

Two days later, at about five a.m., Devon and Brian were in Devon's Jeep station wagon on the Klondike Highway headed to Dawson. The distance between Whitehorse and Dawson was about 300 miles. Without any inclement weather or icy roads, the travel time would be about six hours. Devon had let the family know they were coming.

He hadn't told them about Brian staying on as the local CMP, knowing it would disappoint the family that he hadn't taken the assignment. He planned to stay until after New Year to work with Brian in finding an office and to get things set up. Once they had an office, they would decide what was needed for Brian to do his work, and Devon would have it sent up.

Devon would tell the family after Christmas. The family could totally enjoy everyone being together without a touch of concern and disappointment that Devon hadn't taken the assignment for himself.

The weather held and aside from stops to eat, pour some gas from their gas cans into the Jeep's gas tank and change drivers, the men made the trip in good time and arrived in Dawson early afternoon.

As Devon drove through the small downtown area, he enjoyed the fact that not much had changed since his last trip to Dawson three years ago. He continued along, pointing out things to Brian until they pulled into the family driveway. Devon exited the Jeep and was stretching his cramped body when the front door opened and out rushed his sister Blair, followed by her four-year-old daughter, Rain.

"Devon!" cried Blair as she threw herself into her brother's arms. "We've all missed you so much."

"I've missed you, too," he pulled her under his arm as he reached out for a hug to his niece. "Rain, what happened to my funny, little, curly-headed niece? You've grown up!"

Rain giggled as she snuggled under his other arm. "Maybe you should come home more often."

"Oh, no. You've become your mother." He laughed as he kissed her forehead. Then, remembering that Brian was watching all the family dynamics, he released his kin and pointed over at Brian, who was standing just outside the passenger door on the other side of the car. "Family, meet Constable Brian Stockton."

Blair smiled. "Welcome to Dawson City, Constable."

"Thank you, glad to be here," said Brian.

A light snow had begun to fall. "Devon! You brought the snow!" She kissed him on the cheek, then urged the men to grab their belongs. "Get your things and come inside. I've some fresh scones just out of the oven for you and some hot water boiling for tea. Come." She being followed by Rain, headed back into the house. At the door, she turned. "Hurry on now." Then she was gone.

As Devon opened the back seat door to retrieve his duffle bag, he faced Brian reaching for his from the other side of the car. "Welcome to the Finley-MacDonald clan. Brace yourself, it doesn't let up. In fact, it's going to get crazier."

Devon had regaled Brian with tales about his clan on their long drive. Years ago, Blair had been a teacher in Whitehorse, a few hours away from Ibex Valley, where the family sheep farm was located. Devon manned the CMP office in Whitehorse. Turned out Devon had some CMP business on the coast, so they decided to make a surprise visit to their parents.

Whereby Blair met her future husband for the first time. Arriving late at night, after her parents had gone to bed, she and Devon slipped into the house and headed off to bed. As she climbed into her bed, she found a naked male body sound asleep. The startled man had grabbed the bedsheet and ran out of the bedroom.

Fortunately, Devon had put his gun away before Blair screamed. Their parents ran from their bedroom to calm everyone down and explained that, not expecting any of their three grown children home, they had invited the young man to stay for dinner and spend the night.

Turned out his name was River and he had wandered up a few days earlier just as her father needed some help with his small sheep herd. River had been traveling by horse for a few weeks, so the thought of a soft, warm bed was too tempting to turn down.

There were other fun stories that Devon shared, so Brian hadn't been surprised by Blair's warm welcome to her brother.

Brian smiled. "So, you said. Actually, I thought it was nice. Obviously, they miss you."

"You're right. Just be prepared."

With their duffel bags in hand, they headed up and into the house.

***

The next few days were a blur of family, food, parlor games, and they all usually closed with the menfolk gathered out on the back veranda with their drinks and cigars. Devon and Brian were joined by Mac—Devon's father— and Ian—Devon's brother, River—Devon's brother-in-law—and Tommy—River's father.

Most of the conversations were about the weather, an increase in tourism since the war ended, some mining, and a bit of complaining about one missing family member. River's brother Patrick, co-owner of a small airline down in the States, had some flight commitments over the holiday season and couldn't make it home with his wife and son.

By Christmas, Brian almost felt like a member of the family. He had learned a lot about mining from River and Tommy. And, how it had been Tommy's wife, Abby, who had been determined to head for the Yukon to find gold. He also found out there was a family bar in town, Lucy's Saloon, owned by Abby's sister, Peggy. Peggy and her husband Elmer were semi-retired, but they still worked the bar a couple days a week.

What really surprised Brian was that the upstairs of Lucy's Saloon had rooms rented out to women who worked as bar waitresses and such. Brian quickly figured out what the 'such' was and could see that most of the family was not happy about it.

Brian had enjoyed talking with Ian about his fishing business. Ian's life mirrored Brian's early family life in that Ian had a fishing boat, a wife, and two young sons. Getting the details of Ian's life brought pangs of sadness about the loss of his own family, but thankfully there was never a dull or quiet moment with the Finley and MacDonald clans. That kept the memories to a minimum, allowing Brian to fully enjoy the holiday celebrations.

Brian enjoyed the family camaraderie and felt quite welcome. Christmas Eve was celebrated at Tommy and Abby's home. In addition to the Finley–MacDonalds he had already met, the gathering included Peggy and Elmer, a couple of Abby's brothers and their families, and a young woman who managed Peggy's bar.

Her name was Malie.

As welcoming as the entire gathering was, he noticed that, like him, Malie didn't seem to be blood- or marriage-related to anyone else present.

He was intrigued. It almost seemed as if she were avoiding him. He felt that she was tacitly watching him and, other than when they were introduced, she managed to stay clear of him. She was certainly a beauty with her dark hair, dark eyes, and light beige complexion. He wondered if she was Native Alaskan. As the evening wore on, his curiosity grew, and he could hardly wait to get Devon alone to find out more about the girl.

Christmas Day was a smaller crowd, with just Devon's family along with Tommy and Abby, who arrived around nine a.m. with homemade cinnamon buns, freshly made by their housekeeper Bertie. After gifts were exchanged, the women began working on a turkey dinner to close out the Christmas festivities.

The men headed out to the back porch with the last of the buns and fresh cups of coffee. River and Tommy began hashing over some new orders for minerals from their mine.

The conversation did not interest Devon and Brian, so Devon suggested that he and Brian take a walk down to the Front Street area. He'd show Brian around and maybe check out some possibilities for the CMP office. As Devon opened the back door and told the women they were heading downtown for a little while, Nonie, his mother, rushed over to him.

"Devon, we've hardly had any time to visit. We need to set up some time to talk before you leave."

Devon kissed the top of her head. "We will." He quickly turned and motioned for Brian to follow. As soon as the gate closed behind them, Devon uttered a slight sigh of relief.

"What?" asked Brian. "Something wrong, something you did or didn't do?"

Devon nodded. "Yep. Something I haven't done."

"Want to talk about it?"

"Nothing to talk about. And, to my mother, that goes back to something I haven't done." Devon turned to Brian, raised his eyebrows and uttered a chuckle. "I haven't provided her with a daughter-in-law and grandchildren."

Brian shrugged. "She has that with Ian, and she has grandchildren from him and Blair."

"I agree, but she's a mom. And it seems it's part of a mom's job to see that all her kids find that someone to love and to assure the family clan carries on.

"Well, I think it's nice that you have someone who loves you enough to worry about you and wants you to be happy."

Remembering Brian's lack of family, Devon decided it was time to change the subject. "You're right, I'm lucky to have such a mother."

They walked along in silence for awhile. When Lucy's Saloon came into sight, Brian remembered the dark-haired beauty, Malie. "Sir, I was wondering about Malie, the girl at the Christmas Eve gathering. Is she an Alaskan?"

"No. Actually, she's Hawaiian."

Brian stopped walking and turned to Devon. "Hawaiian? Up here in the Yukon?"

They were just passing the local café. Devon made a suggestion. "Let's get a cup of coffee and head on down to the dock."

Once they had their coffee, they found a bench along the dock where several men and young boys were fishing. Devon began to answer Brian's question about Malie.

"Now, about Malie, it's kind of a long story."

Brian shrugged. "Coffee's good, and we sure aren't interested in learning more about mining."

Devon laughed. "You're right about that." He took a drink of his coffee and began. "See, River's brother, Patrick, served in the Army Air Corps over in Hawaii during the war. Long story short, he met Kathleen, a nurse who was in an abusive marriage to Pete, a Marine corporal stationed in the Islands." Devon paused.

"Patrick and Kathleen met in the mess hall where she and her fellow nurses took their meals. Patrick found he was attracted to her. One morning when he arrived at the mess hall, Kathleen's first lieutenant told Patrick that Pete had beat her up so bad she ended up in the hospital." Devon's shoulders slumped.

"Then, he avoided brig time by being dispatched with his unit for the attack on Iwo Jima. He was told they'd readdress his abuse charges when he returned."

"Wow, what a bastard," said Brian. "Not like any of the Marines I knew over there. Those guys were first-rate."

"He was a disgrace to his unit, that's for sure," Said Devon. "Anyway, Patrick started visiting her in the hospital, and one thing led to another. Eventually, they wanted to marry, and she filed for divorce. Then, Pete was declared missing in action. Everything was put on hold for seven years."

"So, how does Malie fit into all this?"

Devon went on. "Miraculously, Pete was found a few years later, hidden in a cave, by an Army clean-up unit and claimed that he had been a POW. His fellow Marines who had been with him when they landed on Iwo had a different take on his story and never believed him to be a POW, more like a deserter. They reported on some cowardly actions by Pete that had cost the lives of several men in their unit."

"Hard to believe. I served in the Pacific during the war, and occasionally our ship would need some maintenance. We docked in Oahu, and we were given weekend passes. During those nights on the town, we met several Marines. Real stand-up guys, hard to believe one of them would do such a thing."

"He stuck to the POW story. Claimed he had managed to escape and hide for almost a year. When he got back to Oahu, the Brass decided Pete had suffered enough and erased all abuse charges. Unfortunately for Patrick, he and Kathleen ran into him in an Oahu restaurant. Threats were made by Patrick. Later that night Pete was found dead in an alley on the night-life side of town. Patrick was arrested and charged with murder."

"From what you've said, I don't blame Patrick. I think I would have done the same to any man who would put a woman in the hospital." Then he remembered this conversation started with an inquiry about Malie. "But how does Malie fit into all this?"

Devon smiled. "I'm getting to it. Of course, Patrick did not do it. Turns out Pete's Marine buddies had run into him that night and the four of them took turns beating the crap out of him."

"Man, this is crazy," said Brian. "So, his fellow Marines took him out?"

"No. His attorney believed Patrick didn't do it and went out of his way to visit the bar where Pete's body had been found. He found a hooker who had been with Pete earlier that evening and saw what really happened to him."

"Malie was the hooker?"

"Yes. According to her, when the Marines confronted Pete, she was trying to collect her money, but the situation got so tense, she ran back into the bar where she worked." Devon paused.

"But she peeked through the door and watched the confrontation between Pete and the Marines. When they left, Pete was flat on his back. Knowing her boss would not like it if she didn't have the money from her john, she slipped back outside hoping to get hold of his wallet. Before she could touch him, he moaned."

Devon shifted. "Again, she backed off. He managed to get on his feet and started after her, calling her terrible names. As he reached out for her, he slipped on some wet cobblestones and fell flat on his face. When he rolled over on his back, Malie said his face was full of blood and it looked like his forehead was gone."

"My God. That poor girl."

"Amen to that."

"But they arrested Patrick?"

"Malie didn't come forward to tell what happened because she assumed they wouldn't believe anything a hooker said."

Brian shrugged. "Sad."

"Yep. Fortunately, Patrick's lawyer did some deep digging and found her. After she told him what happened, the coroner, due to Malie's story of how Pete got the head wound, revised the reason for death from a beating to a fall. All charges were dropped against Patrick."

"Thank goodness Malie witnessed it. But that still doesn't explain how she got here to Dawson."

Devon smiled. "When Patrick and Kathleen went to thank her, they learned about her past and how she managed to cope with life after a childhood of misfortune. They decided she needed to be around good people, not people who just used her. They offered her the opportunity to relocate here, take some time and be given the chance to start over."

Brian shook his head and frowned. "And she decided Miss Lucy's Saloon was a good place to start over?"

"You know how it's said that timing is everything. Her arrival here was just at the time Patrick's Aunt Peggy was ready to semi-retire from the bar business and enjoy some traveling with her new husband. Malie's knowledge of the bar scene was a perfect replacement for Peggy's."

"What a story!"

"So now you know all the family's dirty secrets."

Brian raised his eyebrows in question.

Devon laughed. "You don't want to know my secrets." He downed the last of his coffee and stood up. "Ready to do some more walking, young constable."

Brian stood up and gave Devon a playful salute. "Yes, Sir."

They tossed their cups in the trash and headed on down the Front Street through town.

***

On January 15th, the sounds of the bald eagles looking for their morning nourishment along the banks of the Yukon woke Brian. Keeping his eyes closed, he stretched his arms and legs awake after another deep sleep in his two-room, one-bedroom apartment. His hotel was along the shoreline and Brian's apartment afforded a picturesque view of the river and the boat docks.

He turned to check the clock and found it was just a little past six a.m. After swinging his legs to the floor, he turned off the alarm set for seven and went to start his coffee. As he waited for it to brew, he took care of morning's nature call, then brushed his teeth, combed his hair, slipped into his briefs, pants, socks and shoes. Grabbing his shirt, he went back to the living room to check on his coffee.

The living room was small but managed to devote the area by the front door to a couch, chair and coffee table atop an oval braided rug. The window side of the room held a small icebox, a one-bowl sink, a two-burner stove and two wall shelves for food items and eating utensils. Below the window was a wide shelf and a stool that served as a kitchen table.

After pouring his coffee, he stood looking out the window at the dark skies. That the sun wouldn't be making its appearance for another couple hours was still a little hard to get used to. The lights along the docking area made it possible for Brian to watch the eagles as they fished, then roosted majestically on the various docking posts.

Eventually, he finished his coffee, rinsed his cup, slipped into his uniform shirt, then headed for his new CMP office. It was amazing what he and Devon had accomplished in the week before Devon headed back to Whitehorse. His apartment was about a block away from his office. It was on the corner of a three unit building along Front Street.

As one entered the office, they faced a desk and chair on one side of the front part of the room and a couple two-drawer file cabinets along the wall on the other side. Atop one of the file cabinets was a hot plate and on the other one was all the fixings for coffee, along with an array of coffee mugs. There was one extra chair set in front of the desk.

For the back half of the room, Devon had hired a contractor to build a small bathroom-size cage on one side of the back wall. The other side offered a real bathroom providing a small sink and a toilet.

Entering his office Brian hung his jacket and hat on a coat rack just inside the door. Sitting at his desk, he lifted his phone receiver.

"Yes, Constable Stockton?" answered the local telephone operator.

"I'm in my office now, Miss Appleton," reported Brian. "Any calls come in during the night?"

"Not a one," answered the operator. "And, aren't you early? It's only six-forty-five."

"Well, I'm out to impress the town folk that I'm here to keep them safe." He teased.

"I can see that. You have a nice day, Constable. I'll be going off duty in an hour or so, but Martha will be here if you need to ring us up for anything."

"Your support is most appreciated," said Brian. "So long, for now."

"Have a nice day," said the operator, then the line went dead.

Brian smiled as he hung up, knowing his early arrival at the office would be shared around town. He knew he needed to prove himself and small things like arriving to work early would help him establish a good reputation.

He looked around the room and shrugged his shoulders. Looked like another boring day. Crime in Whitehorse was low, but here in Dawson it seemed non-existent. The only incident of law breaking reported to Brian since opening the office, was to break up a bar fight between two miners.

By the time he arrived on the scene, the fight had come to an end with no winner, but both men would have a black eye or two and some sore muscles the next day. The bar owner didn't file any complaint as the two men had only broken one chair and a couple whiskey glasses and they had already paid the owner for the damage. No arrests were made.

Brian stood up, grabbed his jacket and hat, then headed out for a walk around town. Despite the cold weather, there were several citizens out buying supplies or heading to one of the local restaurants for a bite to eat.

Smiles were exchanged and occasionally there was a brief welcome to town conversation. He had started along the dock area and was on Front Street heading back toward his office when two elderly women approached him.

"Morning, Constable," said one of them.

"Good morning, ladies." Brian responded.

"Are you settling in comfortably?" asked the other one.

"Yes, I am. A very friendly town you have here."

The one who had spoken first introduced herself. "My name is Mrs. Hilda Brown, and this is Mrs. Sadie Anderson."

Brian nodded. "Nice to meet you. You probably already know my name is Constable Brian Stockton."

"Yes," said Hilda. "So, we were told." She paused, and the women exchanged glances, then Sadie spoke up.

"Constable, we would like to talk with you privately. Are you, by chance, heading back to your office now?"

"I am. Just follow me." Without any other words spoken, Brian led them back to his office. After hanging his hat and coat hat on the rack, he offered to take their coats, but they both declined.

Brian pulled his chair from behind the desk and set it alongside the other chair. "Ladies, please be seated." He walked around and stood behind his desk. "Would you like some coffee?" He pointed toward the file cabinets.

Hilda shook her head no, as did Sadie. "No," said Hilda, "this won't take long."

Brian nodded. "Alright then, what is it you want to discuss?"

With slightly pursed lips, the women again shared a look and a nod of agreement, then Hilda began.

"Constable, I'm sure you're aware that Dawson came to be because of the miners searching for gold in the Yukon."

"Yes, I have read up on the town's history over the past couple of weeks."

"Then you know that certain things were allowed here to accommodate an overwhelmingly male population."

Brain held back a smile from forming. He began to understand the pursed lips on these matrons. "Yes. In my reading, I found Front Street was mainly one assay office, some eateries and a saloon or two."

The woman shared another look, then Sadie took over. "That was fine for those miners, but then some Godly women came on the scene, either as wives who came to join their husbands or a few mail-order brides. They didn't expect to have to deal with the other kind of woman who had beat them to the Yukon."

"Other kind of women?" Brian asked, still stifling a smile.

"Yes," continued Sadie. "Like the hussies that work and live in the saloons, like Miss Lucy's." She paused for a moment then added, "Now, we hope that's not a problem for you."

"A problem? I don't understand," said Brian.

Hilda stepped in. "We know that River Finley is your sergeant major's brother-in-law and the hussy that owns Miss Lucy's is his aunt."

Brian nodded. "Yes, Peggy Finley is River's aunt." Seeing Hilda's shoulders rise, Brian hurried on. "But that has no bearing on what is legal or not legal. If you have concerns, it is my duty to check things out."

"That is a comfort to know." Hilda nodded, then began again. "You see, Constable, there are now many children in Dawson and we do not believe it to be in their best interests to be exposed to such sinfulness."

The ladies exchanged glances again, then Hilda went on. "We want you to know we've tried in the past to discuss this with the mayor. While he says he doesn't approve of them, they aren't harming anyone and they do bring miners from all over the Klondike area to shop and spend money here in Dawson. We want to know if there is any kind of law that forbids their type of work that could force the mayor to take action and have them arrested or run out of town?"

When Hilda finished, Brian took a moment to stroke his chin and look up at the ceiling as if in contemplative thought. Eventually, he nodded. "Ladies, I thank you for bringing this issue to me. I'm not familiar with all the legalities that have been set up in this town, so what I ask of you, is to give me time to do some checking around. I assure you I will not let this matter drop and will get back to you as soon as possible."

He paused and observed their smug smiles. "Now, ladies, how will I reach you when I have some information on this matter?"

"Just call the operator and ask for me or Sadie, she will connect you to one of us."

"I will do that." Brian came out from behind his desk, which brought the ladies to their feet. He opened the office door. "Thank you for stopping by." He forced himself to smile at each of the ladies as they exited his office.

After closing the door, Brian pulled the chair around and sat back down. He shook his head from side to side. This is why they wanted a Mountie stationed here? He wanted to laugh, but here he was trying to make a good impression on the small population and now this. He could see the dividing line already forming.

In the short time he'd been in town, he hadn't visited any of the local saloons. His time was spent working on the office, reading the town history and having his meals at The Nugget, a little café a block down from the office. When he wanted some socializing, he dropped by River's house.

He hadn't seen any hussies bothering anyone. Apparently, they kept to the bar scene. In fact, now and again Malie had crossed his mind, and he thought about dropping by Miss Lucy's for that very reason. But he decided an attraction to a woman was the last thing he needed until he was securely settled in and accepted.

He heaved a heavy sigh. Now, he would probably have to talk to her under the worst circumstances.

Not knowing how soon the ladies would like an update on their complaint, Brian decided to start by going to talk with River.

***

Early that same evening, after a hearty bowl of venison stew and homemade corn bread at The Nugget, Brian headed up to River's house. Rain answered the door.

"Hello, Constable Stockton. Dad and Mom are in the kitchen."

Brian smiled. "Please, when I'm not on official duty, call me Brian."

"I'll have to see if that's okay with my parents," said Rain. She turned and led Brian to her parents. "Look who's here," Rain announced.

"Hey, good to see you," said River as he continued drying dishes. "You just missed supper. Hungry?"

"Thanks, but I just had supper at the Nugget." Brian nodded at Blair who greeted him with a smile and a soapy wave as she continued with washing dishes.

"Ah, their venison stew," said River.

Brian smiled. "Yep."

Rain excused herself to head for her room and do some homework. "It was nice to see you, Constable Stockton."

"Please, like I said, Brian when I'm not on official duty."

Rain looked at her father.

"I guess it would be alright here in the house, but out on the street she should call you Constable."

Brian nodded, then smiled at Rain. "Okay, Rain?"

She smiled. "Goodnight, Brian."

As she left, Brian inquired about River's sons.

"It's Friday night. Movie night." River shrugged. "My aunt Peggy has a large storage area where she stores her supplies. A while back, she curtained off half of the room for her supplies, then set up a few rows of chairs and a small bar for serving soft drinks.

She bought a movie projector and uses the curtains as a screen. Every Friday night, she opens the room up for folks to come and watch a movie. Being way up here, she's not always able get a new movie each week, so often it's reruns, but the young singles like getting together, so it's socializing as well as movie watching."

"Hadn't heard of that yet," said Brian.

River laughed. "It's just kids doing their thing."

"And things," added Blair, but she was smiling.

"So, Constable, what brings you here?" asked River.

"Had a visit today from a Mrs. Brown and a Mrs. Anderson."

Blair laughed. "Dawson's own morals posse," she said as she dried her hands.

"So, it appears," Brian said.

"So, are you going to close certain businesses and run certain ladies out of town?" River asked as he put the last plate on the shelf and closed the cabinet door.

Now Brian laughed. "I take it this is not a new issue."

"We're done in here," said River. "Let's grab a couple beers and head on into the living room."

Not much was said until River and Blair were seated on the sofa with Brian comfortable in a padded rocker.

River shook his head. "So, Hilda and Bertie couldn't get the mayor to act, so now they've decided to call in the law. Busy bodies. They and their old gossip buddies need to find something to do with their time besides being the town conscience."

He raised one eyebrow suggestively and added, "And maybe pay a little more attention to their husbands after supper each night."

"River," said Blair with a slight scold in her voice.

Not wanting to get involved in a husband/wife issue, Brian went back to the issue he was here to talk about. "Now, about those buddies, are there more than just Hilda and Bertie?" asked Brian.

"Not many, but a few," answered Blair.

"They said they're worried about the children seeing so much sin. But, in the short time I've been here, I've not seen, nor heard of, any problems with the saloons and their barmaids. Do you worry about what your children see? Can you fill me in on why they feel it's a problem?"

River shrugged. "Growth."

"Growth?"

"With growth comes more people, and more people tend to bring the less adventurous sort. That usually brings women, and with the women comes the beginning of families and the need for law and order. When that happens, moral codes become important, and that often brings churches. With the churches come good people—but along with those good people come those who become too judgmental, like the Hilda and Bertie types."

"I understand that, but like I said, I haven't seen any SIN-FULNESS such as the ladies are complaining of."

"Neither have we," said Blair.

"So, what do you think they want me to do? Do they really want the ladies run out of town?"

River looked over at Blair. She shook her head and gave River a slight smile as she stood up and said, "Okay, I'll leave, so you boys can have your man talk." She turned to Brian. "Just know that many of us women, wives and mothers, may not like it, but understand; there is often a need for the women in places like Miss Lucy's. Like I said, we may not like it, but as long as they are respectful of women with families and they are discreet, we should just live and let live."

She kissed River's forehead and said, "Now, I'll head upstairs to see what Rain is up to." After a nod to Brian, the men were left alone.

Now, Brian gave River a questioning look. "What was that all about?"

River took a moment to look over toward the stairs, then smiled. "I was sure lucky to find a woman like Blair." He breathed a contented sigh, then turned to Brian and said, "Let me remind you about something you will have to do once you're married with a family. It's all fun and games until they hit puberty."

River smiled and continued saying, "Prior to that it's bedtime stories, sled rides, Easter Bunny and Santa Claus. Lots of fun and myths. When puberty hits, they need information about changes to their bodies. That usually stimulates lots of questions of who, what, why, how, when and where. Blair handled it with Rain and I talked with the boys."

Brian nodded. "Yeah, I remember when my dad had that talk with me." Chuckling, he said, "I think he was more embarrassed by the subject than I was. I already knew some things from my older brother."

"Yeah, it's a one-of-a-kind conversation and the part I found the hardest was to impress upon them the importance of handling it responsibly, like respecting women and the difference between love and need."

"You sound like my dad."

"You and I know that with the pleasure of sex comes possible complications. For instance, shot gun weddings, years of child support and disease." Both men paused to reflect on all that had been said.

After each had downed a little more beer, River went on. "Blair took care of everything with Rain and whatever she told her, Rain must have handled it well, because she's still my little girl. As for my boys, while I didn't tell them the possible advantage of having a first time with a woman who knows how to show a man a good time in bed, I made them aware of it. I cautioned them about being careful, but when the need becomes too strong, it's a good way to satisfy the head between their legs and allow their thinking with the head above their shoulders to return."

"Well said. Close to what my father told me."

"So, as far as the local ladies at places like Miss Lucy's, I think that along with young men, this area is full of single men, of all ages, with needs. And as long as it's kept in adult establishments, I think the morals posse should leave them alone."

"Have Mac and/or Marty frequented—

"Don't know. Don't ask. Did you tell your father about your first time?"

Brian laughed. "Touché." He saluted River with his beer, then took a drink.

River did the same. "But, here's something to think about. And, it needs to stay between you and me, because I'm sort of snitching on my brother Patrick."

"You have my word."

"Let me just say, that when Pat was nineteen, and I was eighteen and we went off to college, neither of us was a virgin. And just to clarify things, before leaving for college, neither of us had been away from Dawson since we were babies."

Brian nodded. "I get it. Believe me, I understand these women serve a purpose. And, from what you're telling me, they keep it in an adult-only area, so townsfolk can only see what's going on if they go to the bars. But when these women aren't working how do they shop or enjoy some time outdoors?"

"Other than maybe a little heavy with their makeup, they dress properly, stay with each other and avoid most contact with the townsfolk."

"So, your family has never had a problem with them?"

"Well, my mother was not happy about her cousin Peggy owning a bar and tried for years to get her to sell it. But Aunt Peggy would have none of it. Story goes that when she inherited the bar ...from her... her... hell, I'm not sure... she was married to Big Jim Thornton or not but, he did leave her the saloon when he died. Rumor has it, she immediately told the barmaids that they were on their own. She wanted no money from them, other than rent money for the rooms upstairs where they lived. What they did in those rooms was their business and as long as it caused no trouble in the saloon, she would leave them alone to live on their tips and the salary she paid them. If they offered their bodies for money, Aunt Peggy stayed out of it."

Brian shook his head. "Your family is amazing. Mining, flying, salooning, fishing, law-enforcement," he paused, "did I skip anything?"

"No, I think you got it all."

As Brian drained the last of his beer, River did the same, then asked, "Want another one?"

"No," said Brian. "But I want to thank you for being so candid. Unfortunately, our talk has pretty much confirmed my thoughts on the issue. Like I said, I've seen no problems, nor have I been called to any situation for what Hilda and Sadie are worried about."

"Like I said, busy bodies."

Brian decided to change the subject. "How are things going out at the mine? Still busy?"

"More than ever."

Their conversation continued as they covered the family mining, Brian's settling in, and how the kids were doing. Brian had just stood up and was saying goodbye when Blair came back into the room.

"Leaving?" she asked.

"Yes, I have to get a good night's sleep so I'm alert to handle all the crime in this town."

She laughed as she swatted his shoulder. "Well, come around any time. We'd love to have you join us for supper any night."

"I'll remember that," Brian said his goodbye and headed back to his apartment.

Brian spent the weekend, typing up his weekly report to mail to Devon, reading, taking long walks and having his evening meals at The Nugget. Again, no calls for his service as a CMP.

After his supper on Sunday night, he decided to stop by a couple of the local saloons. After visiting two of them, he realized Sunday was probably not the best night he could have chosen to check them out. He ordered a bottle of sarsaparilla at each one, then stayed long enough to finish it off and have a brief conversation with the bartenders.

He was not approached by any of the barmaids who serviced the tables where poker was being played. As he exited the second bar, he turned toward his apartment, then decided it was time to check out Miss Lucy's. While he wouldn't mind seeing Malie, he hoped it was River's aunt Peggy he could talk with. He'd met her over the holidays, but places like Miss Lucy's were not a popular topic at family doings.

Walking into Miss Lucy's he was surprised to hear the sound of a piano and to see twice the number of customers than at either of the previous bars he'd visited. Checking out the workers as he headed for the bar, he noticed several barmaids and the elderly piano player. Behind the bar was Peggy's husband Elmer, but no sign of either Peggy or Malie.

"What'll it be Constable?" asked Elmer, as Brian took a seat at the end of the bar.

"Sarsaparilla," said Brian.

"Good choice. My favorite," said Elmer. As he set the bottle and a mug down, he asked, "So, are we passing inspection so far, Constable?"

Brian smiled. "Am I that obvious?"

"Naw, just been expecting you to check us out. Surprised it took you this long."

"Been busy setting up the office and getting a feel for the townsfolk and the area in general." Elmer nodded. "But," continued Brian, "I was really hoping to have a chance to talk with Mrs. … ah, Miss… ah—

"Mrs. Martin, Mrs. Peggy Martin."

"Sorry, yes, Mrs. Martin." Elmer cocked his head to the door at the end of the bar. "She's in our apartment having tea with Malie as they go over our needed supplies list. Want me to let her know you're here? She won't mind. Like I said, we been expecting you."

"No, I don't want to interrupt their work."

"Might as well get it on, Constable. Grab your drink and follow me." He led Brian to the door. As he opened it, he called out, "got a visitor."

Both women were seated at an oak table in what looked like a dining room. Elmer led Brian into a room furnished with a sofa, a padded rocking chair, round coffee table and a radio that served as a shelf for an ornate shaded lamp.

In the dining area, along with the table where the women were seated, was an oak China cabinet stacked with dishes. In addition to the chairs where the women sat, were two extra oak chairs. The door to the kitchen resembled a swinging saloon door.

Peggy was on her feet wearing a friendly smile. "Constable, so nice to see you."

Brian returned her smile. "Thank you." He nodded at Malie who briefly nodded, then looked back down at the list they had been working on. "I didn't mean to interrupt."

"Nonsense," said Peggy who turned to Malie. "Dear, would you go refresh our tea and get a cup for the constable." She looked up at Elmer. "Are you busy out there or can you join us?"

"Not too busy, but I need to be out there to keep an eye on things." He turned and headed back into the bar.

"Have a seat, Constable," said Peggy as she sat back down. Once Brian had complied, she asked, "So how can I help you?"

Brian decided honesty was the best policy, and he felt the woman probably already knew about Hilda and Sadie's complaint. "Mrs. Martin, I–

"Please, Peggy—I'm still adjusting to the Mrs. thing," she said, laughing.

"Okay, Peggy, thank you." He paused as Malie came back into the room with a tray holding a tea pot, cups, sugar and cream.

Peggy poured him a cup of tea. "Sugar, cream?"

"No, just the tea will do."

Once everyone had their tea, Malie returned to focusing on the supply list.

Brian took a sip of his tea, then began the reason for his visit. "Peggy, I had a visit on Friday from two citizens. They voiced concern about what the children are being exposed to due to certain things going on in the local saloons."

Peggy nodded. "Yes, I know how Hilda, Sadie and several other ladies feel about certain things."

It did not surprise Brian that Peggy knew their names. "I'm sorry, but I can't confirm or deny the names you've given."

"I understand." Peggy took a sip of her tea, then asked, "So, Constable, you've been here a few weeks. I'd like to know how you feel about it. And, more importantly, how you interpret the law with respect to what goes on in the saloons, especially mine."

"Personally, I've not noticed any laws being violated. I have checked the laws of Canada, the Yukon Province, and the Dawson Creek laws and nothing seems to stand out as illegal. I have an appointment to meet with the town mayor tomorrow to get his thoughts on the matter, both legally, and from a neighborly standpoint."

Peggy smiled. "This is good news. I've always tried to stay within the law, but once the CMP presence arrived, I must admit I've been concerned about how things would be interpreted."

"Well, right now, I don't have any plans to change anything. But, understand, my final decision will wait until I've met with the mayor."

The door to the bar opened and Elmer called to Peggy. "Need your help for a minute."

"Be right there," answered Peggy as she got to her feet and headed for the door. "If you have anything else, just check with Malie. She's in charge when I'm not here." And she was gone.

As the door closed, Brian looked over at Malie who still had her head down appearing to check things on the supply list. At first, he was annoyed that she was ignoring him, but the attraction to her stirred his curiosity. He wanted to know about this woman.

"So," he began, "at times, you're in charge? Does that mean you're a manager of some sort?"

"I suppose so," she replied curtly.

"I understand you are originally from Hawaii. Quite a change. How do you handle the cold," he smiled teasingly, "let alone the fact that pineapples are a rarity in the Yukon?"

His tease brought her head up, and she glanced at him. His smile caught her off guard for a moment and she smiled back. "Very funny," she managed to say, then refocused on her paper work.

From his first meeting with her over the holidays, there was something about her, something that seemed familiar, that brought with it an attraction. Now, her smile stirred something in him he hadn't felt in a long time, if ever.

But she was a mystery. She worked in a saloon, he'd seldom seen her in conversation at the holiday gatherings, she avoided looking directly at people, and yet she had won Peggy's confidence to manage Miss Lucy's.

Yes, a mystery. He needed to find out the reason for all her reticence.

"So, you manage the bar at night?"

"Sometimes."

"You're aware of what goes on upstairs?"

She raised her head and glared at him. "I live upstairs, so yes, I'm aware of what goes on." Her glare lasted a moment or two, then she looked down. "It's none of your business, so leave us alone."

Before he could answer, Peggy came back into the room. As she sat down, she smiled at Brian. "Some customers are hard to please. One of the old-time miners likes the way I make his miner's mud. He says I'm the only who puts in the right amounts of coffee, bourbon and beer."

Brian grimaced. "Somebody would actually drink that?"

Peggy laughed. "Only the old timers who've been up here for years seem to favor that concoction." She noticed Malie was still focusing on the list. "So, Constable, was Malie able to help with any other questions you have?"

"Yes, she pretty much concurred with what you already told me." He stood up. "I want to thank you for your time. If my conversation with the mayor tomorrow goes the way I think it will, nothing's going to change regarding Miss Lucy's or any of the other saloons."

Peggy stood up and walked Brian to the door. "Thank you. If I can help in any way dealing with anything, don't hesitate to let me know."

"I appreciate that," said Brian, then he turned to look back at Malie. "It was nice meeting you again, Malie."

"Goodbye, Constable," said Malie without looking up.

Brian turned and headed back out into the bar area.

As the door closed, Peggy sat back down at the table. "Did I miss something?" she asked Malie.

Malie looked up. "No, I think we got everything." She ran her finger down the list.

"I'm not talking about the list. Why did you seem to be avoiding the young constable?"

Now Malie stood up. "I wasn't avoiding him. I just wanted to be sure our list was complete." She walked over to the door. "If it's alright with you, I'm going to go upstairs to my room and freshen up, then I'll go relieve Elmer."

Peggy's gut told her there was more than Malie was letting on, but obviously the girl was not ready to share. "That will be fine."

Malie stepped back into the bar. After a quick glance toward Elmer at the bar to be sure Brian was gone, she hurried up the stairs and made her way to her room. It was early in the evening and

Sundays were days of rest for the barmaids so things were pretty quiet.

She refreshed her make-up and patted a few stray hairs into place. She hoped that slipping into her work mode would ease her concern about a certain memory brought to mind when meeting Brian at the family Christmas gathering. A threatening memory that could expose everything and with that the loss of her new lease on life.

After a final look into her mirror, she headed downstairs. The big grin on Elmer's face at seeing his replacement arrive made her smile.

He met her at the end of the bar. "Crowd dwindled when Cyrus' piano shift ended. If the place empties before midnight, go ahead and close up early."

"Thanks, Elmer. I'll take it from here. Go enjoy what's left of the night with Peggy."

He kissed the top of her head as they exchanged places behind the bar. "Have a good night," he said as he opened the door to join his wife.

"You, too," said Malie as she picked up a dish cloth and started wiping down the already clean bar.

Peggy had never hung a clock anywhere in the saloon. She said it was the last thing people out for a good time needed. However, she did keep a small wind-up clock next to the cash register so she would know when they were approaching closing time and she could announce the last call for drinks.

Malie checked the clock and found it was almost nine-thirty, almost three hours until closing time. A quick look around the saloon, showed only five people. Three men were playing poker and one couple sat at a table near the small raised area where the piano sat. Just then, the couple got up, and the woman led the man up the stairs.

During the hours the saloon was open, the girls and their johns could come and go using the saloon stairs. However, when the saloon closed, the doors at the top of the stairs were locked and the johns had to exit via a staircase that led to a door with an exit to the alley behind the saloon.

After watching the couple disappear, Malie wandered over to the poker players to see if any refills to their drinks were needed. None were ordered, but Malie could see that the game was about over. She headed back to the bar and took a seat to wait.

Without anything to keep her busy, her mind traveled back to the few minutes she had been alone with Brian. *Bad timing. And of all the johns, why did you have to show up here in Dawson. Why?*

Malie shook her head in wonder. Her chance to start over was now at risk. Sure, a couple of the Dawson residents knew of her past. Most, even the barmaids in Miss Lucy's, just thought that she was a friend of Patrick and Kathleen Finley, who had invited her to experience the beauty of snow country as compared to the humid islands.

That she had been a prostitute was known only to the MacDonalds and the Finleys and her coming to Dawson was a thank-you from Patrick and Kathleen for coming forward with the truth about the death of the man Patrick was accused of killing.

In the two years she had been in Dawson, she had mostly kept to herself. Other than working in Miss Lucy's, her only time anywhere in the community was buying paint supplies at the local general store and finding places along the river that motivated her discovery that she loved to paint.

Over the years, she had frequently sketched things with a pencil. But, after arriving in Dawson and witnessing the beauty of the mountains, rivers and wild life, she brought a paint brush and began to capture that beauty on various rocks. Now, she had the general store order canvases for her. She hadn't shown them to anyone, just stowed them carefully in her small room above the bar.

A male voice caught her attention.

"Thanks for putting up with us," called one of the poker players to Malie as he stood up. He was joined by the other two in clearing the table of chips and money.

The man who had spoken walked over to the bar and handed the chips and the cards to Malie. "Have a good what's left of the night. See ya soon." He smiled, as all three men stepped out into the night.

Malie hurried over and locked the doors. After washing the glasses from the poker players and turning out most of the lights, she headed up the stairs, locked the doors to the stairs and went to her room. Once she was in her nightgown and snuggled into her bed, she closed her eyes and looked forward to a good night's sleep.

Unfortunately, ever since Christmas, a face appeared. With it, the concern about how the owner of that face could crumble her new beginning here in Dawson. He was even more handsome than she remembered. And, so very respectful.

She sighed and forced herself to relax into her bedding and relive the memory of that night. Her last thought before falling asleep was a 'thank you' as a door closed.

***

At ten o'clock the next morning, Brian arrived for his meeting with Mayor Alexander Webb. The secretary showed him into a small office. The short, portly, bald mayor stood up and welcomed Brian with a handshake, then directed him to a chair in front of his desk.

The office was small and contained only the desk, two file cabinets and four chairs. It strongly resembled Brian's office, but this one had a large window allowing the mayor a view along Front Street.

"So, young man, how are you settling in, here in our little Paradise?" asked Webb.

"Just fine, thank you, Sir."

Webb smiled. "How about we get a little less formal? Let's be Brian and Alex."

Brian nodded his agreement.

"I'm sorry I haven't been by to check out your new office," said Alex. "I was down in the States for the holidays and just got back last Friday."

"So, I heard. Hope you had a good time."

"As good as can be expected when spending time with the in-laws," he said.

"Wouldn't know about in-laws, but being with family is a blessing."

The man studied Brian for a moment, then nodded. "Yes, it is. But, that's not what you're here about is it, Brian?

"No, it isn't." Brian brought the mayor up to date on his visit from Hilda and Sadie. A brief overview of his conversation with River about growing up in Dawson and his visits to the saloons, ended with his conversation with Peggy Martin.

"My, you've been a busy man."

"Well, the way I see it, when a citizen makes a complaint, it's my responsibility to check things out."

"And, what did you find out?"

"Well, first, I checked and found out what the barmaids are doing is not against the law."

"I've tried to tell our local righteous ladies that very same thing."

"I know. They shared your thoughts on their complaint with me."

"Did they also share the fact that as their mayor, while I may agree with their concern that now there are children here in Dawson who could be exposed to the town's night life, there is no law against it. Also, it does bring miners into town and they spend money at many local businesses other than the saloons and the ladies."

"Yes, they did share that."

"Well, Brian, after all the investigation you've done, what is your take, I mean your legal take, on the matter of their complaint?"

Brian smiled. "I have found no wrong doing. I intend to contact Hilda and Sadie and tell them of my findings.

Alex laughed. "Oh, I would love to be there for that."

His words back fired on him. "I think that would be a great idea. I'll set up a meeting with them. Do you want it here or over in my office?"

Alex shook his head. "Walked into that one, didn't I?"

Brian smiled. "Yes, but it would be better if they fully recognize that the law and city government are in agreement on this matter. And, if they question it in any way, we would both be there to address any issues they have with our decision."

The mayor nodded. "Yes, you're right. Let's do it in my office." He looked at a book on his desk. "I have some free time tomorrow afternoon. After you talk with them, let my secretary know the exact time."

He stood up and walked around his desk to stand next to Brian. "Looks like the CMP has done right by Dawson." He offered his hand. "Glad to meet you and have you here in Dawson."

Brian shook his hand. "Thank you. I'll be in touch." He headed back to his office feeling good about how he was settling into Dawson and of his positive interaction with many of the locals. Sitting down at his desk, he picked up the phone.

"What can I do for you, Constable?" asked the operator.

"I need to get a message to Mrs. Brown and Mrs. Anderson."

"Let me connect you to Hilda," said the operator. "Hold on a minute."

Brian tensed up a bit dreading the coming conversation.

"Here she is," said the operator

"Constable? This is Hilda. You wanted to talk to me?"

"Yes. I did some checking around regarding the situation you and Mrs. Anderson brought to my attention last Friday. I have talked with the mayor. Now, we would like to address your concerns, with both of you, in his office tomorrow afternoon at three o'clock. Will that time be convenient?"

"That will be fine. I'll let Sadie know."

"Thank you. I'll see you tomorrow. Is there anything else?"

"No, thank you, Constable. I'll see you tomorrow."

The line was quiet for a moment or two, then the operator came back on. "Hilda has hung up. Is there anyone else you'd like me to ring up, Constable?"

"Yes, can ring up Mayor Webb's office."

When the mayor's secretary came on, Brian gave her the time for tomorrow's meeting.

As he hung up, he finally relaxed back into his chair. With nothing else going on, he began to put together some words for tomorrow's meeting. Knowing that no matter how he phrased it, the ladies would not be pleased. He needed to let the topic rest for now.

All of a sudden, a thought came to mind—his horse. Devon had arranged for Ranger, Brian's assigned horse in Whitehorse, to be shipped up to Dawson. It had arrived a week ago, and he'd only ridden it once or twice since then. Grabbing his hat and coat he headed out for the stable.

More snow was in the forecast starting the next day, so he needed to give the animal some exercise while the terrain was still relatively snow and ice-free. Brian was glad to see Ranger was being well-cared for, and needed no grooming from him. Still, Brian always enjoyed giving the animal a light brushing before and after his rides.

After some idle chat with the stable man, he saddled up and rode along Front Street and up the gravel road toward Midnight Dome. It was too late in the afternoon to ride all the way to the top, but Brian was about a quarter of the way, when the sun dipped out of sight and daylight was quickly turning into a long, dark, Yukon night.

A Stranger in Town

WHILE BRIAN WAS ON his ride, a stranger was coming across the Yukon River on the ferry. Jake Bennett had come over three thousand miles to collect on a debt. But more importantly, he was here to assure his control over the pussies who worked for him. He was the one to decide when one could quit being a money maker for him, not any one of them.

Jake owned a bar in Honolulu, Hawaii and one of his pussies had disappeared one night. She had been working for him to clear up a loan of a little over $3,000 he had given her to clear some personal issues. To provide her with a way to pay the money back, he had arranged for her to waitress in his bar and to please his male customers in one of the six rooms in the back of his bar.

He paid the rent on her small apartment and supplied her with seductive clothing. After servicing a man, she was to give Jake most of the money the customer paid. Jake also demanded that she give him additional money as payment on the loan.

Truth was, she had more than paid the money back, but he never let her know because her beauty and her aura of innocence made her his best money maker. The lonesome military men, so far away from home, seemed to find something familiar about the young girl. His other stock of girls had none of that and didn't bring in half the money that Malie did.

It had taken him awhile, and quite a few bucks, to learn of Malie's connection between the Marine killed behind his bar and the man accused of killing him. It took some persuasion and more bucks to get a bellhop from the hotel where Malie had stayed to tell him about her visits from various military men, included the man who had been accused of the murder.

Jake got the name of the man, Patrick Finley, and learned that he owned an airline in the States. He also learned the man was married, and that he and his wife had taken Malie to the man's home town in Dawson.

As the ferry began docking, Jake was standing at the railing. His eyes raked the small village. He eventually focused on Front Street and identified a couple saloons. He smiled. It may have cost him some bucks and some time, but he was about to get back his big money maker. And, more importantly, he would gain back the complete fear and obedience of all his pussies.

***

Brian was trotting along the river bank about a half mile from town when he spotted a figure just ahead of him. As he got closer, he could see it was a woman, and she seemed to be packing things into what looked like a large picnic basket. She must have heard him coming because she turned toward him. It was Malie.

A smile spread across his face and he slightly quickened his pace. He called out. "Malie, is that you?"

"Yes," she answered as she was closing the basket. She turned and lifted what looked like a picture frame off a large rock.

"Need some help?" he asked as he rode up and glanced down at what looked like a painting. It was already too dark to be sure, but it looked like a boat–a ferry. He dismounted and came over for a better look. "Did you paint that?"

"Yes," she replied curtly as she began walking back toward town.

"Wait, let me help you." He began to follow her.

"Thank you, but there's no need." She kept walking.

They walked along in silence for a few minutes, then Brian decided this was silly. "Malie, why do you seem angry with me. What did I do to bring this on?"

Malie slowed her pace somewhat. "It's nothing, Constable. I just want to get home before it gets any darker."

Brian took a chance. He reached out and grabbed her arm. "I don't believe you. I must have done something. You won't even look at me."

Still looking toward town, Malie took a deep breath. If I tell you what you did—you'll remember that I was just a piece of trash. "I'm sorry. I'm hurrying because I'm scheduled to work in just a few minutes." She wiggled free and continued walking.

Brian watched her go. After shaking his head in frustration, he called out to her, "Okay. Have it your way. Just know, if you ever decide that I'm not the bad guy or whatever you think I am, you can come talk to me anytime."

Malie just kept walking. Her life here in Dawson had been the best two years of her life. She knew if she stopped and turned to him the memory of that night might come back to him. He was her past and her past needed to stay in the past. To do that, she knew she had to avoid Brian. As Miss Lucy's came into view, she hurried her pace and was soon safely out of his reach as she fled up the saloon stairs and into her room.

As she disappeared into the saloon, Brian kicked at the dirt, then looked at Ranger. "Women!" The horse neighed, as if agreeing, which made Brian laugh. He swung back into the saddle and trotted as he got back on his horse and trotted on down to the stables.

***

At a little before three the next afternoon, Brian entered the mayor's office.

His secretary pointed to the mayor's door. "He's waiting for you. I'll show the ladies in when they arrive."

"Thank you," said Brian. He was surprised to see the four chairs had been moved over near the large window. A small round table, laden with a teapot, four cups and a plate of cookies had been placed between the chairs and the window.

"Welcome, Brian," said the mayor, closing the door then directing Brian to one of the chairs. "Glad you came a little early." Once they were both seated, he asked, "Would you like a cup of tea?"

"No, thanks. Just want to get this over with."

The mayor uttered a short laugh. "Brian, you and I both know that no matter what we tell the ladies, it won't be over."

Brian smiled. "I can hope."

"I like your positive attitude young man."

After a short knock on the door, it swung open and the secretary announced the new arrivals. "Your Honor, Mrs. Brown and Mrs. Anderson have arrived."

"Thank you, Nellie. I'll call you if I need you. For now, please close the door," he told his secretary. Wearing a big smile, he turned to Hilda and Sadie. "Ladies, thank you for coming." He pointed to the chairs. "Please take a seat."

Brian managed a smile. "Good afternoon, ladies."

Once everyone was seated, Alex offered the ladies some tea and cookies.

Hilda spoke for them. "No, thank you, Your Honor." Sadie shook her head in agreement with Hilda.

Alex took the time to pour himself a cup of tea, then began. "You, of course, know Constable Stockton."

"Yes," said Hilda. "Good afternoon," she managed with no emotion on her face.

"Well," Alex went on. "I want you to know that I have been most impressed with how quickly and thoroughly our young constable takes his responsibility to our small community here."

"That is nice to know," said Hilda.

Alex turned to Brian with a hint of mischief in his eyes that was not lost on Brian. "Constable, please share what you have learned with these ladies as to your investigation into their concern."

Brian nodded, then began. "The first thing I did was read through my Canadian Law Dictionary. I also checked the Dawson City by-laws. What I found regarding prostitution is that it is against the law for any individual, often referred to as a pimp, or any establishment to offer sexual services for a shared price between the pimp or establishment and the person providing the sex."

This brought smug smiles to the faces of Hilda and Sadie. They disappeared as Brian went on. "However, it is not against the law for a person to offer sexual favors for a price as long as that person is not sharing that price with any pimp or establishment."

The smiles had quickly turned to indignant pursed lips. "So, while the mayor and I understand your concern about what the youth in Dawson may be exposed to, the ladies in question are not violating any laws."

Hilda glared at Brian. "This is not the answer we expected from law enforcement." She glanced at the mayor, then continued. "We already know Mayor Webb's interpretation and acceptance of the disgusting situation of these hussies."

Sadie added, "We felt that by having law enforcement here in Dawson, our young would be protected from the lack of morals these hussies are exposing them to. We raise our children to respect women and that sharing of bodies comes only in the marriage bed. Now, we are being told that what is going on is legal. Shame on you, Constable."

She turned to the mayor and said, "It seems you have convinced Constable Stockton to side with you. Shame on you, Mayor Webb."

The mayor set his tea cup down and shook his head. "Ladies, ladies, please don't be so harsh with our young constable. He is only doing his job to know the laws and to enforce adherence to those laws."

Hilda and Sadie stood up. "This is not over," said Hilda directly to Brian. "We are going to write to your superior in Whitehorse. I'll need his name and address."

Brian stood up and faced the ladies. "His name is Sergeant Major Devon MacDonald. Just address it to him at RCMP Station, Whitehorse, Yukon. He has been a CMP for many years and will diligently look into your stated problem."

Looking a little surprised at the quickness and thoroughness of Brian's response to her request, she managed a slight stutter. "Ah .... Ah ... why thank you, Constable."

After a nod at Brian and a scowling glance at the mayor both ladies left the room.

The mayor's secretary appeared at the door. "I see the ladies left a bit unhappy. Do you need me to do anything?"

"No, thank you, Nellie. Please close the door."

Alex got up and walked over to one of the file cabinets and pulled out a bottle of Hudson's Bay Scotch Whisky. He held the bottle out to Brian. "I think you need a shot of this. I know I do." He poured two glasses and handed one to Brian. Once they were again seated, Alex took a drink of his, then smiled. "You did good, young man. You did good."

"Why don't I feel like I did good?" Brian shook his head, then took a drink of the whisky.

"There was no way we were going to please them. I was hoping that once they realized that their civil servants, and the police were in agreement, they would give up. Obviously, they are not going to let this matter drop." He shrugged, took another sip of his drink, then asked, "How do you think your sergeant major will handle this?"

"He will tell them the same thing we did."

"Well, then I think we just have to wait and see." The men silently nursed their drinks as they worked at putting the situation on a back burner of concern in their minds.

Eventually, Brian drained his glass and stood up. "Well, nothing more we can do. I'm sorry we couldn't bring the ladies to accept, if not like, the law regarding their complaint. Guess you're right, we wait and see how they react to my sergeant major's response."

Alex finished his drink, then got up and extended his hand to Brian. "Like I said, well done. Glad to have you here in Dawson."

Brian returned his handshake and headed back to his own office. On his way, he passed a man who seemed vaguely familiar. He realized he'd only been in Dawson a short time and there were probably many citizens he had not seen as yet. Still, there was something about this man that stood out. They shared a nod, but both walked on without any conversation between them.

When he got back to his office, he had the local operator place a call to Whitehorse. Within minutes, Devon's voice came on the line.

"Brian, surprised to hear from you. Is there a problem?"

"Not a problem, Major, just want to give you a heads up about a couple of local ladies who want some action taken that would be against both Canadian and local law." He went on to give Devon the details about his initial visit from Hilda and Sadie and concluded with the meeting he and the mayor had with the ladies. "So, they wanted your address so they could contact you and have you prove the mayor and I were wrong."

"I'm assuming you did your duty and double checked the laws and have taken the proper legal approach to the problem."

"Yes, sir."

"Well, I thank you for the heads up. Once I get their letter, I'll double check your findings, then let them know they must abide by what you and the mayor have told them."

"Thank you, Major."

"So, Brian how are you settling in?"

"It's a pretty peaceful town. I've been called out to one fight, but it was all solved without any charges by the time I got there. So, I'm faced with lots of police material reading and patrol walks around the city."

Devon laughed. "Sounds like Dawson alright. Seen much of my family?"

"Now and then."

"Tell them I said hello."

"Will do."

"Brian, are you having any second thoughts about this assignment?"

Now Brian laughed. "Occasionally, but overall, I really like the area, the people and the opportunity to prove that your trust in me for this assignment was the right choice."

"Never had a doubt. Now, is there anything else?"

"Not that I can think of. Oh, be sure and tell Ron and Dave that I said hello."

"They're sitting here listening and are sending you a hello wave. It was good to hear from you."

"Good to talk to you, too, Major."

"Now, if there's nothing else, I reckon I'll be signing off now."

"Can't think of anything, so I'm signing off, too."

Brian hung up the phone and leaned back in his chair. He liked many things about Dawson. He thought about the folks he chatted with as he did his patrol walks, and the scenes of the eagles along the dock area and his rides up Half Dome on Ranger.

Then an image came to mind, bringing on a smile. Somehow, someway, he was going to establish, at the very least, a friendship with Malie. Yes indeed. He stood up and checked the clock—it was almost five. After checking in with the local operator to let them know his whereabouts for the evening, he headed up the hill to take River and Blair up on their "supper any night" offer.

***

Earlier, when Bennett shared a nod with Brian, he had been surprised at how young the constable looked. As he headed for a bite to eat at the Nugget, he hoped it would be his last encounter with the local law. His intent was to collect his prize pussy and head back to Oahu as quickly and uneventfully as possible.

After a delicious supper of roasted moose, mashed potatoes and fresh green beans, he leaned back in his chair to savor his third cup of some strong, black coffee. The waitress had tried to strike up a conversation several times, but eventually got the hint that he wasn't interested in chit-chat from his terse answers to her questions about where he was from, how long he'd be in town and such.

After registering at the local hotel as Bill Jones, Jake had talked with the hotel clerk before going to supper and learned when the gold rush was on in the 1890s the population was over 10,000. The city had been alive with many businesses and too many saloons to count. Now, with a population about 1,300, businesses had little competition—and the need for nightlife had dwindled—the saloon count is down to three or four.

When Jake asked in which saloons could a man find some satisfaction. The clerk assured him that in addition to some entertainment and drinks, they all offered the comfort of ladies, for a price.

Now, as he sipped his coffee, he decided he'd hit one every night until he found Malie. He would only do one saloon a night so he wouldn't miss her. Because, if she hadn't changed, she'd be the busiest woman in the saloon's hallway area and not so much in the front area waiting tables. Also, he didn't, and wouldn't, ask for Malie by name. It could draw unwanted attention to him. It was also why he registered at the hotel as Bill Jones. He didn't want anyone to remember him after Malie disappeared.

The Gold Rush Saloon was just down the street from the Nugget. After draining his coffee cup and paying his bill, he chose it as the first place to start his search. After ordering a beer at the bar, he took a seat at a table near some poker players. As he nursed his drink, he tried to appear interested in the poker game, but his mind was on three women who took turns now and then bringing fresh drinks to the players and to several other tables of one or two men.

Two were young, skinny and seductive, a blond and a brunette. One was a gaudy redhead. She was a little older, with a few wrinkles at the corners of her eyes and mouth, but her full figure offered enormous breasts. Eventually, he watched the young blond lead a middle-aged man down a hallway similar to the hallway in his bar back on Oahu. Over the next hour, he watched the redhead make the trip down the hall.

When one of the men playing poker stood up and said he was done for the night, Jake was asked if he wanted to play. He liked the game and was relatively good at it. For the next couple hours, he kept his eye out for any sign of Malie, but enjoyed the ups and downs of some light gambling. When asked his name and where he was from, the players seemed easily satisfied with his brief answers of Bill Jones, and he was taking the long way home to the States, after being discharged from the Navy.

Eventually, the bartender announced closing time was approaching, so no more drinks. One more hand was dealt, then the players cashed in their chips and headed on home.

Back in his hotel room, he slipped out of his clothes and settled himself on the lumpy mattress. The Gold Rush Saloon had not brought Malie back into his life, so it was on to saloon two the next night. His last thoughts of the day, as he pulled the blankets tight around him, was hope of finding Malie in saloon two. He'd had enough of this terrible cold and wanted to be back in the sultry warmth of Oahu.

***

Despite not getting to bed until after midnight, Malie was up and dressed by eight a.m. She had joined Peggy and Elmer for a light breakfast of one egg, a slice of bacon, and a slice of sourdough toast. She filled them in on her uneventful evening while bartending last night, then headed out to the general store.

She was in need of some personal products and she was hoping the order she'd placed over a month ago for a couple more 10x14 canvases and two paint tins had arrived. The owner brightened her day when he told her everything had come in on the ferry yesterday. He bagged all her purchases and said he looked forward to her next visit. Malie thanked him and made her way to the door. As she was about to open it, a man walked by.

The door windows were painted with *Kramer's General Store* and underneath the name was *Open 7 Days a Week–6 a.m. to 8 p.m.* Seeing in or out was impaired somewhat by all the wording, but Malie had no doubt about who had just walked by. She opened the door a crack and watched him continue on down the wooden sidewalk until he entered the Nugget.

"Need help, young lady?" asked the store owner.

"No," said Malie as she tightened her grip on her shopping bags. "I'm fine." She forced a slight smile. "I'm still not used to the weather here and wanted to be sure it hadn't started to snow."

"Always a wise thing to do this time of year," he said as he held the door open for her.

Grateful that Miss Lucy's was in the opposite direction from the Nugget, she was almost at a lope by the time she entered the saloon. Peggy was having a cup of tea at the end of the bar with Elmer.

Fortunately, the saloon was still empty. "I'm back," said Malie as she rushed toward the stairs without another word.

Peggy and Elmer watched her until she was out of sight. "Did she seem upset about something?" Peggy asked Elmer.

"Well, she's never been a big talker, but it did seem like her feathers were a tad ruffled," agreed Elmer.

"Mornings are usually her good times. I do enjoy our morning tea breaks, especially when Blair and Abby can join us."

"The girl has come a long way from the nervous, young thing your nephew, Patrick, brought here at the end of the war."

"Yes," Peggy smiled, "she has."

"And, she turned into a big help for you and me around this place."

Peggy nodded and finished off her tea. After glancing toward the stairs, she lifted the still-warm tea pot off the hot plate and set it on a tray with a couple of cups, some fresh cream, and sugar.

Elmer smiled. "Not going to let it rest, are you?"

"She needs to accept that she's not alone. That people care. That when something is upsetting her, she can talk to us."

Elmer patted Peggy's hand. "If you, or she, needs me for anything, I'm here."

Peggy smiled. "Thanks, love." She kissed his cheek and headed up the stairs. Her knock at Malie's door was accompanied by, "Malie, it's Peggy. May I come in?"

Malie opened the door quickly. "Of course." Peggy almost never came upstairs. It was her barmaids' living quarters, and as long as they caused no trouble, she respected their privacy. Malie looked down the hall, and other than Peggy, it was empty. "Come in," Malie said. "Is there a problem?"

"No problem," answered Peggy. "It's just that we haven't had a morning tea break for awhile, so I thought maybe we'd have one today." She set the tea tray on a petite, circular table near the window. In addition to the table, the tidy room offered a small chifforobe, a chair by the table and a single bed. After pouring two cups and adding the amount of cream and sugar each of them liked, she handed a cup to Malie, then took hers and sat on the edge of the bed. She motioned for Malie to take her tea. "So, how did your trip to the store go?"

Malie took her tea, swallowed a sip, then sat down. "It's good." Peggy's unusual visit still had Malie on alert. She decided to keep her answers short due to a feeling Peggy was angling for something, some information. The women sipped at their tea.

Finally, Peggy's dislike of undercurrents could take no more. She set her cup on the table. "Malie, what happened at the store? You are obviously upset about something. Was something said or done to you because you work for me?"

Now, Malie set her cup down. "No, Mr. Porter is always nice and polite."

"Then what? Whatever you tell me will stay between us. But I really think you need to talk to someone. Keeping things bottled up is never a good thing."

Malie just shook her head. "Peggy, I appreciate your concern, but—

"Malie, stop with the buts. Please, tell me what's bothering you. If I can't help, at least I can listen and let you know someone cares."

"Oh, Peggy, I know you and Elmer care about me. Your kindness in accepting me is something I will always cherish."

"Then let me help. Look, is it something to do with Constable Brian? His presence always seems to make you nervous. Was it him that said or did something to you this morning?"

"No, I didn't see the constable this morning." She sighed, set her cup down, then began to circle the small room. After a couple minutes, she faced Peggy. "You've never asked me about Hawaii or anything about my life there, but I think you know I was … I … …"

"Yes, I know about the prostitution. That was then. My nephew Patrick, and his wife Kathleen, saw something good in you, and they were right. Once I met you, I somehow felt you were intent on putting that type of life in the past. And, if anyone, including the constable, doesn't believe it, that's their problem, not yours."

Malie sat back down, refreshed her tea, then began. "I know, and I appreciate your support and belief in me. It's a major reason I've managed to turn my life around."

Peggy smiled.

"Now, as for the constable, we have met before."

"What? You two knew each other in the past, before coming to Dawson?"

"I wouldn't say knew, but we do have a past. The first time I met him at Christmas, memories flooded over me." She paused.

"Memories?" Peggy's eyes began to widen in understanding. "Oh, my. As I recall, he was in the Navy over in Hawaii. Was he ... I mean did—

"Yes." Malie finished her sentence. "Yes, he was one of my many johns. It was only once, and he had been drinking a bit, so I don't think he really remembers me. Still, I think there's something in the back of his mind that stirs when he sees me."

"But you remember him?"

"Yes." Malie sat back in her chair and actually smiled. "You see, he said 'thank you,' and kissed the top of my head as he said 'goodbye' and left. No one had ever done that before or since. He treated me with respect, no matter the reason we were together."

Peggy was at a loss for words, both due to the smile on Malie's face and wonder that she could remember a single one of her johns so clearly.

"So, now you know why I avoid facing and talking with the constable. I don't want him to remember."

As Peggy tried to think of a way to respond, a thought crossed her mind. She said the constable had not been the reason she had seemed upset earlier when she returned from the general store. She reached across and gave a pat to Malie's hand. "Patrick and Kathleen were so right in seeing so much in you. You are amazing. "

"I see it more as lucky," said Malie. "Lucky that Patrick and Kathleen offered me this opportunity and then having you trust me."

"Well, I think amazing is the right word." She insisted, then risked turning this sharing moment into a pull back by Malie. "I'm glad you trusted me enough to share all this about the constable. But it doesn't seem to explain what upset you on your trip to the general store. If it wasn't the constable, what upset you?"

Concern replaced Malie's smile. "It's another part of my past. This one remembers me. This one can only be here to settle a score."

"A Score?"

Malie nodded. "As I was about to leave the general store, a man walked by. He didn't look into the store, just walked on looking at something up the street. Despite all the painting on the door, I was able to get a good look at him. His name is Jake Bennett, and he was the owner of the bar I worked at in Hawaii."

"He was the owner, so he took a portion of the money paid to his barmaids for sex?"

"Yes. And for me it was more complicated. You see, I owed him some money. In fact, that's how I got started being a prostitute."

"You took money from a pimp?"

Malie nodded. "Like I said, it's complicated."

Peggy poured another couple of cups of tea. "I've nothing to do, so tell me how all this came to be."

"It's a long story."

"Like I said, I've nothing to do. Tell me."

Malie took a sip of her tea and said, "My mother's parents were killed when she was a teenager. A religious sect stepped in and offered her security as part of their family. The sect was male-dominated, and each male had multiple wives. My mother was given to one of them. She was barely seventeen when I was born. Children didn't live with the parents. We lived in a dormitory environment and were cared for by elderly women of the sect."

"Why would the local authorities allow a teenage orphan to be put into such an environment?"

"It was never explained to me. It was all I knew as a child and I was well cared for. Our mothers were allowed to visit us for an hour or so each day, but we never lived with our parents.

Right after I got my first period, I was presented to the leader of the sect at a ceremony attended by his male followers. The leader christened me into adulthood by taking my virginity, then giving me to one of the male attendees who was now considered to be my husband.

I was taught that it was a female duty to please men. I was subjected to training as to what a female must do to please a man. Once I was considered properly trained, I was forced to attend nightly offerings of drug laced tea. After the tea, several of the men would load their wives into a van and drive downtown so their females could please many males.

I didn't know our husbands were paid for the use of our bodies and that the money they were paid is what funded the sect." Needing a moment to gather her thoughts and to try to dull the memories she had allowed to surface, Malie paused and sipped at her tea.

"Oh, my lord," said Peggy. "I can't even imagine. Dear girl."

"It was horrible. My only consolation is that the drugs made everything a blur at times."

"How long did you have to obey that horrible man?"

"Fortunately, not long. One night, the police busted into the hotel where we were being used. The adults, men and women, were arrested. Minors were taken to a local orphanage for temporary safety. The home grounds of the cult were also raided and although the leader and a few men were able to get away, the sect was dissolved and all minor children, boys and girls, were permanently placed in a local orphanage."

"But you said you had a mother. Why were you not given to her?"

"I don't know why, but I did find out that within weeks after the raid, she was found dead of an overdose in a downtown alley."

"Malie, how sad and how horrible for you."

"Yes, she was free of the cult, but sad that she was already so lost that she couldn't make it on her own. But, for me, I hardly knew the woman."

Peggy's heart was breaking for Malie, but she could not think of any words of consolation. She reached over and patted Malie's hand. "If all these memories are too hurtful, I will understand if you want to stop now."

Malie pulled her hand free and reached for a sip of her tea. "These are things I've lived with my whole life. Actually, letting you know my complete past is kind of a relief. I have been so grateful for your confidence in letting me work here in your saloon, but I was always worried about how you would feel about my past." She paused as her eyes met Peggy's. "I trust you and know what I've told you will stay between us." She managed a slight smile. "Well, at least between you, me, and Elmer."

"Yes, it will."

"Now, I need to tell you about Jake."

Peggy nodded for her to go on.

"At the orphanage, we were given housing and food, but it was a cold dormitory environment. Some of the babies and small children were eventually adopted out, but most of us teenagers were considered too damaged to ever be adopted. When I aged out at eighteen, they found me a job and placed me in an apartment with a few other girls from the sect. Life seemed to be improving for me and I actually enjoyed my work in a local garment factory."

"Yet, you ended up working for this Jake."

"Yes. He employed a boy I fell in love with. His name was Kahale, and he was about two years older than me. Like me, he was a child of the sect. He and a couple other boys had managed to escape when the police raided the children's dormitory. They found work loading ships down along the docking area during the day and cleaning saloons at night. On my way home from work one day, we ran into each other. We began dating. He came down with what we thought was a bad cold, but eventually he was diagnosed with tuberculosis and could no longer work. I moved in with him so I could care for him, but we just couldn't afford any medical treatment."

"So, this Jake owned a saloon where Kahale had worked nights."

"Yes, and when Kahale's care took so much of my time, I lost my job. Jake began stopping by and brought us food now and then. When we got an eviction notice, Jake loaned us the rent money and offered to let me waitress at his bar at night after Kahale went to sleep to make some money. Without medical treatment, Kahale went downhill fast and eventually died. Again, Jake came through with money to have him buried."

Peggy shook her head. "This Jake wasn't being a good guy with a loan; he was putting you in a bad situation to repay his loans."

"He began pressuring me to pay him back. I wasn't able to get my factory job back, so I kept working at his club. Eventually, his demands became more insistent, and he told me how I could increase my salary at the bar by entertaining men. Knowing about the sect, he knew I had been trained in how to please men, so it didn't take long before he added that as a way to pay back my debt. Now, I suspect he's here to drag me back to Oahu to repay my debt."

"What a pig!"

"Yes, a pig. However, because he had me prostitute myself, I witnessed how that horrible Marine died and was able to prove Patrick was innocent of his death. It brought Patrick and Kathleen into my life. And for that, I'll be forever grateful."

Both women seemed at a loss for words as each processed all that had been shared.

Peggy spoke first. "Malie, my cousin Abby, has always been my hero, and I've always been amazed at what she has done with her life. But, you, young lady, are even more amazing. Thank you for sharing your past with me. I can only hope sharing it with me," she smiled, "and Elmer, will bring you some peace of mind."

"It has," said Malie.

"Now," said Peggy, "about this pig, Jake! We can't let him harm you in any way."

"I'm not sure what we can do."

"Well, it seems to me, the first thing we need to do is let Constable Brian know—

"No," Malie grabbed Peggy's hand. "No, I don't want him to know about my past."

Peggy knew the constable needed to know what this Jake was planning, but Malie was at a breaking point. She could see concern in Malie's eyes that by sharing her past, this new beginning would all come to an end at the hands of this horrible man.

"Malie, I think you're wrong. The constable should know." To stop Malie's response, she hurried on. "But I'll respect your wishes. However, will you do me one favor?"

Malie looked leery. "And that favor is?"

"I want you to stay out of the bar. Elmer and I will handle things for the next few days. We'll figure out something tell anyone who asks where you are. For now, I'll take you up to Abby and Tommy's place to stay until the monster gives up his search and leaves town."

"Do you think Abby and Tommy will be okay with me staying at their place?"

"Yes. You'll be more than welcome. Now pack what you'll need. I'm going downstairs to tell Elmer we're going up to Abby's, then I'll be back and we'll head on up there."

"Aren't they at the mine right now?"

"Yes, but Gertie will be there."

"You're sure Abby will be okay with this?"

Peggy smiled. "It's what we Finleys do. We take care of each other." She grabbed the tea tray and opened the door. "Now pack." And, she was gone.

Peggy rushed downstairs, glad to see the saloon still fairly empty. Elmer was sitting at the end of the bar reading one of his dime-store westerns.

As she placed the tray on a shelf behind the bar, Elmer asked, "Everything okay?"

She touched his arm. "No, it's not."

Elmer's eyebrows arched. "What?"

"I can't talk now. I'll tell you later. Right now, I need you to stay here and if anyone asks for Malie, tell them she's taking a couple of days off."

"What?"

She came up on her toes and kissed his cheek. "Trust me. I'm taking Malie up to Abby's. Once I get her settled, I'll be back and fill you in on everything."

Elmer managed a slight laugh. "Never a dull moment with you." He affectionally swatted her bottom. "Now git. I'll take care of everything."

Peggy laughed as she headed for the stairs. When she entered Malie's room, the girl was ready to go.

***

Gertie was kneading bread dough when they arrived.

After a quick hug to the woman who was like a dependable, old aunt, Peggy got right to the point of why they were there. "Gertie, Malie will be staying here for a few days. What room do you want her in?"

Having worked for the Finleys for some time, strange arrivals and departures were quite common, so Gertie asked no questions. She told Peggy what room to settle Malie in, then began brewing a pot of tea. The tea and cups were on the table, along with a plate of scones, when the women came back into the kitchen.

Seeing Gertie's offering, Peggy smiled. "How thoughtful of you. But I can't stay."

Gertie nudged one of the chairs out with her foot and gave Peggy that motherly look that always brought any one of the Finleys to pause under a touch of guilt. She was more than an employee, she was family.

The look made Peggy sit down and motion for Malie to do the same.

Once Gertie had joined them, Peggy said, "I just have a few minutes. I need to get back to the bar."

Gertie's face filled with an exaggerated look of concern. "Something's wrong with Elmer?"

Peggy shook her head and smiled. "No, he's fine."

Gertie smiled back as she poured tea into each cup. "That's good. Now, can you tell me anything about why Malie is going to be our guest for a few days?"

"Without details, let's just say someone is in town that she doesn't need to see. In fact, should anyone ask about Malie, tell them she has gone back to the States."

Gertie nodded. "Well, that little tidbit certainly has my curiosity working overtime." Seeing Peggy about to speak, she hurried on. "But I'll wait until you're ready to share more." She handed Peggy a scone. "Now, finish your tea, then you can head back to your bar. Malie will be safe here."

Once Peggy was gone, Gertie could see Malie looked a little uneasy—she decided the girl needed a distraction. "Well, this isn't getting the bread kneaded and supper started. Could you help me a little? Maybe knead the bread?"

"I don't know how," said Malie.

The rest of the day was spent with Gertie getting Malie involved in various kitchen duties.

***

When Peggy arrived back at Miss Lucy's, one of their bartenders had reported for his shift at the bar. After greeting him, Peggy motioned for Elmer to follow her into their apartment. Wasting no time, Peggy filled him in on Malie's past and her concern about this pimp arriving in Dawson.

Elmer, normally a calm, collected non-judgmental man, had moments of rage listening to what Malie had endured. When Peggy ended with Malie's refusal to get the constable involved, Elmer nodded. "No need. When Tommy and River get back from the mine tonight, we'll go deal with this disgusting creature. He'll—

"No! You're so angry and I know Tommy and River will have the same reaction. I'm afraid of what you three would do if he refused to leave Malie alone. Besides, other than you and I, she made me promise I would not tell her story to anyone."

"But we can't allow this bastard to endanger Malie in any way."

"I agree."

"But, dearest, if we do nothing she remains in danger."

"Not if we take this to the constable."

Elmer raised his eyebrows in question, then got up and walked over to the liquor cabinet. He retrieved a bottle of port and a couple shot glasses. He poured a shot for each of them, then motioned for Peggy to join him at the table.

"I thought you said she doesn't want him to know."

Peggy bit at her bottom lip as she sat down. She hated the thought of going against Malie's wishes. After a sip of the port, she began. "Malie has history with the constable."

"How so?"

Peggy filled Elmer in on what Malie had told her about her time with him. She closed by touching Elmer's arm. "She wants to keep her past behind her. She doesn't think he remembers her, and she wants to keep it that way."

Elmer finished his drink. "That poor girl. She feels damned if she allows the constable to get involved and get rid of this Jake, but she's surely damned if the bastard isn't taught a lesson about how us Dawson folks take care of each other." He shook his head from side to side. "So, how do you intend to get the constable involved despite what Malie wants?"

"I'm going to tell him that there's a man named Jake who's staying at the hotel and he has me concerned. I'll say I heard he's a pimp who runs girls in his bar in Hawaii, and he's in town to lure one or two of our local gals to work for him."

Elmer nodded. "Might work."

"I've got to try."

"You have always been a haven for anyone in trouble. But it seems to me this Malie has found a place in your heart."

Peggy finished off her shot. "Yes, she has. Maybe this is what a mother feels like when her child needs help."

"You would have been a great mother."

Peggy stood up and lightly kissed Elmer. "Thank you. Now, I'm going to talk to the constable. God help me, I hope I'm doing the right thing."

Elmer stood up and gave her a quick hug. "Only time will tell. But no matter how it goes. I'll be here for you."

***

On her way to the constable's office, Peggy spotted him walking along the river bank. At the next boardwalk down to the docks, she headed down to catch up with him. When she was close enough, she called out, "Constable!"

He turned and smiled, then waited for her to catch up with him. "Nice to see you, but surprised. Kind of cold for a river walk today."

Peggy gave a slight shiver, then smiled. "Yes, but after living here in Dawson so many years, I'm used to it."

He lifted a small bag and pointed to a nearby bench. "I was about to have lunch, but if you need me for something, it can wait."

"I do need to talk to you about something, but I can tell you as you have your lunch."

They made their way to the bench and sat side by side. Brian opened his lunch bag and took out a ham on rye sandwich. "From The Nugget."

Peggy nodded. "Looks good."

"Want half?"

She laughed and shook her head. "No, thank you. But go ahead and enjoy."

Brian took a small bite, then asked, "So, what do you need to see me about?"

She paused for a few moments to silently ask for Malie's forgiveness, then began. "As the owner of a local saloon, I hear a lot of gossip. Several drinks often loosen lips and things are said that I normally ignore as I dilute future drinks served to the owner of those lips."

Between chews, Brian laughed. "Good idea."

"Well, last night I heard some disturbing gossip and decided not to ignore it. See, it involves some of my barmaids."

Brian's thoughts immediately went to Hilda and Sadie. "Well, if this is about certain claims by a couple local citizens, you've nothing to worry about. I checked things out and found nothing illegal is going on. You've nothing to worry about."

Now Peggy laughed. "I see Hilda and Sadie are still fighting city hall."

"Yes, and unfortunately for them, the law is now in agreement with the city."

"It won't silence them."

"I suppose not. But, does this solve what you wanted to talk to me about?"

"No. The gossip I heard is about a man who has come to Dawson with an ulterior motive that could have terrible consequences for some of our local barmaids."

Brian chewed up and swallowed the last of his sandwich. He wiped his lips with a napkin, then tossed it and the sandwich wrapping in the lunch bag. "What kind of consequences"

"He owns a bar in Oahu, Hawaii, and pimps out his barmaids. I'm worried he might be looking for new girls for his bar."

The word Oahu surprised Brian and set his mind back to his shore leaves spent with his Navy buddies relaxing in the vast array of bars so friendly to servicemen, away from home and family. He finally managed to ask, "And you think he's here to find girls for his bar? Why here in the Yukon? Seems like he could find women a little closer to Hawaii, maybe California."

"Maybe he thinks our local barmaids would be more receptive to the lure of the warmth and excitement of the Islands."

Brian shrugged, but asked, "Do you know the man's name and where I can find him?"

"Yes. His name is Jake Bennett, and he's at the hotel. Can you run him out of town?"

"Whoa, slow down. I appreciate that you are concerned for the welfare of your barmaids, but I'll have to talk with him, and have him explain his reason for being in Dawson in the middle of winter. That in itself might be why some idle gossip guessing got started."

Peggy shook her head. "No. I don't think it's guessing. It's been my experience that gossip usually has some measure of truth. And, if he really is in town to find new women to pimp, I want him stopped."

Brian stood up. "I agree."

Peggy stood up. "Thank you."

As they began walking back toward the Front Street, Brian asked, "Can I ask you something about Malie?"

Peggy tensed, but kept walking. "Malie?"

"She seems upset with me and I have no idea why. I tried to talk to her the other day. I'd been out exercising my horse when I saw her loading up a basket. I think she was painting something."

"Yes, she's very talented and loves the scenery here in the Yukon."

"I offered to help her carry things, but she barely answered me, and just hurried away saying she needed to get to work."

"She's a very private person."

"I know about her past. I know why she was in the alley and saw what happened to the man your nephew Patrick was accused of murdering."

Peggy stopped and looked up at Brian. "She's trying so hard to put that behind her. Her lack of confidence keeps her from trusting people. Don't take it personal. She's very private with most people."

Brian nodded. "I can understand that. It's just there's something about her." He started walking again. They had reached the Front Street. "As to your concerns about this Jake fellow, I'll check into it and get back to you as soon as I know anything."

"Thank you. Please do it soon. I worry about the girls." She turned to head back to her saloon, then turned back around. "And, as for Malie, just give her time."

For a few minutes, Brian watched her continue on down the street, then began walking back to his office. He thought about what Peggy was concerned about and smiled. Actual crime was at a minimum here in Dawson. If it wasn't for the saloons and their workers, he'd have nothing to do.

***

After checking for any messages and adding his conversation with Peggy to his daily log, Brian decided to do some checking on this Jake Bennett.

The hotel lobby was empty when Brian arrived. The small area had a built-in desk on one side of the door entrance and a long wooden bench on the other side. The aisle separating the two was no more than twenty feet wide. Straight ahead was the entrance to a hallway and a flight of stairs to the second floor.

Brian walked over to the desk and was about to tap a bell in front of a sign saying to ring it for service when a gray-haired woman came out of the hallway.

"Can I help you, Constable?" she asked as she proceeded into the desk area and faced Brian.

"Yes. Do you have a guest here by the name of Jake Bennett?"

Without checking the register, she shook her head, "No. No one here by that name."

"Are you sure? Could you check the register?"

"Certainly, Constable, but it won't make a difference." She opened the hotel register and checked a couple of pages, then looked back at Brian. "No, no one named Bennett is registered." She extended her hand. "Constable, we've yet to meet, but my name's Silla Kunuk. Me and my husband, Tulok, own the hotel. We know who our guests are."

Brian nodded as he shook her hand and attempted an apology. "Sorry, Mrs. Kunuk. I didn't mean to be rude."

"That's alright, Constable. You being new in town, I figure you're still getting acquainted." The woman smiled. "Now, what made you think this Bennett fellow was staying here?"

"I had a query from a citizen about his purpose here in Dawson and wanted to talk with him." An idea came to Brian. "Do you have many male guests that are alone without family?"

Without checking the hotel register, she nodded. "A few. Did this citizen say when this Bennett fellow arrived?"

"Didn't say, but I got the feeling it was very recently."

"Well, I have three. One is a geologist who comes up a couple times a year to stay for a week or so to meet with the local miners about what they come across in their digs. The second one is from the Yukon Road Works Department. He comes up every summer and winter to check on our streets. Now, the third one arrived two days ago on the ferry. Never saw him before. Name is Bill Jones. Not much of a talker. Just says he's doing some traveling around."

"How long is he staying?"

"He's paid for a week. Should we be worried? Think he's going to cause any problems?"

"No. It's just part of my job to check out strangers in town."

Silla smiled knowingly. "Right. A constable comes around asking about one of our guests for no reason at all."

Brian shook his head in an effort to dispel her concern. "Just responding to a citizen's query." He smiled. "I haven't been here long, but I already sense how Dawson locals are protective of their beautiful city and strangers make them curious."

Silla laughed. "Yep, we can be pretty nosy."

Brian chuckled. "Not nosy, like I said, curious. I guess I'm beginning to feel like a local because now I'm going to be nosy. Is this Mr. Jones in his room right now?"

"No, he left around lunch time and hasn't come back yet. You want to leave a message for him?"

"No. In fact, don't mention to anyone that I was here asking about that Jones fellow. I'll just keep checking around town."

Silla raised her eyebrows. "Now, you've stirred my nosy up."

Brian laughed. "Nothing to worry about. But, if I find out anything juicy, I'll fill you in on it. Deal?"

She nodded. "Deal."

"Thank you, Mrs. Kunuk. I'm glad we met. Sorry I didn't get by sooner."

"That's okay. Welcome to Dawson and come by anytime."

Brian smiled his thanks and left to continue his search for this Jones fellow. He decided to check out The Nugget. The lunch hour crowd had thinned, and he was pleased to find the eatery had few customers. Sitting at the end of the counter, he spotted the man he had passed on his way to the mayor's office yesterday. A quick scan of the other diners, assured Brian they were locals that he had seen once or twice before around town.

He took a seat two stools down from the man. He gave a slight wave to the owners Jessie, who handled the ordering, food serving and money, and her husband Stoney, the chef. Jessie pointed to the coffee urn and Brian nodded yes.

As Jessie set his cup down, she asked, "Another sandwich, Constable?"

"Not hardly. I'm still full from lunch and your delicious ham on rye. Just the coffee will do."

"Glad you liked it. Just signal if you need a coffee refill." She headed toward the cash register for a paying customer.

Brian, trying to appear casual, glanced over at the man. Again, he felt like he had seen him somewhere other than here in Dawson, but couldn't put it together. His uniform was probably making the man nervous so Brian smiled. "Great food. I eat here a lot."

The man nodded. "Yes, great food."

Brian extended his hand. "I'm the local constable, Brian Stockton."

He shook Brian's hand. "Bill Jones."

"Don't think I've seen you before. New in town?"

"Just visiting."

"Don't get many visitors this time of the year. Staying long?"

Jones stood up. "Haven't decided yet."

"Well, if there's anything I can help you with, don't hesitate to stop by my office."

Jones nodded and headed toward the cash register. Once he had paid and left, Brian waved to Jessie for a refill of his coffee. As she was pouring, Brian asked, "That gentleman come by often?"

"Last couple of days for supper and sometimes lunch."

"He say anything about why he's in town?"

"Not much of a talker. I tried a couple times, but he seems to want to be left alone. He okay? Do we need to keep an eye on him?"

"No. Had a local citizen wondering why he was in town, so I thought I'd check him out. Just trying to stay busy and do my job of protecting the citizens of Dawson." He downed the last of his coffee and stood up.

"Supper tonight? Our special is spaghetti and garlic toast."

"Sounds good, but think I'll have supper with River and Blair."

"Tell 'em I said hello."

"Will do. See you tomorrow," he said as headed out the door.

***

As he left The Nugget, Jake took a quick glance behind him to be sure he wasn't followed. There was something about that cop that made him uneasy, like he had been checking him out. Jake shrugged his shoulders as if to shake his concern away. He hadn't done anything to bring attention to himself. He quickened his pace to the next saloon.

Entering the Puffin Pub, he found it almost empty. Then he remembered that it was only late afternoon, so the night crowd was yet to arrive. Taking a seat at the bar, he ordered a whiskey. "Kind of quiet in here."

The bartender was enjoying a cigar and talked around it as he answered Jake. "Yeah, it's a weekday. Also, it's kind of early. It'll liven up a little later."

Jake nodded, then turned to assess the goings on. No poker games being played, just a few tables where two or three locals were sitting around sharing some BS. He was about to turn back to his drink, when he saw a fiftyish-looking man exiting a hallway as he was buckling his belt. He stopped at the bar and was handed a beer, then he headed toward a table with two men who also looked like they were in their fifties.

"Yer turn, Ed. Just give her a couple minutes."

"No, can't wait. I gotta get home for supper or Sadie will be on my ass." Chubby, overall clad Ed stood up and headed down the hall.

"What's that all about?" Jake asked the bartender.

"Really? You have to ask?"

Jake shook his head and smiled. "Just surprised you've only one working gal."

"Got two barmaids coming in shortly for the night crowd."

"They work the back room, too?"

"If needed." He had just spoken, when two skimpily-clad women came out of the hallway.

Both carried a little extra weight and their dye jobs, one blond and one brunette, were in need of touch ups. The blond began to wander around the tables asking if anyone needed a refill on their drinks. The brunette came to the bar and took a stool two down from Jake.

"Small crowd," she said to the bartender.

"It'll pick up," he said over to one of the tables. "Hey, Mac, piano time."

After a brief wave, one of the table sitters got up and headed over to a piano set up against a wall. As his fingers hit the keys, three middle-aged, overall-clad miners arrived. Within the next half hour, a small blue-collar crowd of men filled most of the bar stools and several of the tables.

Jake kept hoping Malie would wander into the room, but shortly after Ed had come out of the hallway and said goodbye to his buddies, another woman came out of the hall and stood at the end of the bar. The bartender wandered over and took a small stack of bills from her hand.

As he tucked it in his apron pocket, the woman said, "Looks like Lily and Bea will be able to handle things tonight. I'm going to the kitchen to have some of that left over stew for supper, then call it a night."

"You did good today, Roxie."

As she turned around, she spotted Jake. "He been here long?" she asked the bartender.

"Half hour or so. Know him?"

"Not yet," Roxie said with a laugh, then sauntered over to Jake. "Hi, stranger. Looking for some fun?"

"Thanks for asking, but no." Jake stood up and said, "I'm leaving." He nodded then headed for the door without a look back.

Accepting that he probably wouldn't find Malie here, and because it was still early, he decided to try another saloon. A block down the street, he spotted Miss Lucy's Saloon.

When he entered, he noticed it was a little more crowded than either of the previous bars. He found a stool at the bar and sat down. There were two bartenders behind the bar—one was a man—the other a woman. Both carried a little age, but moved with experience in keeping the drinks coming. Hearing men call for refills is how he learned her name was Peggy.

His ears perked up when a man at the other end of the bar asked, "Where's Malie tonight?"

"Gave her the night off," said Peggy as she sat a beer in front of the man. "Besides, I just know you all miss me."

"You betcha, sweetie," he laughed, then looked over at the male bartender. "Damn shame old Elmer here broke our hearts when he made an honest woman out of you."

Several of the men laughed and saluted Elmer with their beer bottles. The miner sitting next to Jake called for another beer.

As Peggy turned toward the miner, something about the man sitting next to him led her to believe he was this Jake fellow. She smiled at the miner. "Coming right up, Zach.

When she turned to grab the beer, she spoke softly to Elmer. "I'm betting that's Jake at the end of the bar next to Zach."

Elmer took the bottle from her hand and headed toward the miner. "Here ya go, Zach." Turning to Jake he asked, "What'll it be stranger?"

Jake nodded at his neighbor's bottle. "Same as him."

Peggy was idly wiping the bar as she laughed and chatted with the old timers that lined her end of the bar, but she was fully aware of the interaction between Elmer and Jake.

As Elmer set a beer down in front of Jake he asked, "So, where ya from, stranger?"

"Here, there, and everywhere."

"In town for long?"

"Don't know. No plans."

Zach entered the conversation. "No plans? Lucky you. No wife, no kids?"

"No," was Jake's answer.

"Well, pardner, if you're looking for work, they're hiring out at my mine. Pay's 20 bucks a week."

"No thanks," said Jake.

Zach shrugged his shoulders, downed his beer, then stood up. "Must be nice to be able to turn down a job. Enjoy your stay in Dawson, stranger." He flipped a coin for his beer toward Elmer. "Thanks. Gotta head on home. Woman's got supper ready. See ya tomorrow."

"Another beer," called out a customer to Elmer.

"Duty calls," said Elmer. "Like Zach said, enjoy your stay here. Come by anytime." Then he headed back towards Peggy.

Glad to be left alone, Jake nursed his drink as he sat hoping that Malie would make an appearance. Time passed slowly as Jake listened to conversations around him, watched a couple of card games in progress and listened to some pleasant piano music. Only one waitress served drinks to the tables and she never left the saloon with anyone. Malie never showed up.

Because it was a week night, the crowd began to thin around nine and by quarter to ten only Jake and two other men sat at the bar.

Elmer raised his voice a little and called out, "Okay, fellows, drink up. Shutting down at ten."

Jake left a couple small bills next to his last beer bottle and got up to leave.

Elmer waved his goodbye. "Come back anytime, stranger."

Jake left along with the remaining two men. They headed up a street toward the housing part of Dawson while Jake went back to the hotel, frustrated at not making contact with Malie. But, at least, he now knew where to find her, so it was just a matter of time.

The hotel lobby was empty and only dimly-lit by a small wall lamp. A sign on the register desk said the hotel was closed, but if a room was needed, knock on the door to room 100, just down the hall. Jake went straight up to his room with a sincere hope that he'd find Malie tomorrow at Miss Lucy's and get the hell out of this cold, barren city.

*****

While Jake visited the bars and finally located where he would be able to find Malie, Brian lucked into a chance to actually talk with her. After leaving the Nugget and his encounter with Jake Bennett, Brian headed back to his office to check for messages, fill out some paper work and do some reading on the law in the Yukon. A glance out the window told him evening was approaching. He decided to log out for the night and take River and Blair's offer of supper, anytime.

When he arrived, Blair opened the door. "Brian, what a nice surprise. Come on in."

Upon entering the house, Brian explained his visit. "Thought I'd take you up on your supper offer." As she led him into the kitchen, he was surprised by how quiet it was and no sign of any food cooking.

"Sit. I'll pour you some coffee."

"Where's River?"

"Probably on his way home from the mine." Blair placed a cup of coffee in front of Brian, then sat down with her own cup.

Brian checked his wrist watch and found it to be just a little after five. "Guess I'm a little early for the supper." He smiled sheepishly, then added, "You did say I could join you anytime."

"Yes and …" She was interrupted as River and their oldest son entered the kitchen.

"Brian," said River. "Nice surprise."

"Hello, Constable," said Mac.

"Brian came by to take us up on our supper offer," said Blair.

River laughed. "Of all nights."

"What?" Brian looked from Blair to River. "You don't eat on Mondays?"

"We do," said River, "but you picked our monthly supper night with Mom and Dad."

Brian stood up. "Oh, sorry."

"Hey, sit back down. I'm going to run upstairs and clean up, then you can join us. They'll be glad to see you again. Those Christmas get-togethers were crowded and busy. I'm sure they'd be glad to get a chance to visit and hear about how you're adjusting to Dawson."

"I don't want to intrude."

"Please?" asked Blair.

Again, Brian looked from Blair to River and back."

River laughed. "She seldom takes no for an answer. Come on. It'll be just Blair, Rain and me. The boys have their own plans."

With his other choice being the Nugget, Brian decided he'd accept their offer. "Okay." He sat back down.

"Great. I won't be long."

At a little before six, Abby opened her front door with a big smile for her son, his wife and her granddaughter. Her eyes lit up when she spotted Brian.

"Mom," River kissed his mother's cheek. "You remember Constable Brian?"

"Of course. Good to see you. Hope there's not a problem."

River laughed. "Only that he's hungry, like me, Blair and Rain."

Abby shook her head as she jokingly slapped her son's shoulder, then stepped back to allow everyone inside. "Come in, come in. Supper's almost ready." She waved for them to follow her into the front room where her husband Tommy and their guest Malie were already enjoying the warm, cedar scented fire ablaze in a large stone fireplace. "Have a seat everyone, while I go and let Gertie know to set another place at the table."

Tommy stood up and shook hands with Brian. "Nice to see you, Constable."

"Nice to see you too," said Brian. "And please... I'm not on duty, so I'm just Brian." He smiled, then focused that smile in Malie's direction. She gave him a quick nod, then looked away.

"Well, good to see you. Have a seat and what can I get you to drink?"

"You're having?" asked Brian.

"River and I always have a beer and the ladies a glass of red wine." He put his arm around Rain. "And our granddaughter here has cola." He kissed her forehead then released her to sit near her mother on the sofa.

"Beer sounds good," said Brian.

Once everyone had their drinks and were enjoying the fireplace ambiance, Abby rejoined them. Talk began covering the weather, Brian's adjustment to living in Dawson and some attention to Rain and how school was going. Eventually, Gertie announced supper was ready.

Brian was seated next to Malie at the table. Friendly conversation continued over the delicious pot roast, mashed potatoes, and mixed vegetables. At one lull in the conversation, Brian turned to Malie who had not yet directly looked at him, nor said a word.

"So, Malie, I understand you are a talented artist."

Keeping her head down, she answered, "Yes. I paint."

"I hear you do some colorful capturing of the scenery around Dawson."

"Yes."

"I'd like to see your work. I'm looking for some color in my drab apartment."

"I'm not ready to show them."

Abby noticed how uncomfortable Malie seemed and broke into the conversation. "So, Brian, after listening to what you've been up to since being assigned here, you sound like maybe living here could be something permanent."

Brian smiled. "In my line of work, who knows. But, yes, I believe I could make this my home."

That brought everyone back into the conversation. Once the dessert of homemade apple pie was finished, the women helped Gertie clear the table, wash dishes and clean up the kitchen. The men went to enjoy the fireside warmth of the living room with glasses of port to finish off the evening. When the kitchen work was done, River, Blair, and Rain said their goodbyes.

Brian stood up as if to join them, but he turned to Malie. "May I speak with you about an investigation I'm working on? It has to do with some things that might be happening in the local saloons and especially Miss Lucy's."

Malie slowly got to her feet, still avoiding looking at Brian. "I'm sure I'd have nothing to offer."

Abby came over and touched Malie's shoulder. "I think you should talk with the constable. I have always wanted Peggy to get rid of Miss Lucy's, but it means the world to her. Please, if it will help Peggy in any way, talk to Brian."

Tommy walked over and offered his hand to Brian. "Glad you could join us for supper. And, like River's offer, you're welcome to supper here any night. But, now, it's been a long day, so I'll say goodnight."

Brian returned Tommy's shake. "Thank you. Appreciate the offer."

The men nodded, then Tommy turned to Abby. "Coming?"

Abby gave a final squeeze to Malie's shoulder, said goodnight to Brian and headed up the stairs with her husband.

Brian took a chance and walked over to stand next to Malie. "Please. Can we talk?"

Feeling trapped, Malie's mind swirled trying to come up with a reason to get out of this room, this house. She should never have let Peggy talk her into leaving her room at Miss Lucy's.

"Malie?"

Her mind came back to earth. Without facing Brian, she answered. "I only bartend for Peggy and I haven't seen anything unusual happening in Miss Lucy's." She was telling the truth because she had only seen Jake on the street, not in the saloon.

"I'm sorry. I couldn't quite hear you." Brian could hear her just fine, but he wanted to somehow cross that line in the sand she had drawn regarding any interaction with him.

At first, Malie's shoulders rose in contention. Then, a picture of Brian flashed before her eyes back when he walked into the Christmas gathering with her saviors, Patrick and Kathleen. For just a moment, she felt like any young girl would feel when a handsome young man smiled her way. But her return smile had been cut short when the memory of their first meeting back in Hawaii surfaced. Now, once again, that memory brought her to turn away and move out of his line of view.

"Look," said Brian, "let the past be the past. I want to talk to the Malie of Dawson, not the Malie of Oahu."

She slowly turned to face him. "You remember?"

"Devon, River's brother-in-law, told me how you came forward to testify for River's brother. That you happened to witness how the man he was accused of killing actually died."

"Then you know what I was doing and why I was in that alley."

"Yes. But, like I said, the past is the past. All I want to talk to you about is a concern brought to my attention by a local citizen."

Malie looked into Brian's eyes. *He doesn't remember being with me.* She took a deep breath and remained facing him.

"What is it you want to know? If it will help Peggy, I'll be happy to answer your questions."

"Thank you." Brian smiled. "What I'm checking out is a report that there is a man in town who is looking to convince some of our local barmaids to come with him to Hawaii to work in his bar. But the concern by a local citizen is that he's really a pimp, and once he gets these girls to Hawaii, he'll force them into working for him as prostitutes."

Malie's eyes widened as she took a step back. *Damn. Peggy said she'd respect my not wanting to go to the constable.*

"Malie?" Brian read the concern in her eyes. "Do you know about this man? I was told his name is Jake Bennett."

Malie fought Peggy's betrayal and managed to set it aside for the moment and deal with Brian's questions. "Yes, I've heard of the man. Who told you about him?"

"I'd rather not identify the citizen who reported the problem. I just want to do my job and keep all Dawson citizens safe."

Malie walked over to the living room window. A full moon was allowing her a view of the moonlit Yukon River rolling along the shores of Dawson, a town she had come to love. Her past haunted her, but she knew there were few secrets in this town. So, in all reality, Malie's past was probably known by almost everyone. And, the only person it seemed to bother was Malie herself. It was time to let her past go and really begin to live for today and, very likely, a good future. She turned around and faced Brian.

"Yes, I know who Jake Bennett is, and I'm pretty sure I know why he's here in Dawson."

Brian cocked his head for a moment in shock. Malie's whole persona had changed. There was still a measure of concern in her eyes, but overall, she looked like someone who had a heavy weight lifted from her shoulders. Like someone exiting a confessional, graced with forgiveness and ready to start over.

"You know why he's here in Dawson?"

"Yes. He's trying to find me."

"You? Not just any barmaid?"

Malie smiled. "Yes, me. And I know it was Peggy who reported him to you."

"And you think this because?"

"Let's sit down. It's a long story." She walked over to the sofa and motioned for him to sit beside her. Once they were both seated, she went on. She told him about Jake being her pimp in Oahu and of her time working in his bar. "But you knew this because of what I saw and how it proved that Patrick did not kill that Marine. I am so blessed to have been given this opportunity to start over so far away from my past."

"Yes, I did hear about your past, but more importantly, I have heard nothing but good things about you here in Dawson. Now, as to this Bennett, how did you find out he was in town and what makes you think he's here for you?"

"This morning, I went to Kramer's General Store. I had ordered some painting supplies and wanted to see if they had arrived. After purchasing them, I was at the door and about to leave when I saw Jake walk by. Fortunately, he didn't see me. After he passed, I peeked out the door. When I saw him enter The Nugget I hurried back to Miss Lucy's. After a quick hello to Peggy and Elmer I hurried up the stairs to my room. Apparently, Peggy could see that I was upset, and she came to my room to see what was wrong." She paused and shook her head. "Nothing gets by Peggy. She got the whole story out of me and tried to talk me into going to you about my concern."

"I wish you had."

"You're right, I should have." A slight smile appeared, and she added, "It seems the Finley family is still looking out for me."

Brian returned her smile. "So, it seems." Then he got serious. "I appreciate your information on this fellow. Now, I have to see how I can handle this. So far, Bennett has done nothing wrong. The most I can do is keep an eye on the situation." He stood up and Malie did the same. "Oh, by the way, you should know he is using an alias around town. He has registered at the hotel as Bill Jones and when asked his name by any locals, that's the name he gives them." He turned to leave, then turned back and said, "Thanks for your input. I'll keep you informed about anything I find out."

Malie touched his arm. "Constable?"

"Yes?"

"Now that you know everything, I don't think I need to stay in hiding. I would just as soon face him and get this over with. I want to go back to my room at Miss Lucy's. I want to go right now. Will you walk me back?"

Brian thought about her request for a moment and decided that allowing Jake to confront Malie might bring this issue to an end more quickly. Still, he wanted to be sure she was safe. "Is that a good idea?" he asked.

"Who knows? But I do know that I'm tired of my past putting roadblocks into my future. I want to face Jake and let him know he no longer has control over me."

"How about I come by in the morning and escort you back to Miss Lucy's?"

"Please. I want to go now. Will you wait while I go get my things?"

"What about the Finleys?"

"I'll knock on their door and if they don't answer, I'll leave them a note. Please."

Brian read the determination in her eyes and had to accept the fact that if he didn't wait, she'd do it by herself.

"I'm not sure I agree, but I'll wait."

She hurried out of the room and was gone less than five minutes. She returned with her valise in hand.

"You told the Finleys?" asked Brian.

She nodded. "Like you, they think I'm wrong."

The streets were deserted as she hurried along with Brian at her side. The full moon provided them with enough light to be able to keep their footing along the gravel road. They passed two men heading up away from the downtown area.

Recognizing Malie, both men smiled and one said, "Missed you tonight. Elmer's smile just doesn't brighten up the place like yours does."

Malie laughed, but kept walking. "See you next time."

"Hope so," said the second man as they continued up the street.

As they turned onto Front Street and headed toward Miss Lucy's, Brian was glad to see the street was empty. Just as they reached the entrance to the saloon, the lights went out inside and outside Miss Lucy's. Malie pushed on the door and it opened almost hitting Elmer who was about to lock it.

"Malie? Is it you?" he asked.

"Yes."

"I thought ... well I ..." then he laughed. "I swear you could be Peggy's daughter. Always expect the unexpected." He noticed Brian. "Constable, is there a problem?"

Brian managed a slight shrug, while Malie walked past Elmer and asked, "Is Peggy still up?"

"Yes."

Malie headed for the door to Peggy's apartment.

"Coming in Constable?" asked Elmer.

"I'd better. At least until Malie explains why she's back."

Elmer motioned for him to come inside, then locked the door. As they passed the bar on their way to join the girls, Elmer offered Brian a drink. Brian declined and followed Malie. She knocked once on Peggy's parlor door, then opened it.

"Malie!" Peggy set down the book she was reading and came to her feet. "Why are you here?" She noticed Elmer and Brian had followed Malie in. "What's going on?" she asked as her eyes darted between Malie and the men.

Malie took one of Peggy's hands. "I told the constable everything. Now, I just want to face Jake and let him know he'll never get me back to Hawaii."

Peggy squeezed Malie's hand. "But I want you safe, out of his reach. Look, I think Jake was in Miss Lucy's tonight. You won't be safe here."

Elmer read the worry in Peggy's face and spoke up. "Peggy, let's all sit down and talk this over." He motioned toward the sofa. "Please."

"Yes," added Brian. "Let's talk about how to handle this."

After a couple moments, Malie led Peggy over, and the two sat side by side on the sofa. Peggy glanced over at Brian as he and Elmer sat in nearby chairs. She turned to Malie.

"You went to Brian?"

"No, he came to dinner at Abby's with River and Blair. When the evening ended, he asked to speak to me." She went on to fill Peggy in on everything that she shared with Brian. "So, I want this over. I want Jake out of town and the fastest way to handle this is to face him."

"Brian?" Peggy's voice reflected her concern.

"She made up her mind to come back here. Do I think it's a good idea? I'm not sure. But this affects her more than anyone, so I think we need to let her do this her way."

"Elmer?" Peggy turned to her husband.

"I think the constable is right and the more I get to know Malie, the more I see traits in her that I see in you. When your mind is made up about something, there's no stopping you. And, it usually works out well. Let's do it Malie's way and just be here to keep her safe."

Brian smiled, then stood up. "Well said." He spoke to Malie. "Now that you're home safe and sound, I'll be leaving. If you need anything, get word to me and I'll be here as quick as I can."

Elmer stood up as did Malie and Peggy.

Malie walked over to Brian and touched his arm. "Thank you for seeing that I got home safe."

Her touch took his breath away and all he could manage was a smile and a nod. He turned at the door. "Goodnight, everyone." Then he and Elmer left the room.

As they walked toward the locked doors, Elmer shook his head and laughed. "Need that beer now, Constable?"

Brian returned his laugh. "Probably, but again I'll pass. I'm going to need a good night's sleep. The next few days may get a little dicey."

At the door, Elmer got serious. "Glad you're in on all this. Thanks."

Brian managed a slight smile. "Keeping Dawson citizens safe, that's what I'm paid to do." He stepped out of the bar, closing the evening with, "Goodnight, Elmer. Probably see you soon."

"Goodnight, Constable."

Brian headed toward his apartment actually feeling pretty good. Malie was now looking at him and talking to him. He wasn't quite sure why that was making him feel good, when this Jake could really mess up her life. However, it was allowing him the chance to spend some time with the beautiful brunette that had drawn his attraction on their first meeting during the Christmas celebrations at the Finley home. He found he was looking forward to tomorrow. This Jake had no idea who he was up against.

***

Once Brian had left, Malie said her goodnight to Peggy and Elmer and went upstairs to her room. Her mind raced with concern about how to handle Jake.

Jake always managed to control her by loaning her money to pay for the needs she could not afford when dealing with Kahale's illness. Then, after he died, she owed Jake so much money she had to keep working to pay off her debt to him.

She shivered and tears threatened at the fear of returning to that life. She wondered how much she still owed him. While working at Miss Lucy's she'd been able to put a little money aside each week and had a small stash of money, she kept in a box in her underwear drawer. Maybe, she could pay him off.

When she thought about how much she had, it occurred to her that Jake had never shared her debt balance with her. Her shoulders rose and her eyes widened at the thought that perhaps it was already paid off and he never told her.

Then, her shoulders relaxed when the thought of who was now on her side. Paid off or not, Brian had assured her he had her back. The law was on her side. As she stretched out on her bed, she let her mind begin a replay of her evening of letting the past go, allowing her to override her concern about Brian remembering what happened in Oahu.

She was finally letting her past go and beginning to look forward to her future. Her last thought before falling asleep was a hope that her future might include Brian.

***

By a little after eight the next morning, Malie was in Peggy's kitchen, having breakfast with Peggy and Elmer.

"Elmer, you make the best French toast."

Peggy smiled at her husband. "Yes, he does. It's why I married him."

Elmer took a drink of his coffee, then raised his eyebrows at Peggy. "That's not what you told me last night."

Peggy laughed.

"All right, you two." Malie stood up and began to collect the dirty dishes. "I think I better leave you love birds alone."

"We'll behave," said Peggy. "Sit back down."

Malie had set everything on the counter next to the sink. She refreshed everyone's coffee, then sat back down. "Let's talk about our schedule for the next few days."

"What's to talk about?" asked Elmer. "One night you tend the bar till closing and I do the day shift, then next day, we switch. Peggy helps out during the busy times."

"But," said Malie, "for the next few days, I will work all the night shifts."

Peggy shook her head, "No, Malie, not the night shifts for a while. It's too dangerous."

Malie reached over and touched Peggy's hand. "I need to do this. I want to do this. I have to face Jake and let him know I'm never going back to Oahu."

"But—

"She's right, dear," interrupted Elmer. "We all need to let this Jake know he's not wanted here. Besides, my bet is we'll be seeing the constable drop by every night." He stood up and continued. "Now, while you ladies clean up my cooking mess, I'll go make sure the bar is well stocked and ready to open."

"Elmer?" Peggy wanted to protest, but his logic rang true.

His answer was to kiss her forehead, then he was gone.

"Malie?"

Malie stood up and also kissed Peggy's forehead, then headed for the sink and the dirty dishes. "It's settled. Come, let's get these dishes done."

Peggy uttered a loud sigh as she got to her feet and went to help. "While I agree you and Elmer are probably right about facing this Jake fellow, I'm still worried about your safety."

"I know. But the sooner I face him; the sooner things will get back to normal."

The women faced each other, then laughed as Peggy added, "Whatever that is here at Miss Lucy's"

They finished the cleanup, then Malie went up to her room. A little after noon, she joined Elmer at the bar. The afternoon went quietly with few customers. One of the barmaids joined them around three. A little before five, Peggy brought out bowls of venison stew and fresh sourdough bread.

The three of them and the barmaid sat at the end of the bar to eat their supper. They had just finished when the first of the evening regulars began to arrive. As Peggy cleared away the remnants of their meal, a poker game started at one of the tables.

Elmer helped Peggy carry things back to their apartment, and the barmaid went to check on the poker players, leaving Malie alone behind the bar. It was a week night, so Malie knew things would be slow. During the next hour, the piano player arrived, along with a couple of regulars who enjoyed his piano playing.

Four young men, barely out of their teens, sat at the bar discussing their work in the mines, sports, and women. Malie filled their mugs when requested, but otherwise stayed at the end of the bar to give them their freedom to talk guy trash.

Hearing the saloon doors creak open, she smiled at the arrival of Brian. When he hung his wool jacket on a peg just to the left of the doors, she was surprised to see him clad in a western shirt, a tan leather vest, Levi denims and cowboy boots. He headed toward the bar and sat down a few stools away from the young men.

She wandered over to greet him. "What can I get for you?"

"Sarsaparilla, please."

As she set his drink on the bar, she smiled. "No uniform. Nice look."

He returned her smile. "Trying for a casual look in case ...well. Thanks." He lifted his glass and took a healthy swallow.

"Thanks for coming. It'll make Peggy and Elmer a little less tense. They aren't happy about me tending the bar."

He smiled. "It's my job." He got serious. "I understand how they feel, but I also see why you want to bring things to a head." Malie nodded her thanks, then Brian asked, "Any sign of Jake?"

"No."

Brian took a few moments to check out the men both at the bar and at the tables. "Good."

"Is he still at the hotel?" she asked.

"I don't know. I haven't checked. I thought it best to stay out of his sight to keep him from suspecting I'd been alerted about his intentions. In fact, probably not a good idea for me to sit here at the bar where he could spot me as soon as he walks through those doors." He stood up. "Think I'll wander over and get to know some Dawson citizens while enjoying the piano man."

During the next hour, a few more customers arrived, mostly to enjoy the piano man and maybe a dance or two. Malie was refilling the mugs of the young men at the bar when the doors swung open and in walked Jake. Malie tilted her head to look as if she was surprised to see him. Jake's face broadened into a wide grin as he took a seat at the far end of the bar.

One of the men she had just served said, "Getting late and gotta work tomorrow, so this is our last brewski. What do we owe so far?"

"A pound and a half from each of you."

They smiled their thanks as they each handed her two pounds and told Malie no change.

"Thanks, guys. Don't work too hard tomorrow."

One of the young men laughed and said, "Tell that to our foreman." Malie smiled her answer as the men went back to chatting among themselves.

She risked a look toward the piano man. Brian stayed seated, but his slight nod let her know he was aware of Jake's arrival. She took a deep breath, then went to face her old boss.

Working to keep fear out of her voice and her eyes, she walked to the end of the bar and asked, "What do you want?"

"Well," smiled Jake, "good to see you, too."

"What do you want?"

"Oh, I think you know what I want, but first I'm a little thirsty. Fix me my favorite drink." When she didn't move, his smile disappeared and his face threatened. "Now!" he hissed.

She turned and poured rum into a glass, then added a small amount of Coke. As she set it in front of him, she managed to say, "Jake, please, leave me alone."

His smile returned as he took a deep slug of his drink. "How can I do that when you owe me so much money?"

"I don't think I do."

"Now, sweet moneymaker, how could you think I would lie to you after all I did for you and Kahale when he was so sick and dying?"

She cringed at the word moneymaker, but refused to let him cower her. "I'll always be grateful at what you did for Kahale, and that he never learned of your real motive in providing the money for his medical care."

Jake smirked. "Motive?"

Malie shook her head. "Just go away."

"Now, you know that isn't going to happen. I can't have my pussies think they can just up and quit working for me. And, don't forget all that money you owe me. So just pack up your things. We'll leave on the ferry tomorrow."

"No."

Jake's eyes narrowed. "Do as I say."

As he hissed his command to Malie, Brian sat down on the bar stool next to him. "Is there a problem here?"

"No," said Jake.

"Now, why don't I believe you?"

"Listen, our conversation is none of your business, so leave us alone."

Brian raised his eyebrows as if asking Malie if she agreed.

She faced Jake with a smile as she answered Brian. "Constable Stockton, this man is threatening me, so no, don't leave us alone."

Her words widened Jake's eyes that now reflected a combination of anger, and a touch of fear. He turned to face Brian. "You're a Mountie?"

Brian nodded. "Yes, I am." He pulled his badge from his shirt pocket and pinned it to his vest. "You now have two choices. Keep bothering this woman, and I'll have to arrest you for threatening one of my citizens, or tell her you're sorry for anything you've said or done. Then, be on the ferry tomorrow leaving Dawson, forever."

Jake's mind raced with frustration. If he was home, one phone call would send this misguided cop on his way. He risked a threatening glare at Malie.

Brian stood up and pulled a pair of handcuffs from his Levis. "Looks like you've decided on option one." As he reached for Jake's wrist, Jake stood up and backed away.

"Hold off, Mountie." Knowing when to hold 'em and when to fold 'em was the reason Jake had been so successful, both in business and life in general. He managed to give Brian a nod of understanding. "I'll be on my way. No need for those cuffs." He turned to Malie and flashed a grin that said 'this ain't over.' Then, without another word he left Miss Lucy's.

As the saloon doors closed, Brian turned to Malie. "You okay?"

"It's not over."

"Oh, I think he got the message."

"You don't know Jake."

Brian reached over and touched Malie's shoulder. "I'll make sure he leaves on that ferry tomorrow. For now, I'm going to follow him back to the hotel. Try to close up early and stay inside."

At that moment, Elmer came back into the bar. One look at Malie's face let him know something had happened. He hurried to her side. "He showed up?"

Malie nodded.

"Yes," said Brian. "I ran him off, but I've got to leave now. I'm going to follow him back to the hotel."

"I'm relieving Malie for the night. She'll be safe."

Brian nodded his thanks, smiled at Malie, then got his coat and headed out to follow Jake. From a block away, he saw Jake enter the hotel. Brian continued down to the hotel. Across the street was a barber shop that provided customers with a bench just outside the front door. Brian sauntered over and sat down. He managed to stay awake and watch for any activity in or around the hotel for the next couple hours. Eventually he went back to his quarters, set his alarm for five a.m., then called it a night.

***

At five-fifteen the next morning, Brian called Miss Lucy's Saloon. "Good morning, Elmer. Sorry to wake you. I just wanted to be sure Malie is alright."

"I think she is. Didn't hear anything. Wait, Peggy is going to run upstairs and check on her."

"Thanks. Like I said, sorry about the early wake up call."

"Just doing your job, I reckon."

While the men waited, Peggy hurried up the stairs and rapped on Malie's door.

"Yes?"

"Malie, it's Peggy. Are you alright?"

The door opened. Malie was dressed in her Levis and a Miss Lucy's tee shirt. "Yes, I'm fine. Did something happen downstairs?"

Peggy smiled. "No. Brian called to be sure Jake had not come back."

"I admit. I was concerned, so I slept in my clothes, but he never came back."

"Good. Now, get some sleep. I need to go tell Brian you're okay." She turned and hurried back down to her apartment. Elmer was slipping into his denims when she entered the bedroom. "She's fine. No one bothered her during the night."

Elmer picked up the receiver he had set on the dresser. "Brian?"

"Yes?"

"Peggy said she's fine. No one came around last night."

"Thanks. See you later today." The line went dead.

"Looks like Dawson's got a good Mountie here to protect us," grinned Elmer as he slipped into a white tee shirt.

"Yes, indeed," said Peggy. "You're not going back to bed?"

"Naw, how about you?" He walked over and gave Peggy a light kiss. "Unless ..."

Peggy stepped back and tightened the belt on her robe, then smiled. "Not a good idea with all the craziness going on, but I will fix you a nice breakfast."

"Guess I'll have to settle for that, you vixen. Come on. I'll start the coffee."

Hand in hand, they headed for the kitchen.

***

A little after five-thirty, Brian walked up to the unattended hotel desk. He was in no hurry, so he didn't ring the little bell to call for anyone. Glancing around the room, he did notice a table with a pot of coffee, all the condiments and a half dozen donuts. While he was filling a cup, Mrs. Kunuk came out of her apartment.

"Constable," she said, "can I help you?"

"Just checking on one of your guests, Bill Jones. Has he checked out yet?"

"No. He's a day-by-day guest, so he pays up each morning if he wants to stay another night."

"So, he wouldn't have to check with you if he decided to leave."

"No, but most guests usually do. See, when they turn in their room key, they get their deposit back."

Brian nodded. "Mind if I have a cup of coffee and take a seat here for awhile?"

"Not at all, Constable. Have a donut or two. I make 'em myself."

Brian smiled. "I wasn't going to, but who can resist home-made." He helped himself to one, then took a seat facing the check-in counter.

As Mrs. Kunuk sat behind her counter, she and Brian exchanged idle talk about the weather and how he was settling into Dawson. She answered Brian's questions about the hotel and how she came to be the owner. Eventually, the conversation dwindled.

Mrs. Kunuk said she had some paperwork to do, but she told Brian he was welcome to stay and have some more coffee. Over the next hour, two guests checked out. Finally, Jake came down the stairs toting his suitcase. Just as he reached the bottom step, he noticed Brian and came to a stop.

Brian smiled as he stood up. "Good morning."

"Why are you here?"

"To escort you to the ferry."

"Don't need an escort."

"Not your choice."

After a go-to-hell glare at Brian, Jake walked up to the counter. "Here's my key," he said as he handed it to Mrs. Kunuk.

She handed him a purple ten-pound note. "Thank you, Mr. Jones. Next time you're in Dawson, come stay with us again." She managed a smile despite the whirl of curiosity she barely managed to hide.

Without another word, Jake picked up his suitcase and strode out the door.

"Thanks for the coffee and donut," said Brian. He smiled at Mrs. Kunuk, then followed Jake.

After they had gone about a block, Jake stopped and turned around. "Mind if I have breakfast before I leave?"

"I'm in no hurry. Go right ahead."

Sitting at separate tables, both men ate the Nugget's daily breakfast special. Within the hour, they were heading toward the ferry. No words were spoken and Brian stayed far enough back to keep any onlooker from thinking they were together. Jake bought his ticket and took a seat to wait for the ferry that was due in about fifteen minutes. Brian stood by the door to wait. There were only five other passengers waiting for the ferry.

"Ferry will dock in five minutes, and boarding will begin in ten minutes," called out the man selling the tickets to all the waiting passengers.

As the passengers boarded, they were greeted by the ship captain and directed to the indoor seating area. Brian followed the last boarding passenger up the ramp.

"Constable, welcome aboard," smiled the captain.

"Thank you, but I'm not boarding. I just have a question."

"Yes?"

"How do your passengers travel after they leave the ferry?"

"Most travelers either bring their cars across on the ferry, or if they're here for just a short stay, they leave their cars in our parking lot. Once a week a tour company brings a group of tourists up on a large tour bus. The tourists leave the bus and ferry across the Yukon River where another tour bus waits on the other side to pick them up for the rest of their tour."

Brian nodded. "I see. Can you do me a favor?"

"I can try."

"Can you make sure one of your passengers boards a car and heads back toward Alaska?"

"Certainly. Which passenger?"

"He's traveling alone, and he's wearing a beige leather jacket. He's using the name Bill Jones."

"I remember the passenger with the leather jacket. I'll see if he picks up a car."

"Thank you." Brian handed him a piece of paper. "Here's the phone number of my office. I'll be waiting for your call."

The raised his eyebrows. "Should I be worried about the safety of my crew and passengers regarding this Jones fellow?"

"No. You've nothing to worry about. He's only a threat to one person and that's why I need to make sure he leaves town."

"Ok, Constable."

"Thanks again," said Brian as he walked back down the ramp and headed to his office.

He spent the morning sorting out the morning mail, answering a phone call about fishing license requirements by referring the caller to the Department of Environment and reading some journals about life in the Yukon, especially Dawson.

Just before lunch time, his phone rang.

"Dawson Mountie Police Office, Constable Stockton speaking."

"Constable, this is Captain Frasier. Just want you to know that Bill Jones drove off in his rental car and seemed headed back to Alaska."

"Thank you, Captain. I appreciate the feedback. Now, can you do me a favor?"

"I can try."

Brian smiled at his honesty. "If he ever shows up again on your ferry, can you give me a call."

"Will do."

"Thanks. And by the way, if you ever need my help on anything give me a call?"

"Thanks, Constable."

The captain hung up as did Brian with a sigh of relief. He stood up and decided to head on over to Miss Lucy's and let Malie know Jake was gone.

Elmer was at the bar when Brian entered Miss Lucy's. "Constable! Is that a smile on your face?" Elmer asked.

"Indeed, it is." Brian glanced around the saloon, then asked, "Where's Malie?"

Elmer nodded toward their living quarters. "She and Peggy are working on the books. Let's go interrupt them with the good news you seem to be bringing." He turned to one of his barmaids sitting at the end of the bar. "Rosie, take over." Then, he led Brian into his living room. "Peggy, Malie, got some good news for you."

The women looked up from the table covered in papers, receipts and books. Peggy smiled at seeing Brian, while Malie looked concerned.

"Yes, I've some good news," said Brian. "Jake is gone. Took the ferry this morning."

"Doesn't sound like Jake to give up that easy," said Malie.

"Well, I escorted him to the ferry, talked with the ferry captain, and had him call me when he saw Jake head back to Alaska."

When Malie remained seated with her face still showing her concern, Peggy stepped in. "Yes, good news. Thank you, so much, Brian," said Peggy as she stood up. "Come, let's have a drink to celebrate."

Brian smiled, but shook his head no. "I'm on duty until five, so no drinks for me. if the offer is still on for this evening I can come back."

"Actually better," said Peggy. "Malie and I will be done with our accounting and I'll fix us a nice supper."

"That would be nice. See you around six?" Brian and Elmer headed back into the bar. "See you tonight," said Brian, then he headed back to his office.

Once the door closed to the men, Peggy sat back down. "Malie, you didn't thank Brian."

Pretending to read a receipt, Malie said, "That's his job."

"Yes, it is his job, but a thank you wouldn't hurt. I know what you're worried about, but you've been around him quite a bit lately." She paused, but getting no response from Malie, she went on. "But, like you said, he'd been drinking. Seems like if he was going to remember that night, it would have happened by now." Again, she paused, but Malie still pretended to be focused on the receipt. "So, he's probably going to be staying in Dawson for a long time and I certainly hope you are, too."

She turned and took Malie gently by her shoulders. "You need to let the past go. For your sake and for Brian's." She gave Malie a slight squeeze, then let her go. After a big sigh, she reached for one of the pieces of paper on the table and moaned, "but, for now, let's get this damn bookkeeping done."

Malie actually smiled. "Yes, let's get it done."

Letting Go of the Past

The rest of the day moved slowly. Sergeant Major, Devon MacDonald, called from Whitehorse to tell Brian he had received the letter of complaint from Hilde and Sadie. After double checking the laws of the Yukon Territory, he agreed with Brian's findings. He would wait a few days, then send them an official reply to their complaint and hoped this would cause the ladies to drop the issue. Brian laughed and told his major he hoped so, too. But Brian doubted the ladies would not back off that easily.

He left the office a little after five to go home, freshen up and change into civilian clothes. A little before six he arrived at Miss Lucy's and headed straight for the door to Peggy and Elmer's living quarters. His knock was immediately answered.

"Come on in," called Elmer as he finished setting the table with plates, silverware, and glasses.

Brian entered and was surprised to see the large table that had held all sorts of bookkeeping papers and books now was covered with a lace tablecloth and lit by two candles, one at each end of the table.

Elmer waved him on in and directed him to the sofa as he set a bottle of wine on the table and fixed himself a drink. "The ladies are finishing things up in the kitchen. Can I get you something to drink?"

Brian looked at Elmer's drink. "Canadian Club on the rocks," said Elmer.

"Sounds good."

Once Elmer had refreshed his drink and poured one for Brian, he sat in a chair next to the sofa. "Cheers," he said, then saluted Brian.

"Cheers," smiled Brian and returned the salute.

"So glad you could join us."

"Thanks for asking me." Brian glanced toward the kitchen.

Elmer smiled. "She's okay."

At that moment, Peggy came through the kitchen door carrying a large platter of venison pot roast, surrounded by a medley of boiled red potatoes and carrots, along with fresh green beans. Malie was right behind her with a pitcher of brown gravy and a basket of biscuits.

"Brian," said Peggy, as she sat the roast on the table. "Welcome. I hope you like venison."

"Love it," said Brian as he and Elmer stood up. "Smells really good."

"Good. Now sit." She pointed to one of the settings across from where Elmer was already standing as he poured wine for each of them. Once Brian was down, she sat between the two men as Malie sat directly across from her.

Catching Peggy's slight nod toward Brian, Malie turned to him. "So glad you could make it, Brian."

Brian took a deep intake of the aroma of the food, then smiled broadly. "Me too."

The room got quiet. No one could think of what to say or do next. As usual, Peggy made a suggestion.

"Brian, we aren't much into the prayer thing, but I think maybe tonight we're all glad things seem to have worked out well. So, why don't we join hands, and have you say a blessing."

"Me?"

"Yes," nodded Peggy. "Please." She reached out and took hold of one of Elmer's hands and one of Brian's.

Elmer followed her lead and took Malie's hand, then Brian took hold of Malie's other hand.

Brian cleared the lump in his throat and began. "Our first blessing is for this great meal you ladies have prepared. Then, we are blessed that the recent threat to Malie has been taken care of. And probably the best thing we are blessed with is that we are here at this table to enjoy each other's company. Amen."

Smiles and a chorus of "Amen" thanked Brian for his words.

Elmer began carving the roast, releasing even more of the tempting aroma of the meat, and Peggy began filling plates. Conversation flowed as they enjoyed the meal, along with sips of their wine. Brief bios were shared on how they came to live in Dawson and of the beauty of the area.

"Well, it is very different." said Brian, when asked how he was adjusting to living in an area of mountains versus living on the edge of the Pacific Ocean. "Both have their attractions and I do still wake up some mornings wondering why I'm not hearing the sound of the waves slapping against the docks, nor the screeching hordes of seagulls swooping about looking for breakfast."

Elmer smiled. "Yep, worked in a bar on Homer Spit for awhile, so I know what you're talking about."

"Yes, it was a good life." Brian paused for a moment as family memories surfaced, but a glance at his current tablemates brought him back to the moment and he went on. "But, the beauty of the mountains, the dry, salt-free air and the small-town atmosphere of the people I've met here in Dawson bring on feelings of welcome, a place of endless possibilities."

Peggy nodded and smiled. "That's just how I felt when Abby and I arrived on the ferry those many years ago."

Brian turned to Malie. "And you? From the tropics to the arctic, that's quite an adjustment."

"Yes, getting used to the cold was an adjustment. But, the beauty of the area, both snowbound in winter and the waving grasses and wildlife in summer, spoke to the part of me that loves to paint. And, the people here have been so supportive. Especially, the Finleys." She paused and glanced at Peggy, then Elmer. "In so short a time, they've become family."

"I can see that," nodded Brian.

More talk about the area resumed among the four of them as they finished their meal. Eventually, after declining help from the men, Peggy and Malie cleared the table. When they returned to the living room, Peggy carried a tray with coffee and all the fixings, while Malie carried a basket of warm blueberry scones.

Brian shook his head. "Elmer, how do you stay so thin with all this fine cooking?"

"Oh, Peggy keeps me busy. Along with some mighty fine exercise now and then."

"Elmer!" Peggy's glare was eased by her devilish grin.

Brian laughed, then bit into one of the scones.

A knock on the door was accompanied by a call for Peggy, who got up and opened the door to find one of their barmaids.

"Peggy, I'm not feeling well. It's a small crowd, but Charley can't handle the bar and the tables."

Peggy touched the girl's forehead. "Yes, feels like you have a slight fever. Go on up to your room. We'll help Charley."

Malie was already on her feet. "I'll go."

Peggy glanced at Elmer, who shrugged. "I can go."

"No," said Malie. "Charley needs someone for the tables, not the bar." With that, she slipped out the door.

Elmer shrugged again. "I swear, it's like I'm living with two Peggys. Good thing you've never been to Hawaii, or I'd swear you were her mother."

Peggy laughed, then looked over at Brian. "Sorry. Once she decides to do something, there's no changing her mind."

"So, I've noticed," said Brian. He finished off his coffee, then stood up. "Well, it's getting late, I better head on home."

Peggy nodded and got up to walk Brian to the door. "I'm so glad you could join us tonight and feel free to come by anytime."

"I really enjoyed this evening, Thanks and I'll surely take you up on your offer," said Brian. He looked over at Elmer. "And Elmer, thanks for a nice evening," he paused, then added, "oh, and about that exercising ..." He just smiled and turned to leave.

Elmer laughed as Peggy poked Brian's arm. "Men!" But she smiled and added. "Goodnight, Brian." She closed the door, then leaned against it and closed her eyes.

Elmer came over to take her hand. "Yes, it's been a long day."

Peggy opened her eyes and smiled. "You think there's any hope for Brian with Malie?"

"Time will tell." He slid his arm around her shoulder. "But, for now ...." He smiled suggestively.

Peggy giggled. "I know. You need to exercise." She allowed him to urge her along in the direction of their bedroom. Thoughts of Brian and Malie disappeared, and no words were spoken as they stripped down and got into bed.

***

For the next month, Brian focused on the people of Dawson as he broke up small fights, answered citizen complaints and concerns and reported in regularly to headquarters in Whitehorse. Occasionally, he'd drop by and have supper with River and Blair, and he'd enjoyed another supper with Elmer, Peggy and Malie at Miss Lucy's. About once a week, usually a Friday night, he'd wander over to Miss Lucy's enjoying listening to the piano player and visiting with Dawson citizens. Malie was often tending bar, but she still kept him at a distance and never allowed them to be alone.

Brian leaned back in his chair. It had been another quiet morning. He had answered some telephone queries, filled out a couple reports and did some reading on the history of the area. He yawned as he glanced at the clock to find it was a little after noon. The sunshine flowing in through the bay window assured him that, for a March Day, a lunch sitting along the river might be nice. After a call to the local telephone operator to let her know, he'd be out of the office for an hour or so, he headed for The Nugget to order a lunch-to-go.

With a brown bag in one hand and a hot coffee in the other, he made his way down to the river's edge and the cement bench that was rapidly becoming his favorite river spot. Other than a few fishermen attending to their boats and catches of the day, the boardwalk was clear of tourists or townsfolk.

He was almost to his bench, when he noticed someone at the end of the boardwalk. What really got his attention was that the person was sitting in the sand, and seemed to be working on what looked like a large pad or notebook. His curiosity got the best of him, along with hope of who it might be.

He passed by his bench and continued on. When he reached the end of the boardwalk, his hope was rewarded as Malie turned to him and smiled.

"Hello, Brian." She glanced at what he was carrying and asked, "Having lunch out in this cold?"

He nodded. "Hello, Malie. Yes, couldn't let this beautiful sunshine go unnoticed. And what about you? Sitting in the cold sand, painting."

"Not painting, sketching." She turned the large pad she was working on to show him a sketch of the ferry boat across the river.

"Nice work. Mind if I join you?"

"Going to eat standing up?"

Brian smiled and stepped down onto the sand and sat beside her. "No, I'll just sit here and watch you sketch while I eat."

"Your uniform is going to get all sandy."

"It'll brush off."

Malie shook her head, then turned back to her sketching.

Brian secured his coffee cup in the sand, then pulled his ham and cheese sandwich out of the bag. He offered it to Malie. "Sorry, didn't realize you'd be here. Want to share?"

She looked at his offer, then chuckled. "No. I had a late breakfast."

"Your loss. Jessie makes the best sandwiches."

"They are good."

Brian worked on his sandwich while Malie worked on her sketch in silence. Eventually, Brian swallowed his last bite, then rinsed it down with a big drink of his coffee.

He wanted to talk to Malie but couldn't find a natural way to ask her to spend time with him—first as a friend, then maybe more. As he brushed a few bread crumbs from his uniform jacket, an idea surfaced. My job involves asking questions, so why not start with that?

He finished off his coffee, then asked, "Am I imagining it, or do you really try to avoid me?"

His direct query, surprised her. She pulled her hand from the sketch for a moment, but managed to gain composure and continued with her sketching. "It's not just you. I prefer being alone."

"Why?"

"Constable, unless you are officially questioning me, I don't think it's any of your business."

"No, it's not official business, so cut the constable, I'm Brian. Can't we just talk. I find that the little amount of time you do allow me, I enjoy your company. You're smart, quick on your feet and always willing to help out at Miss Lucy's."

"You're not going to go away, are you?"

Brian smiled and shook his head no. "I've got about an hour before I have to get back to the office, so, yep, you're stuck with me. So, tell me, why we can't be friends and spend some time together now and then."

Malie continued to sketch for a minute or so. Just as Brian was about to push her for an answer to his question, she stopped sketching and turned to him. "You really want to know why I keep to myself?"

"Yes."

"You won't like it."

"Try me."

"From what I've heard about you; you have lived a life filled with a loving family. Yes, they were taken too soon, but I'm sure you have wonderful memories of them."

"That's true. I've been blessed."

Malie paused and looked out across the Yukon before she began. "Lucky you. I was not so lucky. I was born into a cult. I have no idea who my father is. My mother was forced to take drugs, service men, then died of an overdose. I hooked up with a fellow cult orphan and fell in love, only to lose him to tuberculosis within months."

She turned to face Brian.

"And the best part is that, to help with our expenses while he was dying, his best friend started giving us money—money that came with a payback involving working for him as a hooker."

A so-there expression settled on her face.

"So no, I'm not the least bit interested in making human friends."

She turned away, picked up her sketch pad and pencil, and went back to her drawing.

"All I need is art. Colors, the beauty of nature and animals, interesting structures—those are the only friends I need. They always make me happy and never make demands."

She looked back at Brian.

"They are all the friends I need."

Brian found himself at a loss for words. Eventually, he managed a nod. He let her work for awhile as he tried to gather his thoughts on what she had shared. Eventually, he began to speak to her. "Malie, I can see why you've opted to avoid making friends. But that was then, this is now. Look at the changes in your life this past couple of years. Look at what the support of Patrick and Kathleen have given you since bringing you here from Hawaii. And, look at the relationship you have with Peggy and Elmer. Doesn't that suggest that there are good people who would never think of making you sad or hurting you?"

Malie continued to sketch, but Brian noticed a slight twitch at her jaw line, along with pauses with her pencil, now and then. He remained silent and let her deal with her thoughts. Several minutes passed and, again, just as he was about to speak, she turned to him.

"Yes, the people, especially those you mentioned, have been supportive. They've become very special people to me. But my life has shown me they are the exception, that if I let my guard down, I might leave myself open to more disappointment and hurt."

"That's true. But, isn't all of life a gamble. Nothing is assured. However, if you don't give people a chance, you could be missing out on some of the wonderful things that life often brings our way."

"So, you say."

Brian smiled. She hadn't turned away, and he thought he detected curiosity in her eyes. "Yes, so I say." He took a big risk and reached for her hand. His heart skipped a beat when she let him gently hold her hand. "I have a suggestion. Why don't you start with giving me a chance to prove I can be a friend who won't make demands. Someone you can talk with and maybe have dinner or supper with occasionally."

Malie looked down at their hands for almost a full minute, then looked up at Brian. With a slight smile, she said one word. "Maybe."

Brian gave her hand a slight squeeze before he let her hand go. He smiled. "Okay."

She repeated her okay, then turned back to her sketch. "Do you think I captured most of the ferry's details?"

"Yes. The only thing you might add would be the image of a ship captain at the helm."

She paused. "Maybe, but I usually keep my work to nature or animals or in this case the boat."

He nodded. "Then, it looks good."

They began to share thoughts about the scene and the ferry unaware that they were being watched. Hilde and Sadie had been on their way to the general store, when Hilde stopped and pointed to the beach area. "Isn't that Constable Stockton?"

Sadie actually gasped. "And, look who he's down there with."

"Oh, my word, it's that tramp from Miss Lucy's."

After an, I-Knew-It harumph, followed by a smirk, Sadie said. "Well, I guess we now know why he won't do anything about the hussies."

"Yes, we do." Hilde watched Brian and Malie talking and, occasionally, laughing, obviously enjoying each other's company. Finally, she said, "Yes, we know, but I wonder if his sergeant major knows."

"Well, it certainly doesn't bode well to see the man we expect to protect the community being so friendly with one of the town's hussies. The sergeant major might be more receptive to getting rid of the hussies if he knew Brian was spending time with the type of woman who could corrupt our children, especially our sons."

"You may be right," Hilde agreed. "I think we should send him another letter."

The women shared a nod, then turned and continued on towards the general store.

"Ed said he'd be a little late for supper tonight, so I'll have time to work on the letter after we finish our shopping," said Sadie.

"Yes, Homer's working a bit late tonight too," said Hilde.

Wearing smug smiles, the ladies hurried toward the store, each already forming the letter in their minds.

***

The next few weeks flew by for Brian. Except for the need to right a citizen's wrong a few times, he found time during several of his lunch breaks to sit with Malie as she painted. She had also joined him once for supper at River and Blair's home and another supper at Miss Lucy's, along with Peggy and Elmer. Their times together were casual, no touching or sharing of feelings, just light conversation and a few laughs now and then.

As Brian awoke on Friday morning, his first thought was of what was on his schedule for the day and it was not about work. He and Malie were having their first evening out in public. They were having supper at The Nugget. He tried to focus on what was on his agenda for the day at the station, but thoughts of spending the evening with Malie put everything else on a back burner.

On his way to the office, he stopped at The Nugget for his morning coffee and blueberry muffin. As usual, he found both sitting in a brown bag right next to the cash register.

"Morning, Constable," said Jessie. "That's a big smile. Something good happening today?"

"I'm in Dawson. Something good happens every day."

Jessie laughed as Brian paid her, then grabbed his bag. "Glad you think so, Constable."

Brian gave her a goodbye wave as he headed out the door. After the short walk to the station, Brian set the bag on his desk and picked up his phone.

Immediately, the day-shift operator, Martha came on the line. "Morning, Constable."

"Morning, Martha. Any calls for me?"

"No."

"Good. I'll be here all day, except for lunch around noon."

"Have a good day, Constable."

"You, too," he said, then hung up. He unbagged his breakfast and took a sip of his coffee. He had just taken a bite of the muffin when his phone rang. Taking a moment, he washed the bite down with another swig of his coffee, then answered with, "Dawson Mountie Police Station, Constable Stockton speaking."

"Good morning, Brian," greeted Sergeant Major Devon MacDonald.

Brian smiled. He often missed daily contact with his superior and his peers in Whitehorse. "Good morning, Sergeant."

"How are things in Dawson?"

"Quiet, mostly. You're getting my weekly reports, aren't you?"

"Yes. Nice work."

"Thank you." The conversation seemed a little stilted to Brian. "Why the early morning call?" he asked.

"Well, I have a letter here on my desk."

"Letter? About Dawson?"

"Yes, and about your conduct regarding one of Dawson's citizens."

"My conduct?"

Devon laughed. "Yes. I received another letter from Mrs. Brown and Mrs. Anderson."

"Another letter from Hilde and Sadie? I thought that after our meeting with the mayor they had given up on their complaint about what goes on in the local saloons."

"Apparently not. This letter is to inform me of your association with one of these night ladies, and how it looks to the citizens of Dawson to have their local Mountie in a relationship with a hussy."

Brian had to take a few moments to calm his anger before responding to his sergeant.

"Brian?"

After a loud, frustrated breath, he began. "First of all, in checking out Hilde and Sadie's accusations about hussies in Dawson, I found no violations of any laws. Do some of the barmaids provide more than serving drinks to their customers? Yes. But everyone I checked out follows the law.

As for me being in an association with a hussy, it's a damn lie. Do I spend some time with Malie over at Miss Lucy's? Yes, I do. But it's not an association. And more than that, it is nobody's business who I do associate with."

Brian paused to control his anger, but it won out.

"However, Sergeant Major, if it is an issue for you and a dilemma for Mountie Headquarters, I will turn in my badge. I've done nothing wrong, but I would never want to be a problem for you."

"Whoa," said Devon. "Calm down. Their letter requires my attention, but as for you, Brian, I have no doubts about your integrity and commitment to your responsibilities as a constable."

"Thank you, sir," Brian began to calm down.

"Now, I do need to ask you some questions about their concern over your so-called association with Malie. First, how serious are things between the two of you?"

Brian actually uttered a slight laugh. "On who's part?"

"Well, yours mostly, but both of you."

"Unfortunately for me, Malie just wants us to be friends. As for me, I could be very serious. You know her background and she has been very honest about her trust issues. It took a lot of talking to convince her that we could be friends."

"After all she's been through, I can understand her trust issues. And, quite frankly, it's none of my, nor headquarters, business who you are dating. Other than these two ladies, I haven't had any complaints from Dawson citizens."

"I try to do my best here, sir."

"And, I thank you for doing so." He paused, then went on. "So, how do we mollify these ladies and get them to understand and accept the fact that no laws, regarding prostitution, are being broken in Dawson."

"I wish I knew, sir. I really thought they had accepted everything after our meeting with the mayor."

"I did, too."

"You want to hear something ironic about these women? When I was checking out the local saloons as to their adherence to the law, I saw their husbands enjoying saloon barmaids, if you know what I mean."

Devon laughed. "That certainly explains a lot."

"So, what do you want me to do about the complaint?"

"Nothing. I'll answer their letter and let them know that you are doing nothing wrong. They can rest assured that your first concern is the safety of all Dawson citizens."

"Thank you, sir."

"Oh, by the way, I will be up in Dawson in two weeks. Blair wants to have a big Easter dinner with the whole family, so I'm taking a few days off."

"Great. It will be nice to see you. Tell Ron and Dave I said hello."

"Will do. Take care and see you soon."

"You too, Goodbye."

Brian put the receiver down and shook his head. He wanted to be furious with Hilde and Sophie's complaint, but in reality, he found himself feeling sorry for them.

They always seemed to focus on the dark side of life. He wondered if their way of looking at things was the reason their husbands were getting their pleasures in a saloon. Their men were gone, working long days in the mines, then coming home late after their romps with the barmaids. There's just so much cooking, cleaning and laundry that needs doing while their men are at work, leaving their wives with idle time on their hands.

An idea began to form in Brian's mind. They needed something to do, something positive. Nothing came to him at the moment, but he would keep an eye out for something to occupy the ladies with something that would bring a little brightness into their lives.

The phone rang bringing him back to the moment. He spent the next ten minutes discussing fishing, hunting laws and permits needed in the Yukon with a gentleman from the States who planned on spending the summer in Dawson.

The rest of the day dragged on as Brian found himself frequently checking the slow-moving wall clock. By six o'clock he was walking into Miss Lucy's. Peggy and Malie were sitting at the far end of the bar.

"Welcome, Constable," said Elmer. "Have a seat and I'll bring you your sarsaparilla."

"Thanks," said Brian as he hung his coat on a hook by the door, then took a seat next to Malie. "Good evening, ladies."

"Don't you look nice," said Peggy, as she took in his casual attire of a dark blue blazer, light blue, tie-less shirt and dark blue slacks.

"Thank you. I can spruce up now and then." He grinned as he took a sip of the drink Elmer had brought.

"Apparently."

"And, I must say, you ladies are a sight for sore eyes."

He may have said ladies, but Peggy noticed his eyes were only on Malie. The girl was wearing a full-skirted, yellow dress, with a scoop neck featuring what looked like an Inuit-created necklace of various colored sea shells.

Malie had noticed his attention. "Thank you."

"No, thank you. After a dull day at the office, sitting here with two beautiful ladies is my pleasure."

Peggy laughed. "That's a new line for you."

"It's true." He drained his drink, then stood and held out his hand to Malie. "Now, I'm really hungry. Are you ready?"

Malie nodded and stood up.

"Have a good dinner and a nice evening," said Peggy as Elmer nodded his agreement.

After helping Malie into her coat, the two of them stepped into the cold night air. Fortunately, there had been no snowfall in the last few days, so the streets were ice free. Still, Brian offered his arm to Malie, and she accepted.

"Not too cold tonight," said Brian.

"No, it isn't," agreed Malie. "And look at all the stars. Such a clear night."

"That's something I've noticed here. Dawson's few town lights make the night sky so dark that the number of visible stars is amazing."

"Yes," said Malie.

Brian wanted more of the sound of her voice. "So, how did your day go?"

"As usual. I had the day shift so not too many customers."

"Does it get boring on slow days? I know I've done a lot of reading since taking the constable assignment here in Dawson. There's so little crime that without the reading, I find myself staring at the walls."

"Low crime is a good thing, right?"

"It is indeed. So, what do you do on slow days managing the bar?"

"Well, there are counters to be wiped down, liquor to be inventoried and," she paused and smiled up at Brian, "the latest dime novel I keep near the cash register."

Brian laughed. "Books sure come in handy."

They had arrived at The Nugget. Malie paused and asked, "Are you sure you want to do this?"

"Yes, I'm very hungry."

Malie shook her head in amusement. "You know what I mean. Your reputation is at stake for us to have supper together in a public place."

"Really? You're probably right. Getting a beautiful woman like you to have supper with a plain old Mountie will definitely enhance my reputation."

"Brian, you know what I mean."

He squeezed her arm. "Come on. I'm hungry." He led her into the restaurant, and Jessie seated them by the front window, as Brian had requested.

Jessie set menus on the table for both of them. "Our special tonight is pork roast, with baked potatoes, peas and carrots, followed by apple pie for dessert."

"Malie?" asked Brian.

"The roast sounds fine."

"Me, too," said Brian.

"Good choice. What can I bring you to drink. Coffee, tea, hot chocolate, juice or water?"

"Tea for me," said Malie.

"Just water for me," said Brian.

"I'll get your order in, then be right back with your drinks." Jessie headed back to the kitchen.

Malie glanced around the room. She and Brian were the center of attention. The tables were only half-filled, but it was enough of a crowd to ensure gossip would flow freely over the weekend.

"Let them look," said Brian. "I just—

"You just need to quit worrying and let us enjoy each other's company."

Malie turned back and gave Brian a smile. "You're right. And, I am enjoying your company."

Brian returned her smile. "Good to know."

Jessie arrived with their drinks, then left them alone.

After fixing her tea, Malie asked, "So why was having supper in public so important to you? Peggy made an elk pot roast for supper tonight, so you could have saved some money and," she nodded toward the other tables, "we would have had better company."

"I wanted to have some alone time with you."

She raised her eyebrows. "This is alone time?"

"For me, it is."

"Why?"

"Well, our suppers together in the past have been listening to River and Blair talk about their kids. And, when Peggy and Elmer aren't drooling over each other, the conversation is about the saloon. I wanted an evening of learning more about Malie."

"You know everything about me."

He shook his head. "I doubt that."

She chuckled. Before she could say anything, Jessie arrived with their food. The aroma increased Brian's appetite, and made Malie glad she had ordered the roast.

"Anything else?" asked Jessie.

Malie shook her head no. "Everything looks great," said Brian. "Thanks."

"Enjoy." said Jessie. "Signal when you're ready for your pie." Then they were alone again.

Brian took a fork full of the roast and held it out to Malie. "Cheers."

"Cheers?" she laughed, filled her fork and touched his. "Cheers."

Both downed their first bite. About the only conversation, as they consumed their food, was about how good it was. When their plates were nearly cleared, Brian asked, "Ready for your pie?"

Malie swallowed her last bite. "I shouldn't, but if it's as good as the roast, I can't resist."

Brian waved at Jessie, then pointed to the pie rack.

Jessie came to their table and picked up the empty plates. "Ice cream or whip cream?"

"Just the pie will be fine," said Malie.

"Same here," agreed Brian. "Oh, and Jessie, can you put this on my tab?"

"I'll do that."

"Thanks."

"Let me know if you need anything else," said Jessie, who headed back to the counter and left them alone.

As they ate their pie, Malie commented, "I've always heard how good the food here at The Nugget was."

"Are you saying you've never eaten here before?"

"No."

Brian nodded remembering how she valued her privacy. "Well, I'm glad I was able to introduce you to the fine food here. And, because you seemed to enjoy it, can I hope that we will do this again soon?"

Malie smiled. "We'll see."

When they had finished their pie, Brian asked, "Ready for a walk along the river?"

"Kind of cold and dark for a river walk," said Malie.

"I have to walk you back to Miss Lucy's, so why not along the river? And, there's a full moon to light our way." He stood up and held out his hand.

"You are a strange man, Brian." She laughed, but took his hand.

"Strange? Well, here's hoping you like strange men," said Brian as he squeezed her hand.

She shook her head and smiled as they made their way down to the river walk. There was a slight breeze along the shoreline which brought on a shiver from Malie.

Brian dropped her hand, and put his arm around her shoulder. He smiled when she didn't resist. "You, okay?"

"Yes. It is cold, but the night sky makes it worth the chilly walk."

"Indeed, it does."

They walked along in silence. Brian hoped he was inching into her trust issues, while Malie was intent on guarding those trust issues from any intrusion. At the end of the boardwalk, Malie turned and took a step onto the stairs leading back up to Front Street.

Brian turned her around. The step she was on, brought their faces to the same level. He leaned forward to risk a kiss. A mere second before his lips touched hers, she turned so his lips touched her cheek. He leaned back and looked into her eyes.

"Brian, I'm not ready for—

"I know. I should have asked." To lighten the moment and address the concern in her moonlit eyes, he added, "But it's kind of your fault."

Her eyes widened in question. "My fault?"

"Yes. How could I resist when you look so beautiful?"

She shook her head from side to side.

He laughed and took her hand as he started up the stairs. Nothing more was said until they reached the side entrance to Miss Lucy's.

At the door, she turned and looked up at him. "Thank you, Brian. I had a nice evening."

"Thank you, it was nice."

"About the—

"I overstepped, but..." He paused and touched his lips to her forehead. "Goodnight, Malie. Sweet dreams."

He gave her hand a final squeeze, then turned and headed for home.

She watched him until he reached the street. He stopped, turned and waved for her to go inside. She smiled and went inside.

Once she was out of sight, Brian began walking. After a few steps, he found himself whistling through the big smile on his face.

***

For the next month, Brian and Malie, spent more time with each other. During rides to exercise Ranger, Brian would stop and sit alongside Malie to watch her paint. He took her on short rides on Ranger; they had a couple suppers with River and Blair and several meals together with Peggy and Elmer. They went to The Nugget once. Each evening ended with a kiss to her forehead.

On the Friday before Easter, Brian was filling out his weekly report when the door opened, and in walked his sergeant major.

He sprang to his feet and smiled as he saluted. "Sergeant Major MacDonald."

"At ease, Brian," he returned Brian's smile as Brian came out from behind his desk.

By using his first name, Brian knew it was a social visit, not official business. "Devon, so good to see you. We wondered when you'd be arriving. Blair and River are so glad you're spending Easter with them."

Devon laughed. "That little sister of mine guilted me in to coming, with as she puts it, 'the folks aren't getting any younger and they miss seeing you.'"

Brian nodded. "Your folks are fine. They joined us for dinner last Sunday."

"I know. But I haven't seen them since Christmas, so here I am." He sat down in front of Brian's desk and looked around. "Looks like you've settled in here nicely."

"I learned from you how to set up an office. I'm glad you like it." He walked over to his coffee pot sitting on top of a couple of file cabinets. "Want some coffee?"

"As strong as your KP days in Whitehorse?"

"Yep."

Devon laughed. "Sure. I need some more hair on my chest."

Once the coffee was ready, and the men were seated at the desk, Brian asked, "How long are you staying?"

"I'm heading back Monday morning."

"Short stay."

"Yes, I figure on getting out before Da and Ma start discussing my love life."

"They do worry about you not settling down and—

"Providing more grandchildren," Devon interrupted. Both men laughed.

"Well, no matter how long you stay, I'm glad to see you."

Devon nodded his agreement. After a drink of his coffee, he asked, "Any more problems with the local ladies about the hussies in town?"

"No. Your letter told them it was official protocol not to get involved in a constable's personal life unless something illegal was involved, and their complaint about me didn't address anything illegal. When I see them on my rounds, they answer my hello with a frown, a nod, and a stiff 'Constable.'"

"Sounds like they haven't given up."

"Probably not. But, while trying to find some positive things for them to do, I've had a conversation or two with our local pastor about what he sees as needs for the community."

"He's not worried about the hussies?"

Brian shrugged. "He hasn't mentioned them. His concern is the poverty level of some of the miners. They come up with their families with no money and only high hopes to strike it rich in the mines. As a result, some of the families are nearly starving, and they can't afford to provide winter clothing, which brings on some health issues."

"How does this address the concerns of Hilde and Sadie?"

"Well, their husbands are foremen in their mines, and they bring home enough to take care of their families nicely. And, both women are known for their cooking and sewing skills. The pastor and I are thinking that maybe a local social service office could be established to help the town's needy folks."

Devon drained his cup, then nodded. "Sounds like a good idea for several reasons." He stood up. "Well, guess I better head on up to see Blair."

Brian stood up. "It was sure good to see you."

At the door, Devon turned "Will you be joining us for supper tonight?"

"No, I'm taking Malie to The Nugget tonight."

Devon smiled. "Well, have fun. I'll check in with you before I head back to Whitehorse."

"Thanks," said Brian.

***

Brian and Malie had enjoyed the Friday night special at The Nugget and were now walking along the boardwalk enjoying the moonlit flow of the Yukon River. Brian was in a great mood. Malie seemed a little nervous, but she had been more talkative than usual. And, she smiled more than usual. He couldn't help but hope she was allowing her wall of privacy to begin to crumble. She even allowed him to hold her hand as they walked.

Earlier that afternoon, Malie and Peggy had talked about what was developing between Malie and Brian. They discussed the ups and downs of what Malie was holding back from Brian. In the end, Malie had to agree with Peggy that it was time to tell Brian about their first encounter in Hawaii during the war. Now, as they walked along hand in hand, she knew it was now or never. At the moment, they were walking by a bench facing the river. She halted and looked up at Brian. "Can we sit for a bit? I have something I want to tell you."

"Sure." His heart went into overdrive that she was initiating a conversation. Normally, she only responded to anything he said and, even then, her answers were always short.

Once they were seated, still holding hands, she faced the river. "First of all, I want you to know how much I appreciate how you dealt with Jake."

"It was a group effort. Peggy, Elmer, and you worked with me to get him out of town."

"Maybe so, but I've been a lot more relaxed knowing you all care enough to help me shed the past."

Brian just smiled and gently squeezed her hand.

"Brian, do you remember much about the war?"

"The war?"

She nodded. "Yes, especially your time in Oahu."

He uttered a slight laugh. "Oahu? Now that's quite a bit different from the war memories. War was all concentration to stay alive, dread, disgust and no playing around. Oahu, on the other hand, was relaxation, fun, lots of beer, and blurred memories of boys-night-out fun."

Malie managed a slight smile, and for the first time ever, squeezed Brian's hand as she took a deep breath. "Well, it's your Oahu experiences that I want to talk about."

Brian cocked his head as his brow rose in question.

"Do you remember any particular bar you might have visited during your boy's night outs?"

"No. After we'd have supper, we'd head for the bars. I'm not much of a drinker, so it only took a couple drinks for me lose track of time and place." He paused as a thought occurred. "Did we hit Jake's bar?"

"Yes."

"Often?"

"Just once that I know of."

Wild visions swirled through Brian's brain, and they included women. "Malie, did I ... I..."

She nodded. "Yes."

"Oh my God. Malie, I don't—

"It's okay. You were very drunk and I was sober."

"Yet, you remember me?" He looked down at their clasped hands. "How?

"You said 'thank you' as you kissed my forehead and left. No one has ever done that before or after."

Brian dropped his head and pulled his hands away from her grasp. "Dear God," he moaned. "I don't know what to say."

She grabbed his hand, and with her other hand lifted his head. When their eyes met, he was surprised to see a slight smile on her face, and her eyes held no sign of accusation. "Brian, you don't have to say anything. We were both being forced to do things that we didn't want to. I had my debt to Jake, and most of the military men fighting that horrible war needed those shore leaves to keep them sane. Now, as I work toward turning my life around, I've worried that if you remembered being with me, it would disgust you."

"Malie—

"Please, let me finish." Holding his head between her hands, she continued to force him to look at her. "That's why I avoided looking directly at you, and avoiding any conversation with you. But over the past few months, I've watched you do your job, settle into this community, and most importantly, how you've treated me. My holding back on any true relationship with you just didn't seem to make sense anymore." Her slight smile broadened and she went on. "Because, you see, Brian, I think I've fallen in love with you."

Before he could respond, he felt her lips touch his. As stunned as he was, he reacted by making it a joint kiss. Their lips gently caressed each other until he finally managed to move his head back slightly. "I love you, too." He pressed his lips against hers again and this time it became a deep, moist kiss that neither wanted to end. He put his arms around her, and pulled her body against his, while her hands moved from his face to his back, returning his hug.

Eventually, he ended the kiss, but continued to hold her close.

"Brian," her words were spoken into the soft wool of his coat. "I'm so ashamed—

"Stop." He pulled her even closer. "That was then. This is now, and now is the way we will move forward."

"But—

"No, no buts about the past." He lifted her chin so their eyes could meet. "Our pasts are in the past. We start now." His eyes demanded an answer.

She nodded. "We start now."

They sealed their agreement with another deep kiss as he held them together in a warm embrace. When the kiss finally ended, they continued to sit on the bench while nestled against each other, and silently watched the full moon dominate the sky.

Malie's mind replayed what had happened in the last few minutes bringing her to sigh contentedly.

"I agree," said Brian. "What a night this has been."

Though neither wanted these moments to end, Brian gave her a final squeeze then stood up and extended his hand. "Now, I better get you home before Peggy and Elmer get worried about you. Elmer seems like a nice guy, but I've got a feeling there's more to him than he lets on. And, it's never wise to cross Peggy."

Malie laughed, and she stood up. "Yes, we'd be in big trouble raising their dander."

Brian put his arm around her shoulder and they walked back to Miss Lucy's content with all that had been shared. Brian took her around to the back door, then pulled her into his arms again for a goodnight kiss. When it ended, he opened the door and let her step inside.

Malie came up on her toes and gave him a brief kiss. "This has been the best night of my life."

"Mine, too."

"I'll see you tomorrow?"

"Yes. I've some things I've got to do and now I need to talk with Devon. Our town busybodies keep complaining to him about who I'm keeping company with. So, I want him to know," he paused and kissed her forehead. "That we've moved on from just friendship to love, on both sides."

"Is this going to cause problems for you?"

"No, Devon has assured me my private life is none of the Mountie's business, nor is it the business of the town busybodies." He softly kissed her lips. "Now, go. I want to get home and enjoy my sweet dreams of you."

Malie giggled. "Yes, sweet dreams. Good night." She gave his arm a brief squeeze, then turned and closed the door. She leaned back against it and sighed. As she was about to start up the stairs to her room, she heard Brian begin to whistle as he headed home.

***

A little after eight the next morning, Brian was knocking on River and Blair's kitchen door. He was not surprised when it was Devon that answered his knock.

"Brian, something wrong?"

Brian grinned. "Actually, something is quite right."

Devon's brows rose in question.

"Get me a cup of that great smelling coffee and I'll tell you all about it."

Devon stood aside and let Brian in.

"Where's River and Blair?" asked Brian as he took his coffee from Devon and sat at the kitchen table.

"River's over at the mine and Blair headed on down to the general store. She needed a few more things for tomorrow's Easter dinner." Devon took a sip of his coffee and sat across from Brian. "So, what's so right that it brings you up here so early on Holy Saturday morning?"

"You know that relationship with Malie that I wasn't sure about?"

Devon nodded.

"Last night, after supper, we took a walk along the river and did a lot of talking. Bottom line, we're in love."

Devon smiled. "I'm happy for you, Brian. So is a wedding in the near future?"

Brian laughed. "I hope a wedding is in the future. But truth is, I need to take it slow. She's just learning how to trust, and I don't want to rush her into anything."

"She's come a long way."

The men enjoyed their coffee as they processed Brian's good news.

Finally, Brian asked, "Is this going to cause you any problems with the town busybodies?"

Devon shrugged. "Who knows? But like I said, your private life is yours. As long as you do a good job as the local Mountie with regard to Canadian law, I see no problem."

"Thanks, Sergeant." Brian smiled and gave a loose salute.

Devon laughed as he got up to pour them another cup of coffee.

The Picture, The Letter

At breakfast with Peggy and Elmer, Malie filled them in on the happenings of the previous night. They were very happy for Malie. Questions about a possible wedding came up. Malie handled it about the same as Brian had with Devon. Eventually, talk turned to work schedules and stock inventory. Malie took the day shift, and by ten a.m. she was bartending to the few regulars who came in most weekend mornings to shoot the bull as much as drink beer.

A little after noon, the local mailman dropped off the mail. Malie glanced through what were mostly bills, confirmation of pending orders, and the first ever—a letter for her from Hawaii. The name on the return address was Ruby, one of the girls who had also worked for Jake.

Malie had been too busy taking care of Kahale during the day to socialize with any of Jake's other working girls. But, once Kahale passed, Ruby had quietly managed to show Malie some compassion. They knew Jake frowned on his girls getting too close to each other, but Malie and Ruby had made time each week to take some walks along the beach. They both knew it would not sit well with Jake, so they made every effort to keep it from him.

Around noon, Elmer joined Malie behind the bar to give her a lunch break. As soon as Malie was in her room, she opened the envelope from Ruby. As she unfolded the letter, she found a picture. She managed to hold back a scream as the picture dropped from her fingers to the floor, as if it was on fire. As she began to read the letter, she found it was actually from Jake.

Malie, your actions when I came to get you made me angry. I always knew you and Ruby were friends, so I decided that maybe Ruby could help me make you understand you belong to me. You now have one week to come to me or Ruby will lose more than just a finger. Come alone. No Mountie. I have made my friends in blue aware of who kidnapped you and they are eager to arrest him.

Holding the letter in one hand, Malie reached down and picked up the picture. Ruby's face was covered in misery as she stared down at her hand resting on a blood-stained pillow. The severed baby finger was placed horizontally above Ruby's hand.

As she slipped the picture, along with the letter back into the envelope, her mind raced. Go to Brian — that was her first instinct. But then she remembered Jake had the local police in his pocket. What if they truly believed Brian had kidnapped her? Could they legally arrest him?

And Ruby. If she took any action against Jake, what would happen to Ruby? Tears filled her eyes. No. She couldn't risk Jake doing anything more to her. But how was she supposed to handle this?

Telling anyone would only make things worse. Brian, Peggy, and Elmer would never let her go. And even if she tried, how could she get out of Dawson without them stopping her? To take the ferry, she'd need a car—and she didn't know how to drive.

Then she remembered the delivery planes. They came in often, bringing goods to the local businesses. It was Easter weekend; stores would need holiday stock as well as their regular supplies.

Maybe a plane or two had flown in because of the holiday rush. She could only hope one had — and that she could catch a ride.

She looked around her room. She had found more happiness, peace and acceptance within these four walls than ever before in her life. And, to leave without so much as a goodbye, would hurt her as much as it would Peggy. She looked down at the envelope still in her hand. The look on Ruby's face made her decision for her. She would never be able to live with herself if anything worse happened to Ruby.

After putting the envelope in her purse, she changed into a flannel shirt, a pair of Levi's and her Altra running shoes. She packed a small valise with a change of clothes and a tooth brush. Mali went to the only window in the room and knelt down. After a couple of wiggling pressures to one of the panels below the window, she pushed the panel aside and pulled out a flower-patterned, flour sack. Over the past few years, she had managed to save a few hundred dollars. She pulled the money from the sack and put half of it in her purse. The other half, she put under her foot in her running shoes. Also, in the sack was her passport. Patrick had helped get one when he sent her and his wife Kathleen from Hawaii to Dawson near the end of the war. Hoping it was still good, she put it in her purse.

After a last look around her room, she peeked out into the hallway leading to the backdoor. She hurried from her room. Thankfully, no one saw her. Her heart hurt at not saying goodbye to the two people she couldn't love more.

On her rush to the area where planes landed, she had to share a wave with a couple acquaintances who were out shopping. They were busy getting things for Easter, so none stopped to chat.

When she was almost to the primitive airstrip area, she saw a small plane take flight. Her hope took a severe dip. Please, please let there be another one. As she rounded the last building, her hope rose again when she spotted another plane. She could hear its motors running, but the boarding steps were still in place and the door to the cabin was open.

She recognized the pilot. He flew in once or twice a month with supplies for the general store. After unloading, he would check into the local hotel, have supper at The Nugget, then finish off his day with a couple rounds at Miss Lucy's. He'd sit at the bar and often chat with Malie. He was happily married and had a son and daughter around Malie's age. All in all, a nice man.

Malie hurried up to him. "Luke," she called.

He turned and, at seeing who had called, smiled. "Malie. Nice to see you."

Trying to keep her voice calm, she spoke, "I didn't know you were in town. You didn't stop by Miss Lucy's last night."

"Wasn't in town last night. The Kramers had a run-on food, especially eggs, for Easter and needed some supplies. They're good customers so I agreed to fly them in. But this is a round tripper. Can't miss Easter with the wife and kids."

"How nice of you," she smiled. "Now, I need a favor."

He grinned. "Elmer run out of whiskey?"

She laughed. "No. It's me. I need a ride. A dear friend in Hawaii had an accident and is in the hospital. They aren't sure she's going to survive, so I really need to see her. Do you have room for me to fly back to Anchorage with you?"

"I'm sorry about your friend. Of course you can fly with me to Anchorage, but catching a connecting flight over the holiday weekend might be a problem."

"I'm sure. But I've got to try."

Luke glanced around her and spotted the valise. "Not much luggage."

"No. I just need to get to Hawaii as soon as possible."

After tossing the valise up into the back seat of the plane, he nodded, then pointed to the steps. "Climb in. I was just about to leave."

Within a couple minutes Luke was taxiing down the gravel runway, and Malie was on her way.

***

Elmer glanced at his watch, then at the doors to Miss Lucy's. Malie had been gone almost two hours. This wasn't like Malie. She was usually on time, even frequently early. He was about to call one of his barmaids over to handle the bar, when Peggy came out of their apartment.

As she headed for the bar, she noticed Elmer looked concerned about something. "Is there a problem?" she asked as she joined him.

"Not sure, but something isn't right. I relieved Malie for a lunch break almost two hours ago. Haven't seen hide, nor hair, of her since."

"That's not like Malie. Let me check her room. Her world's been crazy this past month. Maybe she just took a nap."

"Still, not like Malie."

Peggy nodded, then turned to head up the stairs. After knocking a couple times and getting no answer, she turned the door knob. It wasn't locked. Hating to intrude on the girl, Peggy reluctantly entered Malie's room. After a quick look around, she found nothing out of the ordinary and headed back downstairs.

"Find anything?" asked Elmer.

"No. Even her easel, canvases, and paint palettes look untouched. Where could she be?" Peggy called to the one barmaid on the floor. "Have you seen Malie?"

"No, not after she left for lunch."

A man sitting at the end of the bar offered. "Saw her as I was on my way here. About a block or two down the way. I guessed she was out for a walk in her heavy shirt, Levis, and running shoes."

Peggy went over to him. "What direction was she headed?"

"South, toward the edge of town."

Peggy turned to Elmer. "I can't imagine where she would be going."

Elmer thought for a moment, then pointed to a couple envelopes next to the cash register. "She did take one of the envelopes when she headed upstairs."

"She's never received any mail before." Peggy paused to think, then her eyes widened. "You don't suppose that bastard Jake contacted her by mail?" For a few moments, Peggy and Elmer processed the chance that had happened, then Peggy touched Elmer's arm. "I hope not, but I think we should bring Brian in on this."

Elmer nodded. "Go. I'll stay here and take care of things."

Peggy rushed back into their apartment, then clad in a heavy coat, she headed toward the local Mountie office. She was almost to the door when someone called her name. She turned and saw

Brian coming down one of the side streets that led up to Dawson's residential area.

"Peggy, what's up?" asked Brian, as he joined her at his office door.

"I'm worried about Malie. Has she been with you?"

"No, I was up visiting with my sergeant major who's spending the weekend with Blair and River." Brian unlocked his office door, and motioned for Peggy to step inside. He picked up a few envelopes that had been dropped through his mail slot, then set them on his desk. He turned to Peggy. "So why are you worried about Malie?"

Peggy brought him up to date on Malie's long lunch break and that Elmer said she'd received a letter. "This was a first since she's been with us. I can't help but wonder if that Jake wrote to her."

Brian shook his head. "No, I think he got my message, loud and clear, about leaving her alone."

Peggy repeated what one of her locals said about seeing Malie on Front Street near the edge of town and how she was dressed.

"End of Front Street? Maybe she was on her way to do some painting."

"I checked her room. She didn't take any of her paint or canvasses with her."

Brian thought about what Peggy had told him. As he processed it, he sat down behind his desk. Peggy sat across from him. "Did Malie talk to you about what happened last night?"

Peggy smiled. "Yes. Elmer and I always felt there was something between you two. I'm really happy for the both of you."

Brian nodded. "I've been attracted to her ever since I first met her at the Finley's Christmas Eve dinner party, but I could never understand why she kept avoiding me. When she did have to speak to me, she was always curt and never really looked at me. So, after last night, when we laid all our cards on the table, we both had a lot to process." Brian paused in thought, then went on. "You know she never takes things lightly. Maybe she's out walking to clear her mind. We talked about beginning to live for today and look forward to tomorrow."

"That's beautiful, Brian. I can only hope you're right."

He stood up and walked toward the door. "Here's what I'll do. My horse needs some exercise, so I'll saddle up and take a ride around town. She's seen me exercising him before, so if I find her, it won't look like I'm checking on her."

Peggy joined him at the door. "Good idea. I'm sure you're right. She just needed some alone time." Peggy gave his arm a thank you squeeze, then headed on back to Miss Lucy's.

Within a few minutes, Brian had Ranger saddled, and was heading down Front Street in the direction Peggy's customer had last seen Malie. He rode slowly past all the businesses, hoping to catch sight of Malie. After no sight of her, he headed on out of town. Eventually, he wandered over to the Yukon River bank and let Ranger lap up some water, then continued with his search. As he rode along, he noticed what looked to be tire tracks in the gravel used for small plane take-offs and landings.

Remembering that this was Easter weekend, he wrote them off as being from last week and continued on. Ten minutes later he reined the horse to a stop near an area along the river where he knew Malie loved to paint. He stood up in the stirrups and twisted his head in almost a circle to get a wide view and found no sign of her. After a frustrated sigh, he turned Ranger around and headed back toward town.

As he passed Kramer's General Store, a thought crossed his mind. That was where Malie got her supplies for painting. Maybe she didn't take her existing painting equipment, because she was picking up some new material from Kramer's. He dismounted, and tied Ranger to a hitching rail on the side of the building and headed inside.

"Happy Easter, Constable," smiled Mrs. Kramer. "How can I help you?"

"Happy Easter, Mrs. Kramer," he smiled back. "No help needed, just a question."

"Ask away, young man."

"I was out on my morning ride, and I usually spot Malie from Miss Lucy's out painting somewhere along the river, but I didn't see her this morning. I thought maybe she might have stopped here for some paint supplies."

"No, she didn't. But, if you see her, let her know that her latest order arrived today."

"You had a delivery today? By air?"

"Yes, I ran out of so many basic food items—like flour, eggs, sugar, and breakfast meat—that I called my supplier yesterday. He agreed to set up a special delivery for me today. I couldn't believe it. Easter weekend!"

Brian remembered the plane tracks. But surely after last night, Malie would not just walk away from him or her life in Dawson, so he let it go. "That's really something that they would make a special delivery for you." Before turning to leave, he said goodbye, then added, "I hope you and Mr. Kramer have a very nice

Easter." Once outside, he untied Ranger and led him down the block toward Miss Lucy's.

After securing Ranger at the bar's hitching rail, he entered and found Elmer bartending, and Peggy sitting at the end of the bar. Seeing the concern on both their faces, he quickly shook his head no.

"Not a sign of her?" asked Peggy.

"Not a sign," said Brian as he took the stool next Peggy. "And she hasn't come back here yet?"

Elmer set a bottle of sarsaparilla in front of Brian as Peggy shook her head no to Brian's question. All three spent the next few minutes wondering where Malie was, and what she was up to, yet hoping she would walk through the saloon doors at any moment.

Brian was having trouble coming to terms with Malie's disappearance. He felt, no he knew, that they had crossed a line in their relationship last night. After what she had shared with him about his time in Oahu, he felt their agreement of 'we start now' had wiped out the past.

So, why would Malie disappear today? And, in this small town of Dawson, where could she hide, if that's what she was doing. He took another sip of his drink and began to retrace his morning. His ride had been uneventful, with no trace of Malie. Then, he remembered tire tracks in the primitive gravel runway. This triggered the conversation he'd had with Mrs. Kramer about the special delivery she'd had that morning.

"That's it!"

"What's it?" asked Peggy.

Brian shook his head, and gathered his thoughts as he looked over at Peggy. "I didn't realize I'd spoken out loud, but I think I know what she did."

"Did?"

"Yes, for whatever reason, I think she flew out of Dawson."

"Flew out? With who? Why?"

"I still haven't figured out why, but when looking for Malie this morning, I noticed tire tracks on the runway. I assumed they were old. Then, I talked with Mrs. Kramer and found out she had a grocery delivery from her supplier over in Anchorage.

"Luke was in town today?"

"Yes, and I think she hitched a ride to Anchorage with him."

"What the hell? Why?" asked Elmer.

Brian stood up. "I don't know, but I've got to check it out. I'm going back over to Kramer's and get Luke's number."

As Brian turned to leave, Peggy touched his arm. "Keep us in the loop."

"You know I will." He headed for the door, then turned around. "You do the same. If she shows up, let me know right away."

Brian led Ranger to the stable where he boarded him, then hurried back to Kramer's General Store. Mrs. Kramer was behind the counter ringing up a sale for some breakfast items for a young miner.

"What are you doing for Easter, young man?" she asked.

The miner looked barely out of his teens. "Just rest up, I guess. No work tomorrow."

"Think about coming to Dawson Chapel over on 4th Avenue tomorrow around 3 p.m. Some of the local women will be serving a free Easter dinner of ham, potatoes and green beans, followed by a variety of cakes for dessert."

"Free?" repeated the young man.

"Yes, free," Mrs. Kramer smiled. "Hope to see you there."

"Count on it," grinned the young man as he hurried out the door.

Mrs. Kramer looked over at Brian. "Constable, how can I help you?"

"I wanted to ask you about that delivery you got earlier today."

"What about it?"

"Was it Luke, the regular delivery man?"

"Yes."

"Do have Luke's telephone number?"

Brian's question was a surprise and brought a touch of concern to Mrs. Kramer's voice "Yes, of course. Just a moment." She hurried into her small office for a minute or two, then returned with a piece of paper. "Here's his business number and his home number. Giving you this has me worried. Why do you need his number?"

"Trust me, I just need to ask him some questions." Brian felt bad about upsetting this woman. "For now, I need to hurry."

Without another word, Brian headed back to his office. It was already late in the afternoon, so Brian decided to call Luke's home.

"Hello," answered a woman.

"Is Luke there?"

"Yes, may I tell him who's calling?

"Tell him it's Brian Stockton from Dawson City." He purposely left off his title of constable, so as not to bring undue concern to the woman.

"He's in the garage. Hold on a minute and I'll go get him."

After a surprisingly short wait, Luke came on the line. "Constable, how can I help you?"

"You were in Dawson earlier today."

"Yes, a special delivery for the Kramers."

"Were you alone?"

"On the trip up, I was, but I had a passenger on the way back."

"Malie, from Miss Lucy's?"

"Why do you need to know?"

"It's complicated, but I think she may need help."

Brian's words validated Luke's opinion of Malie's leaving Dawson so quickly and without luggage. "Yes, it was Malie. And, she did seem a little upset."

"Did she say where she was going and why?"

"Said she had a friend in Hawaii who'd been in a serious accident, and she needed to get to her as soon as possible."

"Where did you take her?"

"Here. The last I saw of her, she was headed into the Anchorage Airport hoping to catch a plane to Hawaii."

"Thanks, Luke. Sorry to have bothered you this Easter weekend."

"No problem. At least, I hope there's no problem. Malie is a nice lady, and I'd hate to hear of anything bad happening to her."

"Yes, she is a nice lady. I've got to run, but thanks for the information." Before Luke could answer, Brian hung up and had already placed a call to River Finley's house saying he was heading over there to discuss something important with his sergeant major.

Less than ten minutes later, Brian, Devon and River were out on River's back porch. River's wife and daughter were over at River's mother's house getting things ready for their Easter dinner and his sons were off with their friends playing their first baseball game of the season. Brian hurried through the details of Malie's disappearance and where he suspected she had gone. He shared his concern that Jake might be involved.

"I can't imagine Malie leaving," said River. "She's like a daughter to Peggy."

"I know," agreed Brian.

Devon nodded. From the tone of Brian's voice and the concern on his face, he knew Brian either had a plan to find Malie or was desperately looking for one. "So, Brian, got a plan?"

"Nothing specific, I just know I have to find out why she left. And, if Jake is involved, I need to get her back here to Dawson." Brian turned to River. "Is Patrick coming up for Easter with the family?"

River shook his head no. "He's too booked up with travels for the holiday weekend. Mom's not happy about it, but he just can't get away."

"Damn. I was hoping he'd be flying in. I want to get to Hawaii as fast as I can."

"Whoa, my young constable," said Devon. "I know Dawson doesn't have much of a crime problem, but we can't leave them without some sort of law enforcement."

"You're right. Sorry, I wasn't thinking straight."

"Look, I know Malie means a lot to you and to the Finley family, so let's calm down and think this through." After getting a frustrated nod from Brian, Devon continued. "First we need transportation, then a sub for you at the Dawson Mountie office." He turned to River. "Any way of getting in touch with Patrick? He's our best bet for a quick way to get to Hawaii."

"I can call him. I bet he'll get here somehow. Pat will always be grateful to Malie for saving him from the false accusation of murdering Kathleen's husband. I'll give him a call," said River, as he went back into the house.

"Now," said Devon, "if Patrick does agree to come back, I'm assuming you will want to go to Hawaii with him."

Brian didn't flinch as he gave his boss his answer. "Yes. I hope you understand and can give me some time off."

Devon smiled. "You know I will."

"Look," said Brian, "there's not really much crime here. Most are minor citizen's complaints about unruly neighbors, and the occasional young miners in bar fights."

"I know. I get your reports. Still, Dawson needs a law enforcer here."

Brian thought for a minute, then made a suggestion. "Could you deputize River to cover for me?"

Devon raised his eyebrows at the thought, then laughed. "You know, I think he could do it." Before Brian could answer, Devon went on. "But not sure headquarters would approve it. So, I'll stay here in Dawson for a few days. If it takes longer, I'll send for Ron or Dave to come up from Whitehorse."

"You'd do that for me?"

"Special situations require special actions."

Before Brian could answer, River came back out onto the porch wearing a smile.

"He's coming?" asked Brian.

"Yep. When he told Kathleen what was going on, she agreed that they needed to do all they can for Malie. After working things out with his partner, Joe, he'll fly up here. He'll probably get here sometime early tomorrow morning."

"Thanks, River."

River just nodded.

"So now we wait," said Devon.

"Yeah, wait," said Brian. "But, while I wait, I'm going to head back to Miss Lucy's and give Peggy and Elmer an update. Then, I'll pack a change of clothes and come back here."

River and Devon watched Brian take off in almost a run.

"Man, I hope things work out for Brian," said River.

"I do too. He's a fine young man," said Devon.

***

After thanking Luke for what turned out to be a free ride, Malie headed into the Anchorage Airport office. She knew that, because it was Easter weekend, her efforts to get a flight either to Oahu or a connecting airport would be a challenge, but luck was with her. She was able to get a flight to San Francisco within the next hour. Then, after switching planes, she booked a flight to Oahu first thing Easter morning.

Because of the time difference, Malie arrived in Oahu a little after ten a.m. Although she managed a little sleep during her wait in San Francisco and on the flight to Oahu, she was a little groggy, and not ready to face Jake. Then, the picture of Ruby and her hand flashed through her mind, and she immediately refocused and hailed a cab. The ride to Jake's bar was far too short. As the cab drove away, she turned, faced the swinging doors and shuddered. She shook it off, pushed them open, and entered her own version of hell.

Despite it being Easter morning, there were quite a few customers. Some of them drank at the bar and others sat at tables being entertained seductively by scantily dressed women. Malie recognized a couple of them, but several were new.

She headed for the bar and got the attention of the bartender. "Gus, where can I find Jake?"

He shrugged. "Up in his apartment, I guess. Haven't seen him yet today. By the way, surprised to see you back here."

Now, Malie shrugged as she turned toward the hallway that divided eight closet-sized rooms, four on each side, where the men were taken for service. She shuddered as a myriad of memories flashed through her mind. As much as she dreaded going into the hallway, it was also where she'd find the stairs leading up to the second floor. After a deep breath, Malie took the first step and within a little over a minute, she found herself standing at Jake's door. Before losing her nerve, she knocked.

"Yeah?" Jake called out.

"Open the door," she said.

The door opened. Jake was dressed in a loose gray tee, black slacks and wearing flip-flops. An evil grin flashed across his face. "Welcome home, my favorite little pussy."

"Where's Ruby?"

His grin morphed into an evil pout. "Now, is that any way to greet the man who did so much for you?"

Malie slipped into the room and closed the door. "Jake, where is Ruby?"

He glared down at Malie. "Let's get something straight. I ask the questions. I tell you what I want to tell you. You just listen, and do what I say, like in the old days."

His glare no longer frightened her, but she realized that demanding things would get her nowhere with him. When he quit talking Malie said, "I understand."

"Good." He appraised the look on her face and wondered if she was alone. "Sit down. There are some things I need to know." He pointed to a small sofa. Once she complied, he pulled a chair from a dinette set and sat across from her. "Now, some questions. When did you get here?"

"I flew in about an hour ago."

His eyes narrowed with suspicion. "And who flew you in?"

"United from San Francisco."

"How did you get to San Fran?"

"Left Dawson on a food delivery plane headed for Anchorage, then a United flight from Anchorage to San Francisco."

"Not with that Air Force guy?"

"No. I told no one. As soon as I got that picture of Ruby, I came straight here."

"What about that Mountie?"

"I said I told no one."

"I hope so, 'cause if either of them comes looking for you, just one call to my buddies in blue will get them behind bars on kidnapping charges."

"So, you said." Now, Malie leaned toward Jake and demanded, "Where is Ruby?"

The edge of Jake's lip curled viciously. "You belong to me. I decide when we do anything. Got that?"

Malie refused to be intimidated and held her position facing him. "So, you say. But if you want that from me, take me to Ruby."

"Don't demand anything from me. You're lucky you made so much money for me or your fate for deserting me would be much worse than what's happened to Ruby."

Malie sighed and sat back. "Okay. I understand. But, please, let me see Ruby."

"Begging. That's my girl. See, just do what I tell you." He pushed his chair back and stood up. "Follow me. Don't talk to anyone. Just follow me."

He led her out of his apartment, down the stairs, through the dimly-lit hallway and out the back door. To their left, was the door to his parking garage. They got into his Buick, and soon they were headed toward the outskirts of town. He turned into an area that housed several warehouses. Because it was Easter, every place was closed.

At one end of the area was a series of storage sheds about the size of a house, a car, or boat. After telling Malie to sit still, he got out and opened the door to a shed three doors from the end of the units. Motioning for Malie to follow him, he exited the car and the unit, then closed the door.

As he was about to open the door to the next shed, he turned to Malie. "Not a word until I re-close the door. Now, turn around so you'll be backing into the shed."

She turned and did as she was told.

He opened the door, pulled Malie inside, switched on a low-watt light bulb hanging from the middle of the roof, then closed the door. "Okay, you can turn around now."

Malie's eyes swept around the area, and finally settled on a naked woman tied to a chair in one of the corners. A rope secured the woman's chest to the chair, with her arms tied behind her. Both of her legs were tied to chair legs that were bolted to the floor. "No, no, no," she screamed as she ran to Ruby.

The tied-up woman's eyes widened in disbelief at Malie's arrival. The duct tape covering her mouth muffled her words, but she managed a very hoarse scream.

Malie touched Ruby's shoulder as she took in the woman's bondage, then turned to Jake. "Can't we take off the tape and untie her? Please? I came back here like you asked."

Jake shrugged. "There's no one around. That's why I rented these three units at the end. Even if there are people around no one would hear her. The two units on either side of us are mine. So, go ahead. Rip off the tape."

Despite the pain, Ruby did not cry or scream. She just took some very deep breaths. When the tape was fully off, Ruby managed a sad smile up at Malie. "Why did you come?"

The question surprised Malie. "I had to. When I saw what he did to your hand, I couldn't risk him doing even worse like he threatened."

Ruby slowly shook her head. "He lied."

"Lied? What do you mean?" Malie turned to Jake. "You'll let her go now, won't you?"

"Well, yes, I am going to let her go, or I should say she's going somewhere."

"Somewhere? What are you talking about?"

Jake looked over at Ruby. "Are you still mad at me?"

"I'm way beyond mad. I hate you and want you dead."

He looked back at Malie and shrugged again. "She hates me. I think she might tell someone about all this."

"No, we'll keep this a secret. Right, Ruby?"

"It doesn't matter whether I would or not. He isn't about to trust me. I could only wish he'd just kill me and get it over with."

"No! Ruby. We'll help each other through this somehow."

"I wish you hadn't come. He has plans for me. Tell her, Jake."

"Plans? Jake, what's she talking about?"

"It's none of her business—so shut up." He threatened Ruby with a hard glare.

Ruby just laughed. "You don't scare me anymore, asshole." She turned to Malie. "He's been bringing men here, and taking offers from them to buy me, so they can take me to their country for God knows what." She turned back to Jake. "Don't think I didn't hear you talk to that last guy about no one missing me, so I could even be used for terminal sex that men pay a fortune for."

Malie's eyes widened in terror. "NO! Jake no! Tell me you'd never do such a thing."

Jake raised his eyebrows above his malicious sneer. "Not to you, my sweet money maker."

Malie shook her head from left to right in disbelief. She turned to Ruby. "I ... I ... I ..."

Ruby shrugged. "I just wish you hadn't come back. You were my hero. You got away. I was always trying to find a way out like you did. But surely, you now see your coming back isn't going to save me. So, please leave. Right now. Run." Tears streamed down Ruby's face.

"Shut up," yelled Jake as he slapped Ruby's face, then turned to Malie. "Don't even try to run. You know that one call to my guys in blue, and they'll find you and bring you back to me. So, don't even try."

Malie's mind was awhirl. Should she run, obey Jake, attack Jake or try to free Ruby? As each thought crossed her mind, she realized it wouldn't work and went on to the next choice. Eventually, she had to accept that none would work. Still, she could not let Jake win. There had to be something she could do. Eventually, she pretended to comply with his demand. "I won't run. But, can I do one thing for Ruby? Please?"

"What?"

"Can we have a little time to sit and talk—just me and Ruby?" She pointed to a few bottles of water against the wall. "Let us have some water and a few moments to say goodbye. Then, I'll go with you back to the bar, and do whatever you tell me to do."

Jake's better judgement warned him about letting these two women have their moments to say goodbye was not a good idea. Still, letting Malie do this might bring back more of her past submissiveness.

"Okay, but not long. Make it quick."

Malie walked over to the bottles and grabbed two. She was trying to come up with a plan to outwit Jake and get Ruby out of this mess. When she noticed a bucket sitting in one of the corners of the shed, an idea came to her. With her back to Jake, she held one of the bottles to Ruby's lip, then flashed her eyes between Ruby and the bucket and slightly nodded.

Ruby got the message. "No, I can't drink anything. I've got to pee real bad."

Malie turned to Jake. "She needs to relieve herself. Can you untie her so she can use that bucket?"

"There's a hole in the chair, so just slide the bucket under the chair."

"Jake, please, cut her loose. Let her do her thing, and let us say our goodbyes with a hug. Please?"

"No."

"Please," Malie begged. "Look at her. She is in no condition to be a threat to you."

Jake smiled watching Malie beg. She seemed to be slipping back into the submissive pussy he'd convinced needed to pay off her debt for all he did for her old boyfriend, Kahale. Wearing a smirk, he walked over to Ruby. "I'll have Malie untie you for a couple minutes, but don't try anything or you'll be sorry." He pointed to a table that held some tools and a small whip. "You hear me?" He threatened.

Ruby just glared at him.

"You hear what I said?" He threatened.

"Please, Ruby," urged Malie.

After taking a deep breath, Ruby snarled. "I hear you."

"Go ahead," Jake motioned to Malie. "You two have about five minutes."

Malie set the water bottles on the floor, then she managed to untie Ruby. As she reached down to pull Ruby up for a hug, Ruby tried to stand. Her legs, especially her knees protested from their long time in bondage, and she started to fall. Malie pulled her up into her arms.

"Lean against me. I'll hold you," said Malie.

Slowly, feeling began to return. As her blood flow returned, Ruby could stand on her own. She smiled at Malie. "I've missed you."

"I'm so sorry. I should have written," said Malie. "I should have—

"Don't," interrupted Ruby. "You and I both know Asshole wouldn't have let me receive any letter from you." She actually managed a smile. "You look good. Things are going well for you?"

"Yes. Some wonderful people have helped me find a new life. Maybe you can come—

"Don't," said Ruby. "It just makes me sad. My life is over and by coming back yours probably is too."

"No, Ruby. There are people out there who care—

"Enough," said Jake.

Malie wanted more time. "Ruby hasn't used the bucket nor drank her water yet. Please, give us another couple of minutes."

"Fine. Another minute or two."

Malie moved the bucket under the chair where Ruby had been tied.

It was the last place Ruby wanted to sit, but the truth was, she needed to pee. Reluctantly, she sat down. When her release was finished, she picked up a water bottle from the floor and took a long swallow. She kept the bottle to her lips, pretending to drink more. Her eyes never left Jake.

To avoid the hate Jake read in her eyes, he glanced down at his wrist watch.

Recognizing a moment of opportunity, Ruby sprung from the chair, and dove her head into Jake's stomach. The sudden impact caused him to fall backwards, and bump his head on the table that held the tools and whip. He landed on his back as blood began to form around his head. Before he could react, vengeance took hold of Ruby, and she let her anger rule.

She kicked his crotch twice. Before he could curl up in pain and try to turn on his side, she jumped up in the air and landed on his crotch. She continued to jump, and land, on his body from his abdomen, chest, throat and finally on his face. Ignoring his screams of pain, and with a strength she didn't know she had, she rolled him onto his stomach to give his back the same stomping until she heard bones cracking.

As she rolled him onto his broken back, one of his arms moved toward the side pocket of his pants. Several stomps on his arm ended his attempt. Ruby reached down and pulled a small revolver from his pocket.

"You really think I didn't know about this!" She screamed at Jake's broken, bloody body.

It happened so fast, that a stunned Malie was frozen in disbelief at Ruby's attack. At the sight of the gun, she managed to find her voice. "No! Ruby, stop!"

"Not yet," said Ruby as she pointed the gun at Jake's face. He was still alive and moaning in misery. "Look at me. I want you to know who is sending you to hell!" She fired into his right eye, then re-aimed, and shot him in the heart.

His body jerked in reaction, then went limp. Silence reigned.

Ruby threw the gun on his body, then turned to scan the room. On the table, she spotted what she had been wearing when Jake brought her to the shed. She grabbed her muumuu and flip-flops and quickly slipped into them.

Malie finally found her voice. "Ruby, we—

Ruby shook her head. "No. There's no we. But, both of us need to get the hell out of here. I'm going to find a way back into town, then try to figure out my next move. You need to head back to where you came from."

"He's probably dead, but we need to call someone —

"He is dead, so get the hell out of here." She opened the shed door, then turned to Malie. "You and I know the world is a better place without him. Let him lay there and rot. Save yourself." She turned and hurried away from the shed.

Malie took a couple of steps to go after her, but sadly realized there was no way Ruby would listen to her. She turned, and looked down at Jakes's distorted body. Her common sense told her that he was dead, but she felt the need to see if there was any sign of life. A finger under his nose detected no breath.

She pushed the gun away from his heart area and felt his chest. Nothing. She knew she should do like Ruby. Close the shed door and leave. There was a time when she could have, but these last few years of living among normal, caring people had changed her.

A collage of images flashed through her mind including Patrick, Kathleen, Peggy, Elmer and finally Brian. His words of how they needed to live their lives came to mind. 'That was then, this is now, we start now.' She knew what she needed to do.

A Human Being Did It

ALMOST A HALF HOUR later, standing at the shed door, Malie heard sirens. Earlier, she had walked to the shed area entry gate searching for a manager's office. She found it closed, but near it was a phone booth. She told the operator medical help was needed in one of the sheds, as well as the police.

She watched an ambulance arrive and waved it down. Before the attendants opened their doors, a police car arrived. Malie opened the shed door and let the attendants rush over to Jake's body. After a quick check of the body, the attendants informed the police officer, "Dead male. Shots to the face and heart, but looks like he also took quite a beating."

The officer came down on one knee next to the body to verify what he'd been told. Noticing the gun on Jake's chest, he asked the medics if they had a bag for the gun. After securing the gun, the officer checked Jake's pockets and found a wallet. He went back to his car and used his two-way radio to report his find and asked for back-up. Going back to the body, he spoke to the medics. "I need you to leave the body as it is. An investigative team, including the coroner, is on their way."

"We'll wait for the coroner to see if anything from us is needed."

"Thanks," said the officer. "Other than that woman over there, was there anyone else here when you arrived?"

"No, just her."

The slightly chubby, young, dark-haired officer, wearing a name badge identifying him as Reynolds, walked over to Malie. "Ma'am, are you the person who called for help?"

"Yes. I assumed he was dead, but I couldn't just leave him there."

"Ma'am, I have to ask. Did you kill him?"

"No." Malie decided to keep her answers brief to protect Ruby.

"Did you see who did?"

"A stranger." Malie felt she wasn't lying. The woman who killed Jake was not Ruby. Somewhere along the way, Ruby had been replaced by a woman bent on vengeance.

"A stranger? You've never seen this stranger before?"

Before Malie could answer, a car pulled up, and two men wearing dark suits exited the car.

Officer Reynolds turned from Malie to greet the new arrivals. "Hey, guys, got a gruesome one for you. Here's a wallet we found on the victim." Then, he nodded toward Malie. "And, a person of interest."

"Thanks, Reynolds," said Detective O'Brien, taking the wallet. As they were examining it, another car drove up and a gray-haired man dressed in green scrubs, and a woman in gray scrubs exited it and joined in on the body examination.

Malie watched as the men discussed the body. Eventually, the detectives began walking around the shed checking out the table holding the tools and whip, the chair with the hole in the seat, the bucket, and the rope lying at the foot of the chair. O'Brien's partner, Wailani took photos of the area and the body.

The coroner stood up as did his assistant. "O'Brien, did you I.D. this guy?"

"Yeah, found his wallet. Name is Jake Bennett, and his address is on nightclub row." He called over to the officer. "Reynolds, ever hear of a Jake Bennett with an address on nightclub row?"

"Yeah, he owns the Flyin' Hi, a bar on Ala Moana Boulevard."

O'Brien felt Reynolds was holding something back. "And?"

Reynolds shrugged, then added. "Rumor has it he runs a cat house there."

"Rumor, huh?"

Again, Reynolds shrugged as he nodded toward Malie.

They were interrupted when the coroner asked, "Are you done with the body? I need to get it back to my lab so I can finalize the cause and time of death."

O'Brien looked at Wailani. "Need anything else?"

"No, I think we got what we need."

"Okay for us to load the body now?" asked one of the medics.

"Yes," said the coroner. "We'll follow you to the lab."

Once Jake's body was loaded into the ambulance and driven away, the detectives turned to Malie.

"Your name?" asked O'Brien.

"Malie Iona."

"You live here in Oahu?"

"Not anymore."

"Where do you live these days?

"Canada, the Yukon to be specific.

"What brought you back here?"

"Jake had something I needed to take care of."

"So, you knew the victim."

"Yes."

"How?"

"I worked for him a few years back."

"In his bar? A barmaid?"

"Yes."

"Just a barmaid?"

"Among other things, yes."

O'Brien understood and decided to let that subject end. "Officer Reynolds indicated that you might be a person of interest. Does that mean you killed him?"

"No, I did not. He may have been an evil man, but no, I did not kill him."

"But you witnessed who did?"

"Yes."

"And ..."

"It was a stranger."

"How did you happen to be here and see it all go down?"

"He was holding something that I needed to deal with and he drove me out here to see it."

"Holding what?"

"I'd rather not say."

O'Brien took a moment to really look this woman over and think about her brief answers. He noticed her eyes, and how they looked everywhere, except at him. She was obviously holding something back, and so far, she hadn't really excluded herself as the killer.

"Okay, let's get back to the stranger. How did the stranger get here?"

"I don't know. The stranger was here when Jake and I arrived."

"Male or female?"

"All I can tell you is that it was a human being."

"White, black, old, young?"

"A human being."

O'Brien shook his head and raised his voice. "You're being too evasive. Normally, a witness has more details to share. I'm beginning to come to two conclusions. Either you're hiding something, or you did kill him." He turned to Wailani and Reynolds. "What do you think?"

Reynolds shrugged. "I think she killed him."

Wailani also tried to get a look at Malie's eyes, but to no avail. Eventually, he answered his partner. "I guess I agree with you. She's either hiding something, or she's the killer."

"Well, Miss Iona, that means we're going to have to take you down to the station for more questions. Do I need to handcuff you?"

"No. I'll go with you."

O'Brien nodded toward their car. Wailani escorted Malie into the back seat while O'Brien thanked Reynolds and told him they'd get in touch if they needed anything else.

Sitting in the back seat of the detective's car, Malie watched Reynolds drive off and tried to relax as O'Brien started the car to return to the police station. A thought ran through her mind that maybe Jake had won. Her life of being raised in a male-dominated cult, then being forced into a life of prostitution could end with a lifetime in prison, or worse.

***

Brian stood on the Finley's front porch watching the sky ease from total darkness to an ash grey on this Easter Sunday morning. He knew it would still be an hour until the sun crested the distant mountains. He really wanted a cup of coffee, but he was afraid he'd make too much noise trying to find the filters, the ground coffee, filling the coffee pot with water, and lighting the stove to get it brewing.

He almost did it anyway so it would wake everyone, and they could get on their way to Hawaii—to Malie. But common sense won out, and he waited. He knew Patrick needed his sleep. He and his wife Kathleen hadn't arrived in Dawson until after midnight last night.

"Coffee?"

Brian had been so deep in thought, that he hadn't heard the screen door open, so Blair's voice startled him. "Yes, please." He smiled as he accepted a cup from Blair. "You're up early." The coffee was hot, black and was restoring some of the energy that his night of only a few hours of sleep had drained from him.

"Habit," she said after taking a sip of her own coffee.

"Habit?"

"It's Easter morning. Which used to mean hiding Easter eggs and finishing the baskets left by the Easter bunny. Gosh, I miss it."

"Didn't I see three baskets on the table this morning?"

She laughed. "The kids may have outgrown the Easter bunny, but Mom hasn't."

"I guess my mother felt the same. And, I can tell you, my brother and I loved it."

Both silently sipped at their coffee watching the dawn continue to light up the Yukon sky. As Blair drained her cup, she asked Brian, "Need a refill?"

He extended his cup. "Thanks."

She took it and was back in no time and handed him a hot refill.

"Thanks. I really needed the caffeine rush."

"You're welcome." Blair could feel Brian's frustration at having to wait for the others. If it was up to him, she knew he would have jumped aboard the plane, and have Patrick fly right out and head for Hawaii the minute Patrick had arrived last night. "Just try to relax and enjoy the coffee and the sunrise. Patrick won't sleep long. He and Kathleen don't want anything bad to happen to Malie."

"I know. I just want to be there for whatever she needs."

"I fully understand. I felt the same about finding River after he took off to find his birth mother without me."

"I did hear something about that."

"He was on a mission to find her, and wouldn't let anything or anyone, including me, slow him down." She went on to tell Brian about Patrick showing up at her parent's house on his trek to find his brother. She joined Patrick, against his and her parents' wishes. But ultimately, they did catch up with River, who admitted that they were right. He needed them. "So, you see, I think things will turn out okay. Patrick helped me, so I just know he's the one to help you find Malie."

Brian smiled. "Thanks for sharing that part of your past and, by the way, I think River is a lucky man to have you."

Blair laughed. "Yes, he is." Hearing someone call her name she headed for the door. "Speaking of River, I think he's up and wanting some breakfast."

When Brian and Blair entered the kitchen, they spotted River, Devon, and Patrick pouring coffee. "There you are," said River, who gave Blair a kiss on the forehead, then looked over at Brian. "Did you sleep at all last night?"

"A couple hours."

After a much-needed gulp of his cup of caffeine, Patrick sat down at the table. "Well, good morning, everyone. I don't know about any of you, but I think we all need some breakfast as we make some decisions about how we're going to handle our search for Malie. Kathleen is getting dressed and will be down shortly."

"Good idea," said Blair. She and River started to gather everything out of the refrigerator and by the time Kathleen arrived, platters of eggs, bacon, hash browns and toast were on the table. As each filled their plate, Blair topped off their coffee cups, then sat down.

Between bites of food, it was agreed that those going to Hawaii would be Patrick, Brian, River and Kathleen. There was some discussion about whether Kathleen should go, but it was finally settled upon that Malie might need another woman's shoulder to lean on. Blair agreed to take care of Patrick and Kathleen's two children. It was decided that they would fly out within the next hour.

An hour later, Brian was surprised, but pleased, when he felt the rumble of the plane's wheels racing down the gravel runway fade away to the hum of the engine as the plane lifted up into the air. He knew it would still be hours before they reached Oahu. They would need to make a quick stop in Anchorage to fuel up, but they were on their way.

Jack, one of Patrick's fellow pilots during the war, was now working for Patrick's airline. Jack had kept in touch with another war vet, Vernon, who had been a motor pool mechanic stationed in Oahu during the war. He had married and stayed on in Oahu after his discharge. Jack arranged for Vernon to meet them at the airport with some sort of transportation they would need on arrival.

Brian yawned and decided he'd try for a little sleep, but Patrick let them know he was on the approach to the Anchorage airport. They were able to fuel up quickly, and again were on their way. This time Brian reclined his seat, closed his eyes and finally managed to drift off.

For the rest of the flight, he was able to catch a couple hours sleep between hours of staring out the window and wondering what he'd find when they finally arrived. Everyone else, except Patrick, was doing the same thing, allowing Brian's what-if scenarios to race through his thoughts. It occurred to him that perhaps Malie might not want him to chase her down, but the memory of the look in her eyes, and the sincerity of their last kiss assured him the caring was mutual. She had finally opened up to him.

Kathleen made some coffee in the small kitchenette area. She made sure Patrick's cup was always full. She had brought along some snacks, including cookies, small pretzels and a package of fruit flavored hard candy. Other than a cup of coffee now and then, Brian left the snacks to the others.

Evening was setting in when Patrick told everyone to buckle up for their landing in Oahu. Because JP Air Taxi often flew private parties over to the Islands, the airport ground crew was familiar with their pilots and planes. They exited the plane within minutes of arriving. As Patrick informed the ground crew of the uncertainty as to how long they'd be there, River led Brian and Kathleen toward a man waving from the seat of a Jeep.

River, Kathleen and Brian crowded into the back seat of the Jeep. Brian was introduced, then as they waited for Patrick, Vernon inquired about why they were back in Oahu.

"You remember Malie?" River asked.

"Sure." He smiled at Kathleen. "Saved Patrick's ass."

"Yes, she did," said Kathleen

"I thought she went back to the States with you and Pat."

"She did." Kathleen brought Vernon up to date on Jake's visit to Dawson, and how they felt whatever he said or did forced Malie to go back to Oahu. "So, we're worried about her."

Vernon nodded, then smiled. "And here I thought it was because you all missed me so much."

River and Kathleen laughed as Patrick jumped into the Jeep. "What's so funny?" he asked.

"Vern thought we were here because we missed him," said River.

Now, Patrick laughed, "Of course we did." Then, he got serious. "But, did they fill you in on the other reason we're here?"

"Yeah," said Vernon, "looking for Malie."

"Have you seen her by any chance?"

"No."

"Okay, then we're at ground zero. I had my secretary make reservations for us at the Hilton. We'll need to go there and drop off our baggage. How long can we use the Jeep?"

"For as long as you need," said Vernon. "Right now, I'm going to head for my shop so you can drop me off. Just call me if you need me or when you're through with the Jeep."

Patrick smiled. "You're the best. Thanks."

After dropping Vernon off, they headed for the hotel, got checked in, took their baggage to their rooms, then headed down to the hotel restaurant for a bite to eat while deciding on a plan. Over an array of appetizers, they began to throw around ideas on what they needed to do to track Malie down.

It was finally agreed that the first place to look would be at Jake's bar. Patrick remembered the bar scene was only a few blocks from the hotel, so they decided to walk.

The sign 'Flyin' Hi brought emotional reactions to each of them. Patrick, Kathleen and River stopped walking as their stomachs turned just a little at the thought that the woman who had saved Patrick's life might be back under Jake's power to use her body. Brian kept walking hoping to find someone who had seen Malie, and could give them an idea of where she might be.

"Brian," called Patrick. "Wait. Let's do this together."

Either Brian didn't hear him or he was too focused to slow down. He walked into the bar and found it fairly crowded for an Easter Sunday night. Heading straight for the bar, he spotted a couple male bartenders. He approached the older one and got his attention.

"What'll it be?" asked the gray-haired man with the name tag 'Gus.'

"Need some information about a woman I'm looking for."

Gus shook his head. "Sorry. Information isn't served in the Flyin' Hi."

Brian reached into his pocket and laid a twenty-dollar bill on the bar. "Never?"

Gus glanced at the other bartender who was at the end of the bar chatting with a couple regulars while refilling their glasses. He turned back to Brian, then put his hand atop the twenty, slipped it off the bar and into his pocket, then shrugged. "Maybe a sip or two. What woman are looking for?"

"Malie Iona."

"Yeah, she's been gone for awhile, but she showed up this morning."

"She still here?"

"She headed upstairs to talk with the boss. Haven't seen her or him since. Through that door." He nodded toward it. "Take the stairs up to his apartment."

"Gus," called the other bartender. "Need you over here."

"Malie's a nice girl. Hope she's not in any trouble." He turned and headed for the end of the bar.

River, Patrick and Kathleen heard what Gus told Brian. Before they could comment, Brian was heading for the door Gus had pointed out. The other three followed. When they were all in the hallway, out of the view of the bar crowd, Patrick grabbed Brian's shoulder.

"Let's talk about this."

Brian shrugged off his grip. "What's to talk about?"

"We can't just barge in on the man."

"Yes, I can." He was already rapping on the door when the others caught up with him. After several raps, Brian reached for the door knob.

"Brian." Patrick again tried to stop him. "This is private property. We'd be breaking the law by barging in."

Before Patrick could finish, Brian had opened the door and stepped into the apartment. "Jake! Jake Bennett, I need to talk to you." Getting no answer, Brian walked further into the apartment. As he walked into the kitchen area, he called out for Jake. He did the same while looking into a bedroom with an unmade bed and a very messy bathroom.

The others were standing in the entry watching. "I don't know if I want him to find Jake or not," said Patrick. "God knows what he'd do or say."

Brian returned to the others. "He's not here, nor is Malie."

"Sorry, Brian," said Kathleen, "I was hoping we'd, at the very least, get a hint as to where Malie is."

"Damn, me too." He looked at Patrick and River. "Looks like we're back to zero again."

"I'm afraid so," said Patrick.

"Pat," Kathleen offered, "maybe Detective Harrison could help us."

"Detective Harrison, a cop?" asked Brian.

"Yes," said River, "he was a big help to Kathleen and I trying to see Patrick when the police had him in custody. He's been with the Oahu police for a long time and seems to know the area."

"Okay," said Brian, as he headed for the stairs. "Let's head on over to the police station now."

"Brian, stop." Patrick grabbed his arm. "It's Easter Sunday and it's late. He's probably at home with his family. Let's go back to the hotel, get some sleep and head on over there first thing in the morning."

"What if she needs us now?"

"Look," said Patrick. "How about we talk to the bartender again. Tell him we're at the Hilton, and if he sees Malie, he can tell her we're looking for her."

"Brian," soothed Kathleen, "it makes sense. At least, there's an outside chance she'll contact us. If not, we'll go to the police first thing tomorrow."

The last thing Brian wanted to do was stop looking for her, but his common sense told him they were right. This way, the one person who had seen her would be able to tell her they were in Oahu and looking for her. Eventually, he nodded. "Okay. But if she doesn't contact us tonight, it's the police very early tomorrow morning."

Once he was in agreement, they headed downstairs, gave the info to Gus and went to their rooms at the Hilton. Brian brewed himself some coffee, then sat looking out the window at the iridescence of the ocean waves as they rolled ashore under the shimmer of a large half-moon in the sky above Oahu. The beauty of it was lost on him. His thoughts were dark with concern about where Mali could be and was she okay. Nature finally kicked in, bringing him a restless sleep right there in the bedside chair.

***

"That's it? You're sticking with the killer was a human stranger?" asked O'Brien.

"Yes," said Malie.

At that moment, Wailani entered the detective unit and sat down at his desk.

"So, what's the verdict from the coroner?" asked O'Brien.

"Nothing official yet. But it was probably from two gunshots, one to the eye and the other to the heart. However, the victim could have been dead already from his body being stomped on from front to back, head to feet. He did say the gun was a small, double-barrel Derringer.

"What about any clues that could help us, like finger prints or foot size?"

"No."

O'Brien got up. "I'm going over there to—

"No use," said Wailani, "coroner's gone home for the night, and because they only have the one body, the lab is closed until morning."

"Damn." He turned back to Malie. "Unless you can give us more info on the killer, I'm afraid that leaves us no choice but to hold you as the killer."

"It wasn't me."

"So, you've said." He looked over at Wailani.

His partner shrugged. "Like I said before, I think she did it."

O'Brien sat back down and focused on Malie as he pondered whether to officially charge her with the killing or not. Eventually, he reached over, finished off his cold coffee, then stood up and tossed the paper cup into the trash just as two fellow detectives entered the room.

One of them stopped at O'Brien's desk and looked at Malie.

"Busy day?" he asked.

"Not until this afternoon. Then we got called to a homicide."

"This a witness?"

"Not sure witness or killer," said O'Brien. "Going to hold her until the coroner's report is complete."

The man continued on over to his desk. "Okay. We should be here catching up on some paper work. You two look like you could use some shut-eye. If we get a call, we'll get someone from the front desk to keep watch on the cell."

"Thanks. We'll be back early." He stood up, and motioned for Malie to do the same.

"I'm not officially charging you, but I am going to put you in our holding cell until the coroner finishes his report tomorrow morning. Follow me." He led her to one of two small cells against the back wall of the detective unit.

Malie stepped inside and watched him close and lock the door.

"If you need anything just ask Detective Harrison over there. I'll see you early tomorrow morning." He said goodbye to the night detectives, then he and Wailani headed out the door.

Malie looked around the small area. The only furniture was a cot. She decided it would be to her advantage to be as invisible as possible to the night detectives. She sat down, then stretched out on the cot.

Up until now, despite how the detectives were looking at things, Malie hadn't been too worried about being arrested for Jake's killing. Now, being locked up, reality was setting in. She knew she should have been more honest in her description of Ruby. But what Jake did was disgusting, and perhaps he even deserved to die.

When Ruby ran off, Malie knew she should have done the same. She remembered looking down at Jake's body, and not being able to decide if he was still alive or dead. Common decency demanded that she call for help in case he wasn't dead and had a chance to survive. She shivered with the realization that she could, in fact, be arrested and convicted of Jake's killing.

Her mind raced with what she should do. Naming Ruby would be a step in the right direction, but she just couldn't after all the poor woman had endured. She needed to talk with someone. The faces of her new-found family in Dawson flashed through her mind. She smiled thinking of Peggy, and how much her guidance and support would help. Then, she thought of Brian, and how he might know how to convince the law that she was innocent. Her eyes widened thinking about the law. She needed an attorney.

***

At a little after five Monday morning, Brian was about to head out the door when the phone rang. He hurried over to the nightstand and picked up the receiver. "Yes?"

"Brian," said River, "I'm assuming you're up, dressed and ready to head for the police station."

"I was just walking out the door."

"We figured as much. We're on our way. See you in the lobby." The line went dead.

Rather than wait for the elevator, Brian raced down the four flights of stairs. He entered the lobby just as one of the elevator doors opened and out walked Patrick and Kathleen.

"River is on his way," said Patrick as another elevator arrived bringing River to complete the posse.

Brian started for the door, but Kathleen took his arm. "Coffee, Brian. We all need some coffee and maybe a donut or bagel."

"I'm not thirsty or hungry."

"Maybe not," said Kathleen, "but it's not even five-thirty yet. I'm not sure Harrison or any detective would be at the station this early." She nodded toward the hotel coffee bar. "Please. We haven't eaten since we arrived. We need to keep up our strength so we can find Mali." She was fibbing about the eating. River had suggested room service sandwiches when they got back to the hotel, but Brian said he wasn't hungry and went straight to his room. Now, Kathleen tugged on Brian's arm. "Please?"

Reluctantly, Brian followed them to the coffee bar. River told them what he wanted, then said he was going to find a newspaper. Once they had their drinks and food, they found a table for four and began to eat. Brian was surprised how hungry he was and quickly devoured his bagel. Kathleen smiled and pushed half of her bagel over to him. As he gladly began to enjoy her offer, River returned. Before sitting down, he spread the front page on the table to display a picture of Jake under the headline 'Local Nightclub Owner Found Murdered.' The possibilities of those words brought on a shocked silence.

Brian was the first to respond. "She didn't do it."

"I hope not," said River.

Patrick shook his head no as he put his hand on top of Kathleen's. She also shook her head no. "No, I agree, she didn't," said Kathleen.

"I don't want to think so either, but we need to consider it as we try to find her and how we can help her if she did."

"She didn't," insisted Brian. He looked at his watch, then at Patrick and Kathleen. "It's almost six, think your detective has reported for work yet?"

"Maybe," said Patrick. "But, let's read the whole article while River has his coffee and bagel. Then, yes, let's head on over to the police."

The article did not describe the killing, just that the body had been found on the outskirts of town in a storage shed. A person of interest was being interviewed, but the killer had not been identified as yet. Another silence settled over the group as each contemplated the phrase person of interest.

Eventually, Brian stood up. "Let's go."

They joined him and once the table was cleared and trash disposed of, they headed for the police station. During their Jeep ride, Patrick convinced Brian to let him talk with the police. It was almost six-thirty when they approached officer Sam Carter at the main desk.

"Officer Carter, we would like to speak with Detective Harrison please."

"Is he expecting you?" asked the officer.

"No. But, he may be able to help us locate a lost person. My name is Patrick Finley. He knows me, so I'm sure he'll see me."

Carter scanned the group for a moment, then told them to have a seat on the benches along the wall as he tried to locate Detective Harrison. Once they were out of ear shot, he dialed up the Detective's Unit. Harrison answered the call.

"Harrison here. What's up, Sam?"

"Got four people here, three guys and a gal, asking to see you. One of the guys says his name is Patrick Finley. Claims you know him."

"Yes, I do know him. I'll be right out." He hung up, then turned to his partner. "Remember that guy Patrick Finley that we arrested for killing that Marine?"

"Yeah," said Bader. "The case was taken over by the military, and didn't Finley get found not guilty?"

"Yes. The coroner re-examined the body after a witness came forward with an account of how he actually died, so the reason for his death was changed from murder to an accidental fall. And, now he's here and wants to see me."

"Detective Harrison?" Malie was standing at the door to her cell. "He's probably here to see me."

Harrison walked over and really looked at Malie. "You're the hook...the... woman who alibied him?"

"Yes."

"And now you're in here for killing someone."

"I didn't kill—

"Save it." He turned and headed for the door. "Bader, I'm going to check this out."

Bader laughed. "Just be careful and don't let that cute wife of his use another one of her soulful pleas to let her see...Bader said, nodding toward Malie.

"Ha ha," said Harrison as he left the room.

All four members of Malie's posse stood when Harrison arrived.

"Thanks," said Patrick.

"Where is she?" asked Kathleen.

"Is she under arrest?" asked River.

"Let me see her," demanded Brian.

All four had talked at once, drawing the attention of everyone in the station lobby.

Harrison raised his hand in a stop motion. "Hold on. I think we need some privacy. Follow me." He headed down a hallway and opened the door to a room familiar to Kathleen and Patrick. The room contained a small table and four chairs. "Take a seat everyone." River offered to stand, so Harrison sat down across from Patrick and Kathleen and next to Brian. "So, what's this all about?" he asked Patrick.

"We saw today's paper and we think you might be holding a friend of ours as a person of interest in a murder."

"You're talking about the hooker, Malie?"

"Don't call her that," Brian said, his eyes threatening.

Harrison raised his eyebrows and looked at Patrick. "Isn't she the one who alibied you?"

"Yes. But she isn't a...ah..."

Brian stood up and glared down at Harrison. "It doesn't matter what she was. It has nothing to do with what happened to that pimp, Jake. Now, let us talk with her."

Patrick stood up to calm Brian. "You're not helping things. As a police officer, you should understand that Det. Harrison needs clarification. Please, sit down and let's all be civil to each other."

Brian glared at Harrison for a few moments, then Patrick's reminder took hold and he sat back down. "Sorry, Det. Harrison. Patrick's right. It's just that this Jake fellow has harassed Malie and tried to force her to ...well... to go back to work for him."

"When?" asked Harrison. Over the next few minutes, they filled Harrison in on how Malie had gotten to the Yukon and what she was doing for a living these days. After sharing that he was a Royal Canadian Mounted Police Constable, Brian told Harrison how he had run Jake out of town. When they learned that she had gotten a letter from Oahu, it gave them their first clue as to where she had gone. They were shocked that she had returned to Oahu, but they all felt it had something to do with Jake.

Patrick ended the background info with, "Malie took a big chance in coming forward to save me. Now, we want to be sure she's okay. Please, if she's your person of interest, let us talk with her."

"That's quite a story," said Harrison. "Problem is, I didn't catch the Jake Bennett murder investigation. The lead detective for that one is Detective O'Brien."

Brian groaned and before he could say anything, Patrick asked, "Please. Can you get this O'Brien to come join us so we can talk to him?"

"He's on day shift. He won't be in for a couple hours."

Again, before Brian's frustration could alienate any possibility of Harrison helping them, Patrick continued. "So, until he comes in, you're the detective in charge. Please, let us talk with her."

Harrison was about to say no as he let his eyes rove over the foursome, finally resting on Kathleen. Damn. Why do I even look at this woman? Those big, brown, pleading eyes get to me every time. He looked away, but he knew she'd won again. He sighed as he got to his feet. "I'll see what I can do. Wait here."

Once he was gone, River managed a laugh.

"What's so funny?" asked Brian.

"Kathleen. She did it again."

This brought a giggle from Kathleen and a nod from Patrick.

"What the hell do the three of you know that I don't?" asked an annoyed Brian.

"Harrison seems to have a soft spot for Kathleen," said River. "When the OPD was holding Patrick for Pete's murder, she always managed to get Harrison to bring Pat from his cell to this very room. Then, he'd leave us alone for at least a fifteen-minute visit."

While they were reminiscing about Patrick's time with the OPD, Harrison was back in his office filling Bader in on who was back and their request for some time with Malie.

"Did you tell them it's not our case?"

"Yeah."

Bader noticed that Harrison was focusing on Malie. He laughed. "So those big brown eyes got to you again!"

"Shut up."

"You're hopeless. You know it will probably piss O'Brien and Wailani off."

Harrison was already walking over to Malie. "Yeah, proba-bly." He took the key from a ring near the cage. As he unlocked the door, he spoke to Malie. "Listen. There are some people who want to see you. I can take you to them for about a fifteen-minute visit. But I need you to promise you won't give me any trouble and you'll come back with me when I say so."

"Did I hear you say Patrick and Kathleen are in Oahu and wanting to see me?" asked Malie.

"Yes, those two, along with Patrick's brother and a Canadi-an Mountie."

Malie's heartbeat quickened with thoughts of Brian. But, along with the warmth and sincerity she and Brian had shared so recently, having him deal with the slime of her past brought tears to her eyes.

"You promise?"

Harrison's question brought Malie back to the moment. "Yes. I promise no trouble, and I'll come back when you say so."

"Okay, follow me."

"Good luck, hopeless," said Bader bringing Harrison to lift his arm back and give his partner a middle finger salute.

When they got to the visiting room, Harrison paused and told Malie, "Fifteen minutes." Then he opened the door and nodded for Malie to enter the room. Once she was inside, he closed the door and waited in the hall.

"Malie!" Brian stood up, rushed over to her and put his hand on her shoulder. "You're, okay?"

All she could manage was a nod as she smiled at the others.

"We've been so worried," said Brian.

Again, she nodded, while trying to hold back tears that threatened.

Patrick, who had experienced the same flood of emotions when he'd been incarcerated and Kathleen and River showed up, started to rise, but Kathleen beat him to it. She went to Malie and took her hand. "Come. Let's talk." She led her to a chair. Patrick had gotten up, allowing Kathleen to sit next to Malie. Once they were both seated, Kathleen reminded them about their time limit. "Let's use these fifteen minutes wisely."

"I don't know what to say," Malie managed. "That all of you would come all this way to... to..."

"Please, just fill us in on why you came and what has happened here," Patrick urged.

Malie looked around the room, then focused on Patrick as she talked about getting the picture of Ruby's finger, her decision to take care of things without bringing any of the good people of Dawson into Jake's threats and that she had finally managed to help Ruby. As she concluded, she turned to Brian. "I'm so sorry. I know you would... would have..."

Brian nodded and reached across the table extending his hand to her. She reached out and they clasped hands.

Again, Patrick brought everyone back to the moment. "How did you help Ruby? Did she kill Jake?"

If there was ever a time, she needed to accept their help with an honest answer, it was now. But, her disgust and pity for all Ruby had been through, won out and she couldn't bring herself to give an exact accounting of Jake's murder. She lowered her eyes to the table and gave the same description she had given the police. "I did see who killed Jake." She paused, then went on. "It was a human being."

Her words brought questioning looks to the faces of everyone as they waited for more.

Brian was the first to recover. "Malie, male or female, old or young? The police need more. Without it, you're leaving the police with no options. They could arrest you for Jake's murder."

"I can't say any more."

"Can't or won't?" asked Brian.

"Please, all of you, I know you are trying to help, but there are things in my past that you wouldn't understand. My life has been so good these past few years and I don't want my past to bring all of you to think less of me." She turned and looked at Brian. "Especially, you." Tears began to make their way down her face. She stood up and walked over to the door. "You need to go back to Dawson." She turned and opened the door to a surprised Harrison.

After a quick glance at his watch, Harrison said, "You've got another five minutes."

Malie was already walking back towards the cage.

Brian was at the door. "Malie," he called.

She continued to walk.

"Sorry, folks, but I've got to chase her down." He turned and followed Malie, who was opening the door to the detective's office.

Brian turned around and faced the others who looked just as shocked as he felt.

"What the hell just happened?" asked River. "She doesn't want our help?"

"She may not want it, but she's going to get it," said Brian.

Patrick nodded, as did Kathleen.

"Well, as far as I can see, it would be a waste of our time," said River.

Patrick and Kathleen stood up. Patrick put his hand on River's shoulder. "River, all of us have needed help at one time or another and we usually tried to handle it ourselves. You headed out to find your birth mother and didn't want anyone to go with you. Kathleen dealt with an abusive husband and tried to hide his abuse. I didn't want family to know about my arrest for a murder. But what happened in each case? We both got help—from Blair and from you. Kathleen finally accepted help from her First Lieutenant and from me. And as for me, you showed up with the support I needed. So just because Malie says she doesn't want our help doesn't mean we aren't going to help her.

While Patrick talked, memories raced through River's mind of his trek to find his roots. He felt shame for doubting Malie. He nodded. "You're right. Sorry."

Patrick gave his brother's shoulder a quick squeeze, then dropped his arm and turned to the others. "Let's get out of here, get some coffee and make some plans." He smiled at River.

River laughed. "Yes, let's go make plans."

They stopped at the main desk for Patrick to leave a message for Harrison that Patrick and the others could be reached at the Hilton with any updates to Malie's situation. Within the hour, they were back in the hotel dining room and tossing around ideas.

***

Harrison had just locked Malie back in the cage when O'Brien and Wailani arrived.

"Morning," said O'Brien as he walked over to the cage. "No problems last night?"

Bader laughed. "Only my partner's weakness for brown eyes."

Again, he received the middle finger salute from his partner. "Ignore Bader," Harrison said to O'Brien. "No problem with Miss Iona. But there is a problem with the case."

"And that is?" asked O'Brien.

"People have arrived that believe she's innocent and want to work with us. Problem is, one of them has history with me. He talked me into letting him have a few minutes with her."

"And you did?"

Harrison nodded. "I took her to an interrogation room and gave them fifteen minutes."

"What's your history with the guy that wants to help her?"

Harrison gave him a sketchy bit of background, then ended it with a nod toward Malie. "Miss Iona is the hooker who came forward with information on how the man Finley was accused of killing really died. As a result, all charges against Finley were dropped."

"So, did this Finley ask for you to take over the case?"

"No." He paused and looked at Bader, who shrugged, smiled, then nodded. Harrison looked back at O'Brien. "But I think my history with these people could help. So, yes, I'd like to take over the case."

O'Brien turned to Wailani.

"I think she's guilty as hell, but she's making it hard to prove with her lack of details. So, yeah, I don't mind dumping the case."

"Okay," said O'Brien to Harrison. "It's yours. Let's go over to my desk and I'll give you everything we've got so far."

A half hour later, Harrison and Bader had traded shifts with O'Brien and Wailani and now sat in the interrogation room with Malie.

"So," said Harrison to Malie. "No matter how many times I ask, you're going to stick with that you saw a human being kill Jake Bennett."

"It's all I can tell you."

Harrison turned to Bader.

"I've read everything and I feel like there's so much more to what happened in that shed."

"Me too, but she's leaving us no choice. I think we need to charge her and let the lawyers figure it out." As Harrison waited for Bader to answer, he hoped his threat would bring Malie to her senses, but she said not a word.

"Sounds like a plan to me."

They had both stood up, when the door opened and a clerk held out a manila folder. "This just came in for you."

"Thank you," said Harrison as the clerk nodded and left.

"Remain seated," Harrison told Malie, then both he and Bader stepped out into the hall, closing the door behind them. Harrison scanned the document, then handed it to Bader.

"Fingerprints don't lie," said Bader.

"No, they don't," agreed Harrison. He opened the door and both he and Bader reentered the room. "Miss Iona, the gun found on Mr. Bennett's body has been checked for fingerprints. The document that was just delivered to me, verifies that your prints are on the gun. Now, one last chance, please tell us the name of this human who killed Mr. Bennett."

"I have nothing more to say."

Harrison took a deep breath, looked at Bader, who nodded, then began. "Malie Iona, you are under arrest for the murder of Jake Bennett. Do you want us to contact anyone for you?"

"No."

"We'll be taking you down for booking. Tomorrow morning you'll be taken before a judge who will set the amount of bail and, if you haven't already got an attorney, they will assign you a public defender."

Malie took a deep breath and bit at her bottom lip. Her common sense told her to tell the truth about what happened, but the image of a naked Ruby tied to that chair with the duct tape across her mouth tugged at her heart. She stood up.

Her hesitation gave Harrison a moment of hope that Malie was about to come clean, but it was short-lived. He and Bader stood up. He turned to Bader. "You look like you could use some sleep. I can get her booked, so why don't you head on home and I'll see you back here early tomorrow morning."

"You sure?"

"Yeah. It shouldn't take too long. Then I'll head home."

As they left the interrogation room, Bader headed for home, while Harrison got Malie booked and taken for confinement in the OPD jail.

***

During their planning session at the hotel, Brian and the others decided a good attorney was needed. Patrick took a chance and called Hickam AFB. He spoke to a clerk in their legal department and asked if Capt. Hunt was still assigned there. He wasn't, but the clerk put Patrick through to a current attorney. After explaining the purpose of the call, Patrick was given the names of a couple local non-military lawyers, with good reputations, who might be able to help him.

He called the office of attorney Ronald Phillips and set up a meeting at the attorney's office at three that afternoon. With a few hours before their meeting, Patrick and Kathleen thought it would be nice to take a ride out to their favorite ocean side cabana. It had been their place to go when dealing with some rough times relating to Kathleen's ex-husband and Patrick's arrest for his murder.

River planned to go to his room and call Blair for an update on how things were in Dawson. Brian said he had no plans, but would spend some time wandering the tourist shops and checking out the beautiful beach area. They would meet in the hotel lobby at two thirty, then head for the attorney's office.

Brian strolled along a street with a good view of the beach for awhile, then headed up toward the row of restaurants and bars.

He thought he might remember some things from his leave time visiting the area when his ship was docked in Oahu. When nothing seemed familiar, it dawned on him that within minutes of hitting the streets, he and his fellow seamen hit the bars. Brian had never been much of a drinker, so the liquor hit him hard and fast, leaving his actions a hazy blur.

He'd been walking for about a half hour, when he found himself standing in front of the Flyin' Hi night club. He decided to go on in and get something cold to drink. The place was fairly empty this time of day. There were a few couples at tables around the room, but no one was seated at the bar. Just as he took a seat, one of the couples made their way through the doorway he and the others had taken to the stairs leading up to Jake's apartment.

Gus, the bartender who had talked with Brian earlier came over. "Surprised to see you again."

Brian smiled. "Was walking by and needed something cold to drink."

"What can I get you?"

"Anything without alcohol."

Gus laughed. "Got some Coke and ginger ale."

"Ginger ale sounds good. Haven't had that in a long time."

Gus poured his drink, then went to sit at the end of the bar so he could watch the ball game on TV. Occasionally, he'd glance over at Brian to see if he needed anything. Eventually, he noticed that Brian wasn't drinking his ginger ale, and it looked like he was checking the place out. Curiosity got the best of Gus.

"Problem?" he asked as he wandered over to stand across the bar from Brian.

Brian took a sip of his drink. "No, why do you ask?"

"Just seems like you're awfully interested in the layout here. You've been checking out every door, wall, nook and cranny. You lose something when you were here?"

Brian had to smile. "You caught me. But as to losing something when I was here, I'm not sure."

"Well, we do have a box with some lost and found items, but I don't remember finding anything you left behind."

"No, I didn't leave anything, but maybe someone I know did."

"Malie?"

About that time a couple of men carrying large satchels exited the hallway door. One of them came over to the bar and handed Gus a key. "We've pretty much got all we need from upstairs, but the tape is still up across the door to Mr. Bennett's apartment. Don't let anyone have this key other than someone from the OPD."

"Yes, sir," said Gus.

The men left the building without another word.

"They're considering it a crime scene?" asked Brian.

Gus shrugged. "I don't ask questions. They show me a badge and I do what they tell me."

A thought came to Brian. "By the way, was Jake the sole owner of this place?"

"Far as I know."

"Yet, he's dead, and the bar is still open for business?"

"And why do you need to know?"

This made Brian smile and shake his head. "Guess it's the curiosity of the cop in me. Along with concern about Malie."

"You're a cop?"

"Canadian Mountie."

"Never met a Mountie before you."

Brian managed a laugh. "And, now you have."

Gus shrugged and nodded, then began to answer Brian's question. "As to why the place is still open, I called Jakes's accountant about what to do. He said to keep things as they are until he contacts Jake's attorney to see if there's a will and, if so, what the details are." He paused, but when Brian didn't say anything, he went back to Brian's concern about Malie. "So, you're from Canada. How did you know Malie?"

"Yes, Canada. Dawson Creek in the Yukon, to be exact. Malie's been living there a few years now and has made caring friends. When she left without telling us, we decided to see if we could find her and find out why she came back here."

Gus was silent for a few moments, then said, "Yeah, it's easy to like Malie. A lot of us missed her when she disappeared. I always hoped nothing bad had happened to her. Every so often one of the ladies just disappears, like Ruby, who disappeared a week or so ago. It never seemed to bother Jake. However, when Malie disappeared, he was really mad and had our local cops trying to find out what happened to her."

"It's a long story, but she's been in a good place and has made friends that care about her."

"Glad to hear it."

Brian had picked up on the mention of a Ruby, who had recently disappeared. "Hey, you mentioned a Ruby. Were she and Malie friends?"

Gus laughed. "Friends? These girls are too competitive to be friends. Besides, Jake frowned on the girls socializing with each other. But, as I remember it, Malie and Ruby did manage to sneak out for coffee or a walk on the beach, now and then."

"So, this Ruby just disappeared one day?"

Gus nodded.

Brian thought it best not to ask too much more. But the fact that this Ruby person disappeared had to have something to do with Malie's situation. He needed to share this information with the others. That thought brought him to check his watch and found it was time for him to get back to the hotel. He finished his drink and put a couple dollars on the bar. "Got to run. Thanks for sharing things with me."

"I hope things are okay with Malie."

"Me too," said Brian as he turned and left the bar.

***

An hour later, Brian, Patrick, Kathleen and River sat in attorney Ronald Phillips' office sharing all the information they had regarding Malie's situation. They included the information about Malie saying her reason for leaving Dawson had to do with a picture of a woman's severed finger and that her name was Ruby. Now, someone named Ruby has disappeared from the Flyin' Hi' where she worked.

"So last time you talked with Miss Iona, she was being held as a person of interest, but had not been booked?"

Brian nodded.

Phillips picked up his phone and placed a call to the OPD.

"Oahu Police Department, how can I help you?"

"This is attorney Ronald Phillips. I need to speak with Detective Harrison."

"One moment, please."

After a short wait, a man came on the line. "Detective Harrison here, how can I help you, Mr. Phillips?"

"Thank you for taking my call. I have just taken on a client I think you are holding as a person of interest in a recent murder."

"You're calling about Malie Iona?"

"Yes."

"She has been booked for the murder and is now being held in the OPD jail. If you need more information or need to speak with her, you need to contact the Inmate Incarceration Office."

"When was she officially booked?"

"This morning."

"Thank you, detective." Phillips hung up and turned to four concerned faces. "As you heard, Miss Iona has been officially booked for the murder. I'm going to contact the jail and arrange a meeting with her."

"We'll go with you," said Brian.

"That's not possible." He stood up and walked to his office door. "For now, I need to get busy. I'll call you at your hotel as soon as I get a chance to meet with Miss Iona, so you'll know what to expect in the next day or so." He opened his door for them to leave.

Brian and the others stood up. "There's nothing more we can do?" asked Patrick.

"Just let me get busy arranging a meeting with Miss Iona."

Brian was the last to leave. At the door, he stopped. "Mr. Phillips, I'm a Canadian Mountie. I have dealt with both Jake and Malie. I wonder if it would be possible for me to go with you for any meeting with Malie. When we talked to her this morning, ...she seemed... seemed... well, let's just say...it wasn't the Malie we know.

Please, I think between my police background and that I know Malie, I could be an asset in deciding what needs to be done."

Phillips was going to say no, but as Brian went on, he decided it wouldn't do any harm. "Okay, but just you. Once I set up a time to meet with Miss Iona, I'll call you at the hotel."

Brian extended his hand. "Thanks. I'll be waiting for your call."

Phillip gave him a quick handshake, then turned to his secretary. "I've some notes that need to be typed up as soon as possible."

The woman got up and headed in to get the notes. Phillips nodded to the group leaving and followed his secretary.

Brian and the others left the office and headed back to the hotel.

***

By six the next morning, after a restless night's sleep, a casually dressed Brian had showered, shaved and was headed for the hotel coffee bar. On the way, he stopped to get the day's paper. As he reached down to grab one, his arm froze. The headline of the day read 'Former Employee Arrested for Murder.' Next to the headline was a picture of Malie, probably taken during her booking process. Now, Brian really needed that coffee.

After purchasing his coffee, he found a table and sat down. He read the brief article saying Malie Iona had been arrested for the murder of local club owner, Jake Bennett. The details were skimpy and only told of Bennett's body, with two fatal gun shots, being found in a storage shed. Malie Iona was also found at the murder scene. She claimed Bennett was killed by a human being, but would provide no details as to who the human being was.

At the end of the article, Brian closed his eyes and uttered a quiet moan. Opening his eyes he downed half of his coffee.

"Oh no," said Kathleen as she, Patrick and River walked up to the table.

After his quick look at the headline, River said, "Sit down, I'll go get the coffee." He turned and left.

Patrick had picked up the paper. As they sat down, he held it so both he and Kathleen could read the entire article.

"Are you okay, Brian?" asked Kathleen when she read the last word.

"No. I'm frustrated."

At that moment, River arrived with coffee for everyone, including another cup for Brian. While everyone sipped at their drinks, River hurried through the article. "Damn," he said as he set the paper on the table.

"Yeah, damn," agreed Patrick.

"That part about a human being killing him is ridiculous," said River. "Maybe seeing it in print will bring her to give the real details to the police."

Brian shook his head no. "Obviously, she's protecting someone."

"You're right," said Patrick. "After what Malie said about this Ruby and now that we know someone named Ruby is missing, she must have something to do with the murder."

"I think we need to get this information over to Detective Harrison," said River.

Brian glanced at his watch. "Let's head on over there now."

Patrick felt it was too early, but he knew Brian needed to do something. "Okay, but Brian, you need to stay here and wait for the call from the attorney. You don't want to miss the opportunity to talk with Malie."

Brian's jaw twitched. He knew Patrick was right, but just sitting, waiting for the call would be hard. He took a deep breath. "Yeah, you're right."

Everyone had drained their cups and gotten to their feet. Kathleen put her hand on Brian's shoulder. "We'll be back as soon as we can." She patted his shoulder and followed Patrick and River out of the hotel.

Brian got another cup of coffee, then went back to his room to wait for the attorney's call.

***

At a little after eight that same morning, Ruby woke to the strong aroma of coffee brewing in the kitchen. She stretched out and thought about going to get a cup. She had been sleeping on a sofa in Oleen's apartment. Oleen had managed to rise above being a prostitute. She now had a steady job as a janitor at the local hospital. Her small one-bedroom apartment hardly had room for a second person. But, when Ruby showed up claiming she was ready to start fresh and just needed a helping hand for a bit, Oleen could not turn her down.

The rich aroma became too much to resist. Ruby needed that boost a strong cup of black coffee would bring. She got up, removed her shorts and t-shirt, and pulled on her muumuu. After a quick trip to the bathroom, Ruby headed for the kitchen. She poured a cup, then sat down at a table centered in a combination living room and kitchen.

Taking her first sip, she sent a silent thank you to Oleen, who had already left for work. The last couple of days of running and hiding had helped her avoid the police, but she knew she still needed to find a way off this island. It seemed like the best way to start over or, at least, keep her from getting caught for Jake's murder.

She shook her head and took another drink of the coffee. Not now. I'll think about an escape plan later. For now, I need to relax, clear my head. A folded newspaper across the table caught her eye. Taking another drink, she pulled it over and flipped it open. She nearly spit the coffee out but managed to swallow it as she read the headline, then the whole article.

Damn, damn, damn! Malie, I told you to get the hell out, to go back to where you came from. What the hell have you done?

This brought on a whole new set of problems. What she should do warred with what she wanted to do. Her sense of decency insisted she go to the police; Malie was clearly taking the blame for Jake's murder.

Why is it when I think my life can't get any worse, it does! She took a deep breath and thought about her past. Her mother was Hawaiian, her father an American dock worker who was killed in an accident on the job when she was only ten years old. Her mother could never accept his death and drank herself to death when Ruby was twelve.

Her mother's sister took Ruby in, but treated her as a servant rather than a niece. She moved out on her eighteenth birthday and took a job as a file clerk in the local school board headquarters. After a year or so, Ruby decided with the war on and so many military men in Oahu, she could make more money as a cocktail waitress.

At first, it didn't pay much more than being a file clerk. She found herself in debt and was about to get evicted from her apartment, when Jake offered her a way to make some extra money. Servicing men in the back rooms of the Flyin' Hi' paid better. Most of the men were either young, inexperienced kids or crude, fat, old men.

One day, as she was preparing a round of beer to serve to some young sailors, Jake walked by and nodded up towards his apartment. She nodded back, then after delivering the beer, she headed up to Jake's apartment. He got right to the point and told her he had a job she might be interested in and it paid a lot more than she was making now.

She would teach women how to service men rather than be a servicer herself. Sounded good to her. Jake told her to tell no one about his offer and to go right downstairs and tell Gus she was going to run an errand. Then Jake would pick her up a block away and take her to the house where she would be staying while instructing the women.

What happened next ran through her mind like it was happening again. Jake drove to an area of storage sheds, then parked in one of them. He got out of the car and told her to follow him.

"I thought you said we were going to a house?"

"We will. For now, just follow me," said Jake.

He closed the shed door and opened the door to the next shed. As she entered, he had pushed her face against the wall. Before she could react, she felt a knife at her neck.

"What the hell?" she managed.

"Just do what I say and I won't hurt you."

He had reached over and picked up a glass of some very cloudy water from a table holding a variety of tools and a whip. "Drink this." He held it to her lips and forced her to drink until the glass was empty.

Ruby remembered that immediately she began to feel dizzy and soon lost consciousness. When she woke, she was naked. Her hands, torso and legs were tied to a cane chair with a hole carved out of the center of the seat. Her mouth was taped shut.

The rest of her memories, until Malie arrived, were of dark nights, visits by Jake to give her some muesli and water. Every so often he brought men to check out what they would be purchasing. Now, as she sat looking at the newspaper, she knew she had a decision to make. If she turned herself in to help Malie, another worse episode of her life would surely happen. But, if she didn't turn herself in and manage to get off the island, there was a chance her life could get better.

"Why me?" she screamed out loud. "Again! Why me?" She threw her head back in frustration while slowly coming to a decision. She stood up and refreshed her coffee, then went to stand at the only window in the apartment. Surprisingly, it was a nice view of Diamond Head. It was beautiful as was most of the scenery in Hawaii. As she drained her cup, she actually smiled. "Hope my cell has this good a view."

After rinsing her cup, Ruby returned to the bathroom. She washed her face and hands, brushed her teeth, combed her hair, then slipped into a tee-shirt, cotton slacks and a pair of flip-flops. She found a note pad and pencil next to the phone in the living room and left Oleen a brief note of thanks.

Fifteen minutes later, she found herself standing in front of the OPD building. She paused and did a complete circle, taking in what she assumed would be her last look around the city as a free woman. After a deep breath, Ruby walked through the main door and up to the information desk.

"How may I help you?" asked an OPD Sergeant.

"I need to speak to whoever is handling Jake Bennett's murder case."

"May I tell him your name?"

"Ruby."

"Just Ruby?"

"Yes."

The officer's eyes scanned the attractive, but ragged looking woman for a moment or two, then picked up the receiver. When it was answered, he turned his back on Ruby. "Got someone here at my desk who wants to speak with whoever is handling the Bennett murder case." He paused for a moment, then answered Harrison's question. "Says her name is Ruby." Another pause. "Yep, just Ruby." After another pause, he said, "Okay." After hanging up, he turned back to Ruby. "Take a seat on the bench over there. Detective Harrison will be out as soon as possible."

Once seated, Ruby began to glance around the station, but soon had to quit. Every time she looked at the main door, it was all she could do to keep from getting up and running. After about a ten-minute wait, she spotted a tall, middle-aged, casually dressed man heading her way.

"Ruby?"

"Yes."

"I'm Detective Harrison. You wanted to see me?"

"Yes. I need to talk to Malie Iona before we go any further."

"I'll need more information before I could arrange that." Harrison hoped he looked and sounded calmer than he was.

Ruby glanced around the busy station and while she didn't feel anyone was watching her, she wanted some privacy before she shared her confession. "Is there somewhere we can talk privately?"

Malie's words "It was a human being" came singing back to Harrison. "Yes. Follow me." He led her to a small room just down the hall. After the door was closed and they were seated, he came to the point of her visit. "Do you know something about Jake Bennett's murder? You know, we have already arrested Miss Iona for it."

"Yes, I know. And, that's why I'm here. See, you've arrested the wrong person. I killed Jake."

"And why should I believe you? Maybe you're here to confuse the situation and put doubt on the arrest of Malie Iona for the murder."

Ruby cocked her head and looked at Harrison like he was an idiot. "Are you for real?"

Now, Harrison gave her the same look. "I wouldn't be a real detective if I believed everything without verifying it—now, would I?"

Their stare contest lasted another couple of seconds, then Ruby managed a slight smile. "I'm sorry for the sarcasm. It's just this is so hard for me."

"Okay. Let's start over. You say you killed Jake Bennett. Why are you just now turning yourself in?"

"He was an evil bastard and deserved to die. And, I really thought I could get away with it. Then, I saw today's paper. Jake was evil to a lot of people who, I'm sure, are not sorry to hear he's dead. But it definitely wasn't Malie. Yes, she was there and saw me kill him, but she took no part in the killing."

"Why would she not tell us you killed him?"

Ruby placed her hand with the still-bandaged missing baby finger on the table. "He wanted Malie to return to Oahu and work in the Flyin' Hi. At one time, she was his highest earning working girl. When she left, he felt his reputation as a man not to be crossed took a hit. Apparently, he found out where she'd gone to and decided to use me to bait her back. Malie's known for being a caring person, always someone who you could go to for help. So, he sent her a picture of my severed finger and told her if she didn't come back within a week, he'd cut off another piece of my body."

Harrison looked down at Ruby's finger. He'd been a detective for a long time and seen a lot of bad things. This story of hers rated right up there with the worst of them. "So, she came back?"

"Yes."

"Why would she do that? Were you two good friends?"

"I wouldn't say good friends. Just a small sisterhood of women used by Jake. But, once she suddenly disappeared, nobody in Oahu ever heard from her again. I was surprised as anyone when she showed up at the shed where Jake held me."

"If she wasn't involved in—

"Hey." Ruby glared at Harrison. "You said if I gave you more information, you'd arrange for me to talk to Malie. I've told you how it all went down. Now, let me see Malie."

He stood up. "Wait here. I'll go see what I can do." He turned and left the room. On his way back to his desk, he hoped she wanted to see Malie bad enough she'd do what he said and wait.

His partner had been on the phone talking to the District Attorney's office when Harrison got the call from the front desk. The D.A. needed information regarding a previous case the two of them had worked on. Bader was deep in conversation. Harrison couldn't get his attention, so went to meet with Ruby without his partner.

Now, off the phone, Bader looked up as Harrison reentered the room and headed straight for a chair at Bader's desk.

"You are not going to believe what just happened."

"What?" asked Bader. "Must really be something to get you to look that unnerved."

"Yeah, something."

Bader laughed. "What the hell?"

"I've got a woman sitting in an interrogating room who just admitted to killing Jake Bennett."

"What the hell?"

"She wants to talk to Malie."

"You believe her?

"I don't know what to believe. I accused her of admitting to the killing to confuse things and bring doubt as to who actually did the killing."

"Shit."

"Yeah, shit."

Bader picked up the folder with the fingerprint info. "Well, says here there were other prints on the gun. Could they both have killed him? One causing all those body wounds and one with the gun. After all, Bennett was shot twice."

"There were three sets of prints on the gun. Malie, Bennett and one unidentified."

"Well, this is getting interesting." Bader uttered a slight laugh. "Maybe she's the human being Miss Iona keeps referring to."

"That's what I was thinking."

"Should we arrest her? It's not everyday someone walks in off the street saying they killed someone."

"Like I said, maybe they're just trying to confuse the situation. I'd like to see them together. Let's take this Ruby over to the jail so we can arrange for her to talk with Miss Iona. Then we can decide to arrest her or not."

"I can't go now." Bader picked up a pile of folders. "The D.A. wants these in his office right now."

"Okay." Harrison stood up. "I'll take her. After you drop the files off, come by the jail."

Both men left the office minutes before Patrick, Kathleen and River arrived at the OPD.

The trio had stopped for breakfast at a shoreline restaurant, then headed over to share what Gus had said about Ruby's disappearance. They were disappointed to have missed the detectives. They left a message for them to call the hotel. They did not give details, just said they had additional information that might help Malie's case.

On the way over to the jail, Harrison made Ruby understand that the only way he would arrange this meeting with Miss Iona was if he remained in the room with them. When they arrived at the jail, Harrison told the Sergeant in charge he had additional questions for Miss Iona for his investigation. Within minutes, he and Ruby were waiting in a small room with a table and two chairs.

He told Ruby to sit in one and that he would remain standing, leaving the other chair for Miss Iona.

***

After Harrison dropped Malie off for booking the night before, Malie had been in a daze. She barely remembered being photographed, the fingerprinting process, the body search, putting on the orange jumpsuit and being led to a cell with two cots, a sink and a toilet. She had not uttered a word, unless required to answer a question from the people involved in the process. She managed a couple hours sleep, despite the guards talking and jingling keys as they made their hourly walk-throughs checking on the few inmates being held.

Now, as she stretched out on one of the cots, her mind kept bringing back the happenings in the shed and how shocked she had been to see what Jake had done to Ruby. She had to admit that there were moments when she wanted to do something to Jake to make him account for what he had done. Malie even wondered if Ruby hadn't killed him could she have stepped forward and done something to Jake so he could never hurt anyone ever again.

She shook her head no and stood up. This was getting her nowhere. She knew she should tell the police who killed Jake. But, even now, the look on Ruby's face as she sat tied to that chair and told Malie what Jake had done and was planning to do brought on a shiver of disgust. No, she thought, Ruby has gone through enough. Malie knew she had been lucky to have been offered a way out with her move to Dawson. These past few years were an awakening as to how good people lived and acted. Ruby deserved a chance to experience something like that.

As Malie paced the small cell, she passed by the breakfast tray, delivered hours ago. It still sat in the door slot. The only part of the breakfast she had consumed was the coffee and a dry slice of toast. The lone sausage patty, scrambled egg and spoonful of hash browns sat cold and untouched. Surprisingly, her stomach growled. She couldn't remember the last time she had eaten anything other than that piece of toast, so she took the tray and sat back down on the cot. The food was cold and unseasoned, but seemed to satisfy her hunger pangs and silenced her stomach.

She was setting the tray back in the door slot when a jailer approached her cell. "Detective Harrison needs to talk to you," he said as he unlocked the cell door. "Follow me."

Malie followed him out and down the hallway. The jailer stopped at a closed door marked Interview Room. As he opened it, he said, "I'll be waiting here in the hall to escort you back to your cell."

The first person she spotted was Ruby. Her eyes widened in shock. "What are you doing here?"

Ruby managed a slight smile, then shrugged. "Your picture on the front page of the newspaper."

"My picture was in the paper?"

Harrison interrupted. "Miss Iona, please sit down. Your friend here has presented us with a new twist in the Jake Bennett murder case."

"Oh, Ruby, you didn't."

Harrison walked over and pulled out the chair. "I need you to sit down."

Feeling that her knees were about to give out, Malie complied, then looked directly at Ruby. "What did you tell him."

"The truth."

"Why? I never told them anything."

"Still, the paper said you were arrested for Jake's murder and that you were in jail."

"They were just trying to make me name the human I said committed the murder. They had no proof. I was sure they'd have to let me go."

"Actually, we do have proof," said Harrison. "If you remember, your prints were on the gun found atop Bennett's body."

"But I'm sure there were other prints on the gun," said Malie. "The only thing I'm guilty of is not naming the person who did the murder."

Harrison grimaced. "Yeah, a human being did it."

Ruby banged her fist on the table. "Stop it! I did it. I killed the son-of-a-bitch."

Harrison wanted to believe her. Yet, the thought that perhaps these women were working together to bring doubt on who was the actual killer was dogging him. Malie interrupted his mental debate.

"Ruby, don't do this to yourself," she pleaded.

Ruby touched Malie's arm. "Enough. I appreciate you trying to help me get away with killing Jake, but I can't let you do it. Jake deserved to die and you know it. As I sat there for days tied to that chair, I began to wonder if he could do this to me—maybe he has hurt other women. Maybe by killing him, I made him pay for things he did in the past and kept him from continuing to do evil to women in the future." She patted Malie's hand. "Let it go. Tell them what you saw me do."

"They'll arrest you and take away your future, maybe even your life."

"My life has been a mess for years. And, somehow being in prison doesn't sound near as bad as what he had planned for me."

"Ladies," interrupted Harrison, "please, I need some details. As I listen to the both of you, this Bennett is sounding less and less like an innocent victim."

Malie shook her head no, but Ruby shook her head yes. "I may be a lot of things, but I'm not bad enough to let you go down for what I did." She turned to Harrison and began. She told him about Jake pretending to offer her the job to teach young prostitutes, then taking her to the shed and tying her up on a chair with a hole in the seat like a toilet. He left her tied up for days, and taped her mouth shut when he was not in the shed.

She described the men Jake brought to the shed who wanted to buy a woman that could be killed during sex and not be missed by anyone. When Malie arrived and talked Jake into untying her so she could drink some water, she realized this could be her only chance for survival.

Ruby went into detail about how she attacked him and ultimately killed him. Malie had no part in what she did. She had told Malie to leave when she left and was surprised when she opened the paper this morning and saw Malie had been arrested. When she finished, she reached over and wiped a tear from the corner of Malie's eye. She turned back to Harrison. "So, now you know the details. I killed Jake. Let Malie go."

Harrison now had no doubts. Ruby was the killer. As he was about to speak, the door opened and his partner walked in.

One look around the room, let Bader know he had arrived at a crucial moment. "What did I miss?" he asked Harrison.

"Miss Iona's human being has been identified." He nodded at Ruby.

"You believe her?"

Harrison glanced at Malie, then Ruby, then nodded to his partner. "Yes, I do."

"Well," laughed Bader, "that's going to make the attorney out in the lobby very happy."

"An attorney?"

"Yeah, when I went up to the information desk to ask where I could find you, there were two men already talking to the sergeant in charge. I heard one of them identify himself as Malie Iona's attorney, Ronald Phillips, and he was there to speak with Miss Iona."

"An attorney for me?" asked Malie.

"That's what he said," he answered Malie. Then he turned back to Harrison. "I told the sergeant I was one of the detectives who had arrested Miss Iona and that if he told me where you were, I'd see where things stood. Then I asked Phillips to wait in the lobby and I would go find out what was currently going on with Miss Iona's case."

"I think we're going to have to drop the charges against Miss Iona," said Harrison. But, before we do that, I need to get some finger prints." He turned to Ruby. "I'm going to need a couple of things from you. First, your last name and second, will you let us fingerprint you?"

"My name is Ruby Kent, and yes, you can fingerprint me."

Harrison turned to Bader. "Can you take her to be finger printed, then back to our office until we can verify her prints are on the gun. After I get an okay from the desk sergeant to let the attorney in here to talk with Miss Iona, I'll bring the attorney up to date on these recent developments. And, that it's possible once Miss Kent's prints are identified as to being on the murder weapon, we'll be dropping the charges against Miss Iona."

Bader turned to Ruby. "Miss Kent, will you please come with me?"

Ruby stood up and so did Malie who touched Ruby's arm. "I'm so sorry. You've already suffered so much."

Ruby managed a slight smile and shrugged. "At least Jake will never hurt anyone again." She put her hand over Malie's hand on her arm. "Thank you for trying to cover up for me." She gave a squeeze to Malie's hand, then turned and followed Bader out of the room.

"Miss Iona," said Harrison, "please be seated. I'm going to talk with this attorney, then bring him here to talk with you."

Malie just nodded, then sat down.

After telling the guard at the door where he was going, he headed toward the information desk. The desk sergeant told Harrison it was fine for him to take the attorney to talk with his client, then pointed at the two men sitting on a bench along the wall. Harrison walked over and introduced himself.

"I'm Detective Harrison. Which one of you is attorney Phillips?"

"That would be me," said the attorney.

Harrison turned to Brian. "I remember you. You and several other people came to see Miss Iona the day before yesterday."

"Yes. My name is Brian Stockton. I'm a Canadian Mountie and I'm here to help Mr. Phillips with Malie's situation."

"I see." Harrison turned to Phillips. "Yes, about Miss Iona's situation. Someone else has just come forward claiming to be the person who killed Jake Bennett. We're in the process of verifying her claim. Once we have actual proof that this new person is telling the truth, all charges against Miss Iona will be dropped."

"You're going to release Malie? When?" Brian jumped to his feet.

Phillips also stood up. "Someone has admitted to the crime for which you have arrested Miss Iona?"

"That's what it looks like."

"Then, I demand you release Miss Iona immediately."

"Not so fast. There are procedures that need to be followed. Now, do you want to talk with Miss Iona or not?"

"Yes," said Brian.

"Of course," said Phillips, "but just know, I'll be filing the papers to have all charges against Miss Iona dropped."

Harrison nodded, then said, "Follow me." He led them to the room where Malie waited. Brian was the first to enter the room.

"Brian!" Malie came to her feet and allowed Brian to give her a hug.

"Take as long as you need," said Harrison to Phillips. "I'm going to find my partner and move things along as quickly I can to arrange for Miss Iona's release. In the meantime, when you finish your visit, this guard will escort Miss Iona back to her cell." He nodded, then turned to head down the hall.

As Phillips entered the room, he uttered an "Ahem."

This brought Brian to release Malie and introduce the attorney. "Malie, this is attorney Ronald Phillips. Patrick and I have hired him to represent you."

"Thank you," said Malie. "But I think they were going to assign me a public attorney because I can't afford—

"Don't worry," said Brian. "Patrick and I will take care of it." He touched her shoulder urging her to sit back down. Once she complied, he sat next to her and took hold of her hand as Phillips sat across from them.

"Miss Iona," began Phillips, "I'm sure you're aware that someone has come forward admitting to the murder. This means that you will probably be released very soon."

"Yes," said Malie. "Ruby Kent has come forward."

"And, you know that she is telling the truth?"

"Yes, I was there. But—in all fairness—it was more an act of self-defense than murder."

"Can you tell me, in detail, what you witnessed?

Malie looked up at Brian. "It was so horrible."

Brian took her hand. "Tell him. Give him all the information he needs to get you released. Maybe he can even help Ruby Kent in proving it was self-defense like you said."

Malie nodded, then turned to Phillips. She started at the beginning about getting the picture of the severed finger and ending with Ruby tossing the gun onto Jake's body and running out of the shed.

"Will your recount of the actual murder match any statement made by Ruby?" asked Phillips.

"Yes. What I told you exactly matches what Ruby confessed to Detective Harrison."

Brian asked, "If they have a confession from the actual murderer why isn't Malie walking out of here right now?"

"As a lawman yourself," said Phillips, "what would you do in this case? You have one woman who was at the crime scene saying she witnessed who murdered the victim, but won't give the name. Then another woman comes forward and says she did it. Puts the police in a conundrum until they can verify which woman to believe."

Brian nodded. "Yes. I guess I'm thinking about things personally–not professionally." Still holding Malie's hand, he asked, "Why did you hold back on telling them it was Ruby even after they charged you?"

"You wouldn't understand. These last few years I've lived among decent people who have never experienced what people like Ruby and I have lived among all of our lives. When I saw what she had been put through, I just couldn't name her. I couldn't bring myself to bring even more misery into her life. And because I didn't kill Jake, I never imagined that the police would arrest me. Then, even when they did, I always felt that eventually they would realize that I didn't do it." She managed a sad smile, then added, "and I was right." She shook her head sadly. But I never wanted them to find out it was Ruby. Brian, if you had seen what I saw in the shed, you would agree it was self-defense."

Brian squeezed her hand, then turned to Phillips. "What do you think? Is her self-defense claim feasible?"

"From what Miss Iona has related, I tend to think it may be, but I'd need to talk with Miss Kent to be sure."

Malie's eyes lit up. "You would take on Ruby's defense?"

"I'll have to talk to Patrick. But when he finds out how much it means to Malie, I believe he'll want you to defend Malie's friend." Brian smiled at her.

Phillips nodded. "Okay, then. I'll take on Miss Kent's defense. But, at the moment, I'm seeing a lot of ifs that have to be addressed. If they arrest Ruby Kent. If they release Miss Iona."

He stood up. "For now, I'm going to go back to my office and file the papers to contest your arrest. I will contact Detective Harrison to fill him in on the fact that if Miss Kent is arrested, I will be her attorney and will need to speak with her before she discusses any more of the situation with him or any other law enforcement personnel.

Miss Iona, for now, I'll leave you with the guard outside who will take you back to your cell." He turned to Brian. "I can give you a couple minutes alone with Miss Iona while I tell the guard my interview with her is over. Keep it quick." He left them alone, closing the door behind him.

Brian stood up and pulled Malie to her feet and into his arms. "It's almost over. Be strong and know that you'll be out of this awful place real soon." They shared a light kiss that begged for more, but both knew it would have to wait.

"Brian, I ... I ... Brian, I... I..."

"I know. I—

The guard opened the door. "Your time is up. Please follow me."

Brian kissed the top of her head as she turned and followed the guard down the hall.

Brian and Phillips watched until they turned out of sight.

"Well," said Phillips, "let's go. I've got a lot to do and you need to fill your friends in on all this new information and that it looks good for Miss Iona."

Wearing a smile, Brian followed Phillips out of the jail.

Freedom

Arriving back at the hotel, Brian found his friends in the restaurant having a late lunch. The big smile on his face was a welcome sight to the dour-faced threesome.

"Well, at least someone is having a good day," Patrick noted.

"Indeed I am."

"Want to share with us?" asked River.

Still grinning, he began. "I just left the jail after Malie and I shared a kiss and a hug."

"What? You were with Malie and the two of you were able to touch?" asked an excited Kathleen.

About that time a waiter arrived. "Can I get something for you, sir?" he asked.

Brian glanced at the plates of food on the table. Kathleen's salad looked good, but the hamburger and fries in front of the men won him over. He looked up at the waiter. "I'll have one of those." He pointed at Patrick's food.

"And to drink, sir?"

He nodded at the beer in front of Patrick's hamburger. "Same."

When the waiter was gone, River excitedly asked, "Let's have it. Your grin has us thinking things are going well. Fill us in on details."

"You're right. Things are going very well. Phillips and I went to the jail and as luck would have it, Detective Harrison was already there meeting with Malie."

"But he didn't release her?"

"Not yet, but the story he shared with me and Phillips was that someone had come forward and admitted to killing Bennett."

"They have the real killer?" asked Patrick.

"Yes, and believe it or not, it was this Ruby that Gus said disappeared a couple of weeks ago."

"So, if they have the real killer, why hasn't Malie been released?" asked Patrick.

Brian went on to tell them Harrison's concern about Ruby telling the truth and that he and his partner were working on validating Ruby's claim. He told them about Phillips working on getting Malie released and ended with Phillips taking on Ruby's case that was looking like self-defense. "I said we'd cover his fee; like we were covering his fee for Malie." Brian paused, glanced around the table and was happy to see a nod from all three about paying Ruby's fee.

Brian's food and drink arrived and for the first time in days their meal was enjoyed over light conversation, laced with a feeling that maybe the worst was over. When they finished, Patrick and Kathleen left to enjoy visiting some of their favorite spots in Oahu. River went to his room to call the mining office and bring himself up to date on how things were going. Brian went to his room to wait for the call to go pick up Malie when she was released.

***

Harrison and Bader's long experience in working with the fingerprinting techs got them some priority over other things the techs were working on. By a little before four that afternoon, they had what they needed. Ruby's prints were on the gun. They had just informed Ruby of the results and told her they would be taking her over to the jail for formal booking right after they notified Phillips. Earlier they had gotten the call from Phillips saying if Ruby was arrested, he would be her attorney.

Harrison dialed the attorney's number and was put right through.

"Mr. Phillips, this is to inform you that we are formally arresting Miss Kent for the murder of Jake Bennett. We will be taking her over to the jail within the next few minutes."

"Tell Miss Kent I'll be over to see her within the next hour or so."

"Will do."

"Detective Harrison, are you also in the process of releasing Miss Iona?"

"Yes, we will do that while we book Miss Kent."

"I'll call Officer Stockton and let him know. As I said, we will be there within the next hour."

When Harrison hung up, he and Bader took Ruby over to the jail. When they arrived, Bader started the booking process while Harrison asked to see the sheriff about getting Miss Iona released. Both tasks were complete in about the same time. As Harrison and Bader were leaving the building, they met Phillips and Brian arriving.

"What's happening?" asked Phillips.

"We've booked Ruby Kent for the murder of Jake Bennett. They are processing her now," said Harrison. He turned to Brian. "The sheriff is getting Miss Iona released as we speak."

"Thank you for the update," said Phillips.

"Do you need anything else from my partner and I?" asked Harrison.

Phillips turned to Brian who asked, "How long until Malie will be released?"

"I don't know," said Harrison. "Anything else?" After getting a no from Phillips and Brian, Harrison and Bader said their goodbyes and left.

Phillips and Brian approached the information desk and asked when Phillips could meet with Ruby and when Malie would be freed. The sergeant at the desk told them to take a seat on the nearby benches and he would check. Within ten minutes a jailer approached Phillips and said he would take Phillips to an interview room and a guard would be bringing Ruby to him shortly. He had no information on Malie's release.

"Officer Stockton," said Phillips, "I don't know how long I will be with Miss Kent, so if you're not here when she and I are through talking, I will call you at the hotel with the status of her situation." He turned and followed the guard.

Brian sat back down and waited. Phillips hadn't been gone very long when a door opened and Malie entered the waiting area.

Wearing a nervous smile, the first person she spotted was Brian. The smile turned into pure joy. They met in the middle of the room for a brief hug. It only lasted a couple seconds as each of them wanted out of this place and to breathe in some cool, fresh island air. Hand in hand, Brian led her down the steps and down the street. Once they were about a block from the police station, he stopped and pulled her into his arms.

She snuggled against him for a couple of moments, then looked up. "Brian, why?"

He smiled. "I had no choice." He released her, pulled her toward the curb and waved down a passing cab.

Entering the cab, Brian told him to take them to the hotel as he and Malie relaxed into the leather seats.

"Brian, what did you mean about having no choice?"

"Remember, I told you before all this happened that I love you."

"Still? After—

Brian nodded toward the cabbie, then took her hand. "Later."

She squeezed his hand and rested her head against his shoulder. "Okay, later."

For the rest of the trip, no more words were spoken. After paying the cabbie, Brian asked, "Are you hungry?"

His question surprised her and she was even more surprised to realize that she was indeed hungry. "What about the others? Shouldn't we let them know what's going on?"

"Yes. But I'll bet they're already having supper or they'll find us before we've even ordered our food. Come, let's get a table." He led her to the dining area. As he was talking to the hostess, he spotted the posse already seated.

Smiles and hugs were shared as Brian and Malie joined them and took their seats at the table.

"So," Patrick started, "fill us in. You've been released. Have all the charges been dropped?"

"Yes," said Malie with a bit of sadness in her voice.

"And yet," asked Kathleen, "You seem a little upset?"

"Not upset, just a little worried about my friend, Ruby."

"She's in good hands," said Brian. "We've hired attorney Ronald Phillips to represent Ruby. He comes with excellent references. In fact, he's already looking into a plea of self-defense."

Malie's eyes lit up. "Really? He thinks it could be self-defense?"

"That's what he's working on."

Their waiter arrived and took their food and drink orders.

When they were alone again, Malie excitedly said, "Oh, it truly was self-defense." She went on to tell them about the conditions she found Ruby in, and of Jake's plan to sell her for sex that could end up in her death.

Fortunately, their drinks arrived. Everyone was at a loss for words that such a thing could be done by one human being to another.

It was Kathleen who managed to say, "What a truly evil man."

Patrick put his hand over Kathleen's and with his other hand, he raised his cocktail. "Here's to a brave young woman who has now come forward to help two people caught in bad places. I'm sure Ruby thanks you and I, sincerely thank you, Malie."

The others raised their glasses with words of agreement. The food arrived as they set their glasses down.

Brian picked up his fork and nodded for the others to do the same. "For now, let's just relax and enjoy this food over the fact that Malie is free and here with us. Any plan for what comes next can come after we hear from Phillips." He took a bite of his food and the others agreed by following his lead.

The conversation over supper was about the food, how Kathleen and Patrick had spent their day and River's report on how things were going in Dawson. After a desert featuring a couple of pieces of pie shared around the table, Patrick paid the tab. They agreed to meet at eight the next morning for breakfast.

"Malie, do you need us to get you a room for the night?" asked Kathleen.

"She already has a room," said Brian.

"Okay, then. See you tomorrow morning," said Patrick as he quickly took Kathleen's arm and led her toward the elevators.

"Yes, see you tomorrow," said River, as he headed for the stairs.

Malie looked up at Brian. "I have a room? Where?"

He took her arm and led her out of the dining area. "I'll show you."

They took an elevator to the fourth floor and down the hall to a room at the end. Brian used a room key and opened the door to a room featuring a small bathroom to the right as you entered, then a fairly large room with two double beds and a large window with a great view of the shoreline, awash with the ebb and flow of the Pacific Ocean.

As Malie entered, she noticed an open closet where a couple of men's shirts and slacks were hung. She turned to Brian. "This is your room?"

"Yes." He walked over to the small refrigerator near the closet and pulled out two soft drink cans. He held one out to Malie. "Can we talk?"

All Malie wanted to do was to rush into his arms and hold him as close to her as she could. But she knew she wanted more than just his arms around her. He said he loved her, but would he feel the same, if she .... No, she decided, he wanted to talk. Finally, she smiled, took the offered soft drink and followed him to a table with a couple of chairs set under the large window.

Once they were seated, they enjoyed the ocean view for a couple minutes, then Brian began. "You asked what I meant about having no choice."

"Yes."

"I love you."

"Still? I ran off without telling you why or where I was going. We had just agreed that we are in the this-is-now stage of our relationship, but I took off and went back to the that-was-then.

"I admit I was a little confused at first. But, that conversation about the then and now kept repeating itself in my mind, along with the memory of that last kiss we shared. I just knew it had to be something serious for you to leave Dawson and all the people who have grown to love and trust you. When I talked to River, he called Patrick. When Patrick heard about you disappearing, he was all in for finding you. We all were worried and afraid something bad was happening to you. You see, it's not only me who loves you, it's Patrick, it's Kathleen, it's Peggy and Elmer and many others in Dawson."

As he talked, tears filled Malie's eyes. "I don't know what to say."

Brian reached over and took her hands. "So, you see, I had no choice. My heart refused to lose you, to lose the words of love we shared."

She squeezed his hand, stood up and pulled him into her arms. Their deep kiss along with warm caresses reaffirmed their love. No words were needed.

Eventually, Brian ended the kiss and put some space between their bodies.

"Brian?"

He smiled. "Yes, I want to take this further." He took hold of her hands. "But I want something first."

"Anything," she whispered.

"Marry me."

"Yes," she answered without hesitation and reached up to pull his face down for a kiss, but he held back.

"Tomorrow."

"You can make it happen tomorrow?"

"I may have to move mountains, but I will make it happen." He kissed her forehead. "For now, let's get some sleep." He took her hand and led her to the bed by the window. "You sleep here and I'll sleep there." He pointed to the other bed.

"Brian?"

He grinned. "Look, you're going to need a good night's sleep, because tomorrow we'll only be using one of these beds, and neither of us will be getting much sleep." He gave another kiss to her forehead, then went to pull back the covers on the other bed and sat down. He took off his shoes and socks. He stood up and pulled off his shirt, then smiled at Malie. "Can you step into the bathroom for a couple minutes? When you come out, I'll try to keep my eyes closed while you settle into your bed."

Malie shook her head and laughed as she went into the bathroom. When she came out wearing a lite terry robe, Brian was on his side in the bed next to the wall. She slipped into the bed near the window, keeping the robe on. When she was settled in, she smiled over at Brian. "You can open your eyes now."

Brian turned and their eyes met. He recognized the same want in her eyes that he was feeling so he knew he had to keep their goodnights brief. "Goodnight, Malie."

"Goodnight, Brian."

They both turned on their sides with their backs to each other.

"I love you," said Malie.

"I love you," said Brian.

Surprising both of them, they snuggled into their bedding and fell into a deep sleep that neither of them had experienced in a long time.

***

Brian woke first. He grabbed his tee and Levis from the foot of his bed, got his small suitcase out of the closet and hurried into the bathroom. In just a few minutes, he'd brushed his teeth, ran a wet washrag over his body, pulled on fresh underwear, then into yesterday's tee and Levis. When he reentered the bedroom, he found Malie, wearing the terry robe, sitting at the table with a cup of instant coffee.

"Good morning," She smiled and pointed to a cup for him on the table.

"Good morning," he said as he kissed her forehead, sat across from her and picked up the cup. "Sleep well?"

"Yes, and you?"

"Best in ages."

Malie nodded in agreement.

After a glance at the clock on the radio sitting between the two beds, he noticed it was almost 7:30. If he was going to make this wedding happen today, he needed to get moving. As he was about to stand up, Malie spoke.

"Brian, I did some thinking last night and then again this morning."

Brian's eyebrow rose with a look of concern. "Thinking about what?"

"That maybe we're rushing things."

"Rushing? About what? Our love? Getting married?"

She reached over and put her hand over his. "No, not about our love or marriage. I just worry about how such a quick marriage will affect your job. Don't you have to get some kind of approval from your sergeant major? And what about the town biddies that have been giving you so much trouble?"

He pulled his hand out from under hers and covered her hand with his. "First of all, marriage is not included in my job description. I can marry who I want. I don't need approval from Devon."

"But won't he be concerned about how the community will feel about the town constable going home each night to a bar... a former... a—

"It's none of their business."

"But, the town biddies, Hilda and Sadie, they're sure to have a negative reaction."

Brian stood up and pulled Malie up with him. "The only thing that matters to me is you. If our marriage annoys the Canadian Police Dept or the town biddies, I can find other work. Look, I was raised a fisherman, I became a sailor, and now I'm a constable.

I'm flexible. I really don't believe that my marriage to you will affect my job, but if it does, so be it. I'll have you and I'll find another job." He kissed her lips lightly. "I love you. Now, marry me. Today."

Malie shook her head from side to side in a smile. "How did I ever find you?" She kissed him. "Yes, let's get married today."

He pulled her into his arms for a more serious kiss that was neither light, nor short. Finally, it was Malie who pulled back.

"Don't you need to go make it happen?"

He laughed as he loosened their embrace and stepped back. "Well, what almost happened just now was tempting, but you're right. I need to get busy." He walked over to the door. "I'll be back as soon as I can." He turned and left the room.

Malie walked over and touched the door. "I love you," she said as she patted the door a couple of times, then turned and headed into the bathroom. While taking care of her morning needs, she decided to get dressed and see if she could hook up with Kathleen, and maybe even head on over to see if they could meet with Ruby.

***

Brian's first stop on making things happen was at Patrick's hotel room. After getting the details about how Patrick and Kathleen got married on the Pacific Ocean shore, the two men took off to see if they could find the same preacher and to check out the shoreline picnic area where the ceremony took place. They even made a quick stop at a jewelry store to purchase two gold bands.

The women met up and after being denied a visit with Ruby, they stopped at a department store. They found two dresses that, while not being traditional wedding garb, would look nice at the ceremony.

By a little after four that same afternoon, it was all arranged. Brian and Malie had even managed to get to the court house and get a marriage license. At sunset, with Patrick as best man, and Kathleen as maid of honor, the preacher stood with his back to the ocean facing the young couple.

The minister posed the age-old wedding ceremony question to the groom.

As Brian stared into Malie's eyes, he responded, "I do."

The question was then posed to the bride.

"I do," said Malie.

Next, as they placed gold bands on each other's hands, they confirmed their commitment with the words, "With this ring, I thee wed."

The ceremony ended with a kiss after the preacher uttered the words. "I now pronounce you husband and wife. You may seal your promises with a kiss."

Although invited, the preacher declined, so it was the five of them who went to a steak house with an ocean view for their wedding supper. The food and drinks were good, the conversation consisted of what had brought them to Hawaii, but more importantly how much all of them looked forward to returning home. They parted with an agreement to meet for breakfast the next morning at eight, after having packed for their trip home. Patrick planned to be in the air no later than eleven a.m. Goodnights were exchanged as each headed off to their own rooms.

When Brian and Malie reached the door to their room, Brian opened the door, then turned and carried a surprised Malie into the room. He kicked the door shut and continued to carry Malie over to the bed by the window. Slowly, all clothes were shed and the young couple spent the next couple of hours confirming the promises made during their wedding ceremony. Eventually, their emotionally and physically satisfied bodies relaxed. Malie turned on her side allowing the warmth of Brian's body to snuggle up against her back.

Before Brian slipped off into the arms of Morpheus, with his lips against her neck, he mumbled, "I love you."

"I love you, too," said Malie as her hand reached back and caressed his hip.

Before long, Malie felt Brian's body totally relax into sleep. She wanted to do the same, but her mind was alive with thoughts of what was, what is and anticipation of what was to come. Then, thoughts of Ruby appeared. At first Malie was afraid those thoughts would bring a dark cloud into what had been a perfect day. But her anticipation of what life had in store for her brought on feelings that all would be okay for Ruby, too. She felt sure that this episode in Ruby's life would bring on a change much like what meeting Patrick and Kathleen had done for Malie.

She smiled and eased her body back against her future and joined that future in the arms of Morpheus.

Epilogue

Seven months had passed since the wild and crazy happenings over in Hawaii. As the wife of the town constable, Malie knew she had to get ready for the Community Center Christmas Party. But she was cold after her walk home after visiting with her doctor. She decided she needed a hot cup of cocoa. She had stopped by the post office on her way home and found several Christmas cards in their mail box. Once the hot cocoa was ready, she sat at the kitchen table and checked out the cards. Her eyes lit up at seeing an Oahu postmark and a return address for Ruby.

Shortly after their return from Hawaii, Ruby had put through a call to Malie at Miss Lucy's Saloon. Attorney Phillips had managed to present enough evidence from the Flyin' Hi and the storage shed where Jake had held and abused Ruby to have the murder charges against Ruby changed to self-defense. Ruby had been released. Phillips' fee had not been cheap, but Patrick, Kathleen, River and Brian paid up with sincere gratitude.

Malie opened Ruby's card to find a letter inside. As Malie read along, she discovered that Phillips had represented Ruby in a lawsuit to have all of Jake's assets awarded to Ruby in payment for the abuse he put her through. They had won, and now Ruby owned the Flyin' Hi and a substantial amount of money.

Ruby thanked Malie for all she and her friends had done for her and to let her know if she could repay them in any way. Her life these days was better than she ever hoped for and there was even the possibility of a genuine love in her future. Bartender, Gus, had been a real help as she learned all that was necessary to run a bar.

She was in no hurry to make a commitment, but she enjoyed her private moments with Gus and felt that perhaps there was more to their relationship to come. She closed by wishing everyone that had come to her rescue a very Merry Christmas and a Wonderful New Year.

Joyful tears filled Malie's eyes as she closed the letter and set it on the table with the card. A glance at the return names on the other couple of cards let her know they were from friends in Dawson, so she set them aside and took a drink of her now cooled down cocoa. Another glance at the clock let her know, she needed to get ready. Brian would be home soon.

Once dressed in a soft, wool, red dress, she added a Christmas angel necklace, applied her make-up, brushed her hair and stepped into her black pumps. As she checked herself out in the full-length mirror attached to the closet door, her hand began to caress her stomach.

Was it a boy or a girl and did she really want to know until she could hold it in her arms. She smiled. She was giving Brian a Christmas present he would never forget. Should she tell him when he got home, at the party, or later tonight when they would have the privacy and many hours to themselves. She decided on later that night.

"Malie, I'm home."

She heard the back door close, then Brian's footstep on the wooden floor leading to their bedroom.

As he entered the room, he smiled. "Malie, you look beautiful."

She smiled back as she touched her stomach. "We're going to have a baby!"

About the author

Sharon Poppen resides in Lake Havasu City, AZ. She was born in Chicago, IL and over the years has resided in Albuquerque, NM, Simi Valley, CA, and Livermore, CA. She is the mother of two children, and has three step-children and five grandchildren.

A retired telecommunications manager, she is a graduate of URL, the University of Real Life. Sharon is also a graduate of Mohave Community College in Lake Havasu City, AZ where she earned an AA in Literature.

Sharon has won awards from the Arizona Authors Assoc. and the National League of American Pen Women.

Her novels are available in print and e-book from Amazon Books.

Her short stories and poetry have appeared in such publications as The Today News-Herald, A Flasher's Dozen, Desert Treasures, Skive, Offerings from the Oasis, A Long Story Short, Apollo Lyre and Laughter Loaf

Sharon's workshops on Journaling, Novel Writing, Short Story Writing, and Blogging bring rave reviews.

Preview

An excerpt from

Irish Girl

I hope you enjoyed reading *A New Flower in the Yukon*. As a thank you, I want to share with you the opening chapter of another one of my recent novels, *Irish Girl*.

Lancaster

"Damn, Meara, does every meal have to be boiled? There are frying pans in the cupboard." Adam shoved his bowl of corned beef and cabbage across the table. The bowl was pushed with such force that it banged into Meara's bowl and shoved it off the table onto her lap. The hot broth scalded her thighs and brought her petite five-foot two body up on her feet. Her thick copper-colored head flew about her shoulders as if caught in a windstorm. She pursed her lips tightly to hold in a painful scream.

Adam sighed and ran his fingers threw his thick, brown hair in frustration for a moment or two. Then, the hurt in her hazel eyes brought on a wave of shame. No one deserved to feel such pain and rejection. He got to his feet and rushed over to pick her up. He carried her to the bathroom, sat her in the tub and turned on the cold water. As it filled the tub, he pulled her dress over her head. He had to fight the bile threatening to erupt as he watched bright red scald marks forming on her thighs.

As the cold water somewhat eased her pain, Meara looked up at Adam. "I'm sorry. I won't do it again." She touched his arm as her eyes begged for forgiveness.

"Damn it, Meara. I didn't mean to hurt you. I just ..."

She touched his arm again. "I know." She started to rise out of the tub. "I'll go fry up some hamburger for you."

The reddish blisters on her legs still ate at the shame he felt at hurting her. He put his hand on her shoulder and urged her back down. "You need to let the cold-water work on the burns. We'll worry about supper later." As she settled down into the soothing water, he opened the medicine cabinet to see if he could find anything to ease her pain. Finding nothing, he turned back to her. He winced at the thought of his commanding officer hearing about another display of his short temper, but at the sound of her muffled moans, he knew what he had to do. "I don't see anything to put on the burns. I think I should take you to the med-center."

"No," she shook her head and again started to rise out of the tub. She avoided his hand as he reached out to urge her back down. "No med-center. They'll have to make a report and your sergeant might, might ..." She stopped speaking. They both knew any record of this would not sit well if reported to his sergeant. She stepped out of the tub and reached for her robe hanging on the bathroom door. "Come. We just need some sliced potatoes."

"Potatoes?" Adam now worried that the pain was making her crazy.

"Yes." She took his hand and led him back into the kitchen area. A shelf along one of the walls held a variety of grocery dry goods and a sack of potatoes. After grabbing a couple of potatoes from the sack, she pulled a potato peeler from the utensil drawer, then handed Adam a knife.

"I'll peel; you cut the potato into slices."

"What?"

"Please." The pain on her thighs was becoming more intense.

As soon as the potatoes were peeled and sliced, she sat on a kitchen chair and began to cover her thighs with the potatoes. Then she remembered another of her mother's homemade remedies

"Honey, I need that jar of honey," she told Adam.

At this point, he decided it was pointless to question her requests. He got the honey off the shelf. When he handed her the jar, he noticed she had removed the potatoes. Taking the jar, she gently covered her thighs in the thick, golden liquid. Once the honey was in place, she eased the potato slices into the thickness.

Adam watched and had to fight with himself to keep from grabbing her and taking her to the med-center. He knew this incident would add to his short temper reputation. Overall, he loved his military life. But he was so used to getting his own way, that occasionally, dissension from his peers irked him enough to incite flare ups. So far, no penalties other than an extra KP or latrine duty, but he knew scalding his wife would not sit well with his Sergeant.

Meara's voice interrupted his thoughts. "I think the honey and potatoes are working."

Adam looked down at the mess, then began to shake his head. "I still think we should go and have a doctor look at those burns."

"I'll be fine." Meara managed a slight smile. She looked over at the table and the floor, still dripping with what should have been their supper. "You must be hungry. Get me the bread and the bologna and I'll fix you a sandwich."

Adam shook his head. "I lost my appetite. Just sit there and let that concoction, whatever you call it, do its thing." He retrieved a dishrag from the sink and began to clear away the dirty dishes and wipe off the table.

"Adam, I'll take care of that in a little while."

He continued with the cleanup. "You just sit there. I'll take care of it." With the table back in order, he looked around the room for a mop. Finding none, he asked, "Where's the mop?"

Meara started to rise, but Adam quickly put his hand on her shoulder and eased her back down.

"Sit. Just tell me where the mop is."

She told him and he found it outside the kitchen door on their small back porch. After wetting it down in the sink, he began to mop the floor under the table.

"Adam ..."

"Hey," he interrupted. "I've done some KP mopping from time to time. I can handle this."

All she could do was nod.

Once the kitchen was cleaned up, Adam sat down next to Meara and looked at her thighs. "Still hurt real bad?"

"No. The honey and potatoes seem to be working."

The couple sat in silence for several minutes. Each working through what had happened and why. Meara was at a total loss. It seemed nothing she did satisfied Adam. Her mind wandered back nearly two years, to May of 1955 when a handsome, six-foot, brown-eyed American Air Force corporal smiled at her and her friends as they enjoyed a girl's night out at the Foggy Bottom, a local pub in Cambridge, England. He was at the bar with several

US Airforce men stationed at nearby RAF Alconbury. By the time the pub reached closing time, the men and women had shared a couple pitchers of ale and several dances.

The following Saturday night, the girls arrived at the pub to find the airmen had already secured a large table and several pitchers of ale were waiting. Week by week, the group settled into couples and Meara was pleased Adam was attracted to her. They dated exclusively for the next year. Adam had even joined her for a week-end trip back home to Waterford, Ireland to meet her family. When his papers came through for reassignment back to the States, they married. Within a week of arriving at Edwards Air Force Base in Lancaster, California, he sent for Meara. They settled into a small apartment near the base. Meara so enjoyed her new life in this new country as Adam's wife. But, just after their first anniversary, she began to notice his displeasure of almost everything she said or did. She tried to talk to him about it, but he said it was just the stress of his work assignment and didn't want to discuss it.

Coming out of her reverie, she noticed that a couple of the potato slices had fallen from the honey. The burning sensation was still there, but the honey seemed to be alleviating it somewhat. She turned to Adam. He sat looking down at his hands resting on the table. He may have been within inches of her, but she felt his mind was miles away. And from the occasional twitch of his jaw line, it wasn't a pleasant place. Not sure if she should try to bring him back to the moment, she held back speaking to him and refocused on putting the fallen potato slices back into the honey.

Adam was indeed in another place; He was reliving his first meeting with Meara. For him, she stood out from the other girls. Her reddish-brown hair framed an angelic face blessed with alabaster skin, big hazel eyes and full lips that begged to be kissed.

Her innocent smile had a way of bringing him to recognize she was quite different from the type of girls he usually found in bars, whether back in the states or here in England. As they began dating, her positive attitude and interest in him, his family, his schooling, his interests outside of his military life and of America in general made every evening he spent with her increase his attraction to her. Eventually, he realized he was in love for the first time in his life.

Within a month of bringing Meara to the states, Adam asked for a four-day pass and took her home to meet his family, a father, mother and two older sisters who lived in Albuquerque, New Mexico. Although a little leery of Adam's, what they considered rash, rush into marriage. Meara quickly won them over and they were sad when Adam's pass ended and the couple returned to base.

Six months into their marriage, the bliss of coming home to his new wife each night, began to pale. She seemed content to keep to her Irish, everything gets boiled, cooking recipes, and added to that, her problem adjusting to the desert landscape of the area surrounding the base and their apartment. Daily, he had to listen to how she missed the greenery of Ireland along with the cool, misty, often foggy days she would walk around her village. Now, it was so dry and often so hot, walking anywhere was out of the question. She hated that and the fact that when she did walk anywhere the busy streets bustled with loud and often smelly vehicles.

As the months went by, he dreaded the boiled dinners and the constant comparison of the dry, desert Lancaster to the lush green of Ireland. Having been raised as the only son in the family, he was spoiled by his parents as well as his older sisters. Whatever Adam wanted; Adam was given. He had never learned that relationships were give and take. He raised his head and looked over at

Meara and wondered why she didn't enjoy making him happy, like his family always did.

"Adam?" asked Meara when their eyes met.

"Sorry, I let my mind wander." He looked over at her thighs. Covered in the honey-potato concoction, he couldn't tell if the redness was still there. "Are you still in pain?"

"Just a little. I'll be alright."

Another awkward silence settled over the couple. Adam was at a loss as to what to do or say. Finally, he decided enough was enough. He took a deep breath and took the first step of deception in their marriage. He needed to get out of the house.

"Meara, I didn't get a chance to tell you before we sat down for supper, but I drew night duty tonight." He glanced down at his watch. "I need to report for sentry duty by ten o'clock." He stood up. Guilt tried to intervene. "But, if you need to go see a medic, I'll —

"No, I'll be fine." She glanced at the wall clock. "It's already after nine. You'll need a clean shirt." She started to get up.

He shook his head. "No stay there and let the honey do its thing. I'll try to get someone to come relieve me and be home as soon as possible." He headed for the bedroom and within a couple minutes, he was back in full uniform. He kissed her forehead. "I'll be back home as soon as possible." Then he was gone.

Meara stared at the closed door for awhile as tears formed in the corner of her eyes. The quietness of the small apartment closed in on her. Just as she was about to give in and let her tears fall, her grandmother's Irish words of wisdom came to mind. 'It is better to bend than to break.' She closed her eyes and took a deep breath. When she opened them, she looked at the picture of them taken a few weeks earlier when Adam had taken her to Santa Monica

Beach in Los Angeles. The smiles on their faces brought back the fun of the day and his handsome face reminded her of how much she loved Adam.

She reached down, removed the potatoes and stood up. She had too much to lose if Adam was unhappy. Glancing up at the ceiling, she smiled.

"Thank you, Grandma. There is no way us Irish girls break, we may bend now and then, but breaking in not an option."

Despite the slight stinging of the red splotches on her thighs, she gathered the potato slices and put them in the trash. Adam had done a good job of cleaning up the mess, but she felt another wipe down of the table and floor was necessary. After completing her chores, she smoothed another thin layer of honey on her thighs, then headed for the bedroom and a long, lonely night without Adam.

(To read more of *Irish Girl* it is available as an e-book and print book at Amazon.com)

www.ingramcontent.com/pod-product-compliance
Lightning Source LLC
Chambersburg PA
CBHW031026310726
48969CB00007B/1885